Sayulita Sunset

A NOVEL

G. CARLOS SMITH

Copyright © 2024 by G. Carlos Smith

All rights reserved. No part of this publication may be reproduced or transmitted in any form or by any means, electronic or mechanical, including photocopy, recording, or any information storage and retrieval system, without permission in writing from the author. The characters and entities herein are fictional. Any resemblance to a real person or entity is purely coincidental.

PERPETUAL
An imprint of Perpetual Books, LLC, of the author

ISBN References:
HC: 979-8-9905553-0-3
PB: 979-8-9905553-1-0
eBook: 979-8-9905553-2-7

*To my dearest
Keith, Olivia, Evelyn & Lia*

Chapter 1

THE SUN GLIMMERED OVER THE VAST HORIZON OF THE DEEP, BLUE Pacific Ocean. While sipping his coffee, Francisco scanned the vista's expanse from the living room under the thatched *palapa* of his family home in Mexico. An early breeze warmed the coastline with a misty, salty scent as the morning waves, crashing gently against the damp white sand of the beach below, punctuated the home with the peaceful rhythm of their constant flow. He smiled, reflecting. The sound of the waves, the primordial smell of the sea, the touch of the warm sand, the wonderous enormity of the ocean, and the broad array of memories they'd built living there—they grounded him, in an almost instinctive way. He walked to the edge of the palapa and leaned against the bamboo beams of its railing. It was early, but the clouds were already coalescing above him, probably from the tropical humidity. *The quiet before the storm?* he thought. Well, he hoped not. There would be choppy waters for his family ahead; he was sure of that. But come what may, he knew that Sayulita would always feel like home, their home, and that left him with a satisfying sense of comfort and completion. He took another sip of his coffee and continued his gaze across the bay.

In the distance, the tourists' fishing boats trudged slowly from their docks in the marina on their way to the open sea, as they did every morning. But that morning, several of the boats had stopped, circling in the distance instead. *Probably dolphins*, he thought. He walked to the dresser, pulled out his binoculars, and searched the ocean. The calm blue of the morning sea spanned infinitely and unadulterated, until the spray of a whale emerged as the crest of its tail broke the water's canopy. Francisco refocused the binoculars and quickly realized that there actually were two. One looked huge, but the other seemed relatively small. *A mother and her calf?* he thought. He'd watched these whales pass through the bay for decades; still, the mass and vibrance of their bodies continued to amaze him. As quickly as the two emerged, they again descended, disappearing into the depths of their dark ocean habitat.

As expected, the fishing boats continued circling the area where the whales had been, waiting for another peek at the mammals while keeping a safe distance so as not to disturb them. When the whales reappeared, the baby came up first, spinning its fully emerged body in the air, followed quickly by its mother, who showered a nearby boat with the spray of her blowhole and the splash of her tail. He could see the vessel toss with the displacement of the waves while the fisherman's passengers laughed at their unexpected shower. As the whales again submerged, the boats quickly moved, anticipating the next location of the animals' return while circling for the best possible view.

Five minutes passed—then a few more. But the water remained calm and unbroken. When the whales didn't reappear, the fishermen gave up and resumed their journey out to sea. *No*, Francisco thought. *You just need to give them more time—have a little patience*. He reluctantly shook his head and grinned. He knew the instructions were intended for him, not the fishermen. He just hoped he'd be able to follow them.

He set the binoculars down on a coffee table near the palapa railing and scanned the sea with his naked eyes. As he searched, he wondered how long it would take the baby whale to reach adulthood. Would it come back to the bay without its mother? Or would she show him the way, at least the first time? He wondered if she'd have another calf by then, or if this would be her last—her last baby, her last journey south? *Maybe*, he thought. He knew from experience that the journey north was a difficult one. He'd done it. Was it as hard for them? As treacherous? He had no idea. But with a final leap, the two animals again broke the bank of the sea, cresting into the air, before diving into the depths of the ocean.

And so it goes, he thought, *the cycle of life*. The characters are replaced over time, as one generation moves on or away, leaving the next to take its place. But the plot and venue remain more or less unchanged? He hoped so. He wanted the baby, like his own, to be safe and to return in a natural succession. He wondered if the calf would make it. The life of the small whale probably wasn't easy. Perhaps surviving life's hardships was part of what made the animals even more beautiful, vibrant, and good. And all of it, God's creation—His plan? *Well, maybe*, he thought, chuckling to himself. *And maybe not.*

To the right of Francisco's home were the cliffs above the village of Sayulita, which at the early hour remained quiet. Directly below was the long shoreline of the beach. The cafés lining it were still closed, with the curtains of their shop tents rolled down and their colorful wooden chairs neatly stacked. A handful of early morning walkers strolled leisurely along the beach, and the first surfers of the day headed out. Because the sun had yet to fully emerge over the back of the sea cliffs behind his home, the cool freshness of the morning surrounded the beach. That, he knew, would quickly flee with the arrival of the afternoon heat. Shortly thereafter, the wind would begin, bringing the crash of the afternoon waves against the rocks of the coast to the left of the beach below.

"*¿Viste tu correo?*" Consuela asked. *(You saw the mail?)*

Francisco gazed up at the mildly wrinkled face of his housekeeper and longtime friend. He smiled. "Not yet."

Her brow furrowed. "*Sí*, Francisco, *sí!* I left it for you yesterday, and you didn't even look at it."

"Something for you?" he asked.

"*No, es para ti. Es en serio.*" *(No, it's for you. Seriously.)* Her voice embodied her earnest concern. She loved him; it was transparent.

"For me?" he said, pointing at himself in mock surprise. "Well, then, it couldn't be that important." He knew he was teasing her but couldn't seem to help himself.

Consuela scuttled into the kitchen and started banging the pots—her customary way of expressing displeasure. Francisco listened with mild amusement. He didn't know exactly how old she was, but he knew she was at least a couple of years ahead of him, making her just over sixty. Her hair was graying, but she religiously dyed it. She wasn't overweight, given her age. But her very short stature made her look as if she were. It didn't matter, and she didn't care; her being radiated joy in the simple pleasure of life. It was her nature.

"*¿Huevos rancheros?*" she asked, smiling. "*Con chilaquiles de pollo.*" *(Mexican eggs with chicken, beans, and chips.)*

"*Sí,*" he responded, smiling back.

Francisco knew chilaquiles were her favorite breakfast dish and that his desires, whatever they may be, were inconsequential. But he didn't mind. After the many years they'd shared, he loved her company much more than her cooking. While he paid her as the cook and housekeeper, those roles were as incidental to their relationship as they were for any mother taking care of her own family. While now she was his housemate and friend, he couldn't deny that she had, in many ways, been the mother of his children and a stabilizing force in their lives. He loved her—they all did.

"Don't you give me that smile, Francisco," she said, pointing at him with her wooden spoon. "You're ignoring me all over again."

"How long have you been cooking your *huevos increíbles* for me?" he asked, changing the subject to her amazing eggs.

Consuela again held up the wooden spoon, directing it at him as she formed her words. "Forever," she said. "Why? *Me lo pregunto una y otra vez.*" *(I ask myself over and over again.)* She paused. "*No sé.*" She shrugged her shoulders to emphasize she didn't know the answer.

Francisco smiled back at her.

"Maybe you'll wake up tomorrow, and *I'll* be gone. Then what would *you* do?" she asked.

"Probably eat cereal," he answered. While he understood the irony of her statement, he chose again to ignore it.

"*Ay,*" she contested, before turning back to the bowl to stir. "*Ay ya yai.*"

Her focus on the bowl made it clear that the conversation had ended. *"Me vuelves loco. ¡Eres increíble!" (You drive me crazy. You're unbelievable!)* Francisco took another sip of his coffee before glancing around the palapa. Their home was a grand villa in the traditional Mexican style. The thatched straw formed a dense ceiling that arched to a tall peak in the center of the open living room and tented the stunning panoramic views of the ocean below. All of the floors were made of natural beige marble that created a cool freshness at any time of day when touched by bare feet. Thick beamed pillars supported the palapa with wall-to-wall windows of glass, which opened like sliding doors, framed in the same dark wood. When left open during the mornings and evenings, they allowed a natural ocean breeze to pass through the entire home, but they closed completely when desired to protect the home during the hottest hours of the afternoon heat or the annual tropical storms. To the right was the kitchen, made of the same dark wood, where Consuela continued with breakfast. The appliances, while showing their age, were all of high quality, complete with a Wolf range and a Sub-Zero refrigerator. As he looked at the rust on the range's hood and the graying straw of the palapa roof, he realized that it was time to replace at least some of these items. *But not today,* he thought. *And not on my watch.*

Adjacent and to the right of the home was his restaurant, the *Vista Linda,* or Pretty View, which Francisco had owned and run for quite some time. The restaurant palapa, framed in the rear by the bluffs, primarily catered to the wealthy customers of the nearby Four Seasons Hotel, who were looking for an authentic but more upscale Mexican dining experience. With seating for about thirty, the restaurant was known for its fine seafood cuisine and spectacular views of the Pacific Ocean. Complementing the experience for special occasions was a Mexican *sinfonia* with mariachi singers, two violins, a guitar, a trumpet, a vihuela, a folk harp, and a stringed bass.

Below the home and restaurant were the white, glistening sands of the Sayulita beach, accessed by a narrow path winding down the cliffs from the buildings above. To the left of the main palapa of the living room was a short staircase that led to the four bedrooms of the home. Behind them were the living quarters for Consuela and her husband of many years, Guillermo. When he'd first arrived, Francisco had actually lived in Consuela's tiny apartment. He smiled, remembering what the prior owner had said years later when he'd bought the home: "Oh, and by the way, the housekeepers are included." At the time, he'd thought they sounded like someone who needed to be freed or a liability he'd have to manage. But he'd been so very wrong.

"Will Guillermo join us?" Francisco asked.

"No," Consuela answered. "He went out on his boat."

"Fishing?" he asked.

"*Sí*, fishing," she answered, while rolling her eyes sarcastically.

Francisco chuckled. While Guillermo's job was to help maintain the home and take tourists fishing, he liked to take his boat out alone from time to time. When he was successful, the fresh fish he caught made a wonderful addition to the restaurant menu. But as often as not, Guillermo took the boat out to drink his beer and smoke his pot pipe, away from the critique of his wife's vigilant gaze.

"Maybe he'll bring us back a fish," Francisco said hopefully. "Something special?"

"*No creo*," she answered with another scowl, circumventing any chance at humor. *(I don't think so.)*

"Now, eat your eggs, and open your mail." She dropped the plate abruptly in front of Francisco before heading back up to her quarters.

Francisco slowly ate the eggs, savoring the taste of each bite as if it were his last, while intermittently sipping his coffee and enjoying the view. But he knew he was stalling. He finished the meal and placed the dishes in the dishwasher, slowly and deliberately. Then he walked to the entry hall of the home, where the mirror above the entry table caught his eye. He wasn't young anymore, but he was still handsome. His thick brown hair remained, save for some light streaking in gray. His strong jaw, speckled with a day's growth of beard, had only hints of a falling skin line. But the all-white whiskers clearly exposed his increasing age. The wrinkles of his brow were firm, but the deep brown of his eyes remained warm and vibrant, even penetrating. Through his T-shirt, his arms remained lean and muscular, and in his shorts, his legs looked firm. And while his skin bore the tan of a beach life, its lighter Latin coloring was healthy and void of scars. He'd been blessed.

As he neared the entry table, he noticed again how his head exceeded the mirror's height. He smiled. He'd always been taller than others here, even in his own home. While his look was clearly Latin, his height revealed his European roots: Spanish on his father's side, with Spanish and some French on his mother's. As the mirror could attest, he looked like the others but didn't quite fit in.

He glanced down at the table under the mirror and perused the pile of mail that had previously arrived. Most of it was the usual: bills, advertisements, and the like. At the top was the letter Consuela had obviously noticed from the *Clínica Médica Central de la Ciudad de México*, or Central Medical Clinic of Mexico City. He reluctantly opened the letter before noticing its date: October 15—the same day their lives had forever changed exactly twenty-three years earlier.

Francisco watched Derek, his husband, as they drove through the almond groves and headed toward the California interstate in their silver Audi. The trip to Yosemite National Park had been a mistake; there was no doubt about it. While the falls were spectacular, the twins, age two, were too young to appreciate them and had to be carried almost everywhere. As a result, they'd stayed in the Yosemite Valley, a short walk from the limited parking, or they'd taken a shuttle bus from place to place. While sleeping in cabins had seemed like an adventure, navigating the distant public facilities while removing the mud following an early rain proved to be too much with the girls. After leaving a day early, getting back on the road to the Bay area seemed like a welcome escape from a rustic nightmare.

Derek was older than Francisco by five or so years, making him about thirty, but they looked about the same age. At six foot one, Derek was a little taller than Francisco. Derek's skin was pale and White; his hair was blond, and his eyes were a translucent blue. While Derek carried ten more pounds than Francisco did, both of them were fit and muscular. And while their clothes—blue jeans and a T-shirt for Derek with jeans and a polo shirt for Francisco—were traditionally masculine, the cut of their hair and their attention to grooming suggested to a perceptive viewer that they weren't straight.

"Smell that?" Francisco asked as the car proceeded along the freeway.

"No," Derek answered while scrunching his nose.

"You're just saying that because you know it's your turn to change a diaper," Francisco answered.

"That doesn't change the accuracy of the answer," Derek said.

"Seriously?" Francisco answered, but Derek didn't respond. Francisco pressed his lips. Derek was in a mood. He could feel it. Because of a scratching sound under the wooden floorboards of their Yosemite Park cabin, no one had slept the night before. Derek had pretended it was nothing, but Francisco was pretty sure it had been a rat.

"Why don't you pull the car over?" Francisco suggested. "It's lunchtime anyway."

Derek smirked. "Okay," he answered. "What're you thinking?"

"Any place that's fast but not drive-through?"

As they continued up the interstate, they realized that their options were going to be limited. "There's a Denny's," Francisco said.

"Are you kidding?" Derek asked.

"I know you're hungry because you're getting super crabby," Francisco answered. "And the stink that you claim doesn't exist is just going to get worse."

Derek frowned at Francisco before changing lanes and heading for the exit. "I'm *so* ready for this vacation to end," he said, as he pulled into the lot behind the back side of the Denny's near a large, institutional garbage bin.

Francisco unbuckled Elena's car seat and pulled her out while Derek pulled Rebecca out of hers.

"Shit," Derek said, holding Rebecca away from him. "That is so rank."

Francisco didn't respond but instead picked up the diaper bag and unzipped it while checking for snacks. Then Rebecca started to cry.

"Got a pacifier?" Derek asked.

"Sure," Francisco answered, searching through the bag as Rebecca's cries grew more intense. "She really needs a change. I'll do it once we're inside."

When they reached the Denny's entrance, Francisco pulled at the front door while holding Elena's hand, but the door was stuck. He put down the diaper bag and lodged Elena in Derek's other hand. With a firmer tug, he opened the door, and they entered.

"Classy place," Derek said, passing Elena's hand back.

The restaurant's decor was as expected for a Denny's, with faux wood Formica tabletops on the bar behind an unattended sign saying, "PLEASE WAIT FOR YOUR HOSTESS TO SEAT YOU." The entrance had a handful of patrons sitting on a bench, patiently following its instructions. After a while, the hostess returned, took their names, and told them they were third on the list with a wait of "about ten minutes."

"I'll change Rebecca and be right back," Derek said.

"Are you sure?" Francisco asked.

"It's my turn, right? I'll do it," Derek responded curtly.

Francisco apprehensively nodded.

After changing Rebecca, Derek returned from the restroom to the hostess station. When Elena's pacifier fell on the floor, she started to cry.

"So we're next?" Derek asked the hostess.

"Yes. They're clearing a table right here in front," she answered. "Will the wives be joining you today?" She looked at the girls.

Francisco smiled. "No, just the four of us."

It was a common mistake. People just assumed that two guys with kids must have wives. When Francisco held Elena, a Latino man with a Latina child, and Derek held Rebecca, a White man with a White child, the assumption was even more reasonable. But Francisco had given up correcting people. Why bother?

The hostess stepped away just as another couple entered the restaurant. Francisco had heard the loud rumble of a Harley-Davidson moments earlier and, from the appearance of the couple, presumed the motorcycle was theirs. The man had a scruffy, graying beard, and the woman's dark hair showed the white lines of a bad dye job. Their look was severe, likely reflecting a life of hardship: The man's complexion was pimply and uneven, and the woman couldn't stop grinding her teeth. Francisco presumed they used drugs, possibly meth. Both of them were big, with the man being physically large and the woman being both large and obese. Each of them wore black leather. From their odor, Francisco assumed they'd been driving in the hot sun for quite some time.

When Elena started crying again, Rebecca started to cry as well. Placing Rebecca on the floor with a toy from the diaper bag to distract her, Derek took Elena from Francisco's arm and began rocking her. Francisco noticed the dirty diaper smell again before seeing a streak of feces along the top of Elena's leg and Derek's wrist. He reluctantly pointed to Derek's hand and then to Elena's leg.

"Crap," Derek whispered, audibly enough for the other guests to hear, while reaching for the wipes.

Francisco just raised his eyebrows in response while smothering a chuckle.

The biker couple noticed that a table up front was opening up, and with the hostess absent, started walking over to take it.

"Excuse me," Derek said. "But I think that table's ours. Can you wait for the hostess?"

When the biker turned around, his brow furrowed, and his face reddened. "We're here," he said, "and we're taking it."

Hearing the commotion, the hostess returned to see what was happening.

"We're next in line," Derek said, "and we've got two hungry kids." He nodded down to Elena and over to Francisco, who now held Rebecca.

"Didn't you hear me?" the biker responded. "I said no." Then he looked at them more carefully, scrutinizing them from top to bottom. His girlfriend also watched, as Francisco handed Derek the diaper bag.

"Them kids yours?" the girlfriend asked.

The tone of her voice was critical, so Derek didn't answer. The woman looked at her partner and made an effeminate gesture with one hand while pointing to Derek with the other.

"It's Adam and Eve, not Adam and Steve," the man said. "At least that's what my Bible says." He laughed at his own joke while his girlfriend gave a supportive chuckle.

"No kidding," Derek responded. "I hadn't heard that one before."

The couple's faces soured at the sarcastic response, and Francisco grimaced. Derek wasn't one to back down from a confrontation, but these people didn't seem like the type to confront.

"It's okay," Francisco whispered to Derek. "We can eat at the bar." Derek didn't respond. "Derek, she's got an anklet," Francisco pleaded.

When Derek glanced down at her parole anklet, the woman noticed, and her eyes angrily narrowed. "If God wanted you gays to have babies," she whispered to Derek, "he'd have given your boy toy a pussy."

"You should try it sometime," the man audibly added. "Pussy." He slapped the buttocks of his girlfriend, and she laughed with him.

Derek challenged her by looking directly into her eyes. Then he watched as the man proceeded with his girlfriend toward the open booth.

"Fuck you, faggot," the man quietly said as he passed Derek. "We're eating now."

Noticing a disturbance, the manager quickly came over to address it. "Can I find you guys another table?" he asked Derek. "I'm sorry for any inconvenience."

Francisco couldn't tell if the manager's use of the words *any inconvenience* was genuine, but he knew Derek wouldn't buy it.

"It *is* an inconvenience," Derek said. "We have two toddlers who're hungry, and we were here before them." He nodded to the motorcycle couple, who were watching him from the booth. "So, I think you need to tell *them* to move and apologize to *them* for *any inconvenience*."

The manager looked at Derek and then back at the couple, weighing his options. Noticing the commotion, the other patrons in the restaurant started watching him as well, waiting to see what his response would be. Recognizing that Derek wasn't going to back down, the manager directed a waitress to finish cleaning another table before walking over to the motorcycle couple sitting at the booth.

"I'm sorry," he said, "but this is a table for four, and we need it for this other family who got here first." He nodded back to Derek and Francisco. "I've got another table for two that's almost ready. Can I show you to it now?"

The man put his menu down and angrily looked up at the manager. "*Family?*" the man said sarcastically. Then he looked over at Derek, who stared directly back at him. The man's face quickly reddened. Then he slammed his hands on the table, knocking over a water glass as the table shook. When he got up from the booth, his girlfriend followed him. Everyone in the restaurant watched silently.

"You might like to fuck guys," he said to Derek, stopping briefly as he passed. "But you just fucked the wrong one." He pointed his index and middle fingers at his own eyes before pointing them threateningly at Derek's.

Derek nodded without answering, and the man and woman proceeded with the manager to their table for two. A waitress then led Derek, followed by Francisco and the girls, back to the first table, which had already been recleaned. After Derek took his seat, Francisco fastened Rebecca into her booster seat before heading quickly to the restroom to change Elena. Upon returning and securing Elena in her seat, Francisco sat down as well and tried to decompress. He knew better than to say anything further but was unable to stop himself.

"I can't believe you," Francisco said. "Are you crazy?"

Derek looked up at him. "I'm not putting up with that kinda bigotry anywhere, even on I-5 in the middle of nowhere," he said.

When Francisco didn't respond, Derek just opened his menu and started to read it. Francisco was furious. Engaging with the motorcycle couple had no upside, and the attention from the customers had been humiliating. But he knew better than to criticize Derek further.

The waitress returned after a while and took their order without making much eye contact. Once the meal had been prepared, she left their plates on the table without inquiry. Derek's cheeseburger seemed safe enough, but Francisco's turkey plate wasn't. He ate a little bit of it and stirred the mashed potatoes and stuffing, ignoring the soggy green beans. While eating, they intermittently fed the twins from their own plates along with some of the toddler food they'd brought.

Throughout the meal, Francisco noticed that the Denny's patrons continued to sneak glances at them while pretending as if nothing had happened.

When they were finished, the waitress left them the tab without clearing their table. "You pay upfront," she said, forcing a smile before heading off toward another table.

"What's her problem?" Francisco asked.

Derek shrugged. "You lost her when you couldn't produce a wife."

Francisco smirked. "Why don't you go ahead and pay it?" he asked. "I'll clean the twins up and meet you at the car." He pulled out some wipes and handed Derek the baby bag.

"Sure," Derek said, getting up from the table.

"Hey," Francisco said, stopping him. "Let's drop it with the motorcycle couple, okay?"

Derek looked at the table where they'd been sitting. "They left," he said. "No big deal."

Francisco wiped what remained of the lunch from the girls' mouths by dipping a napkin in his water glass. Then he cleaned up the mess they'd left on the table and floor. After unfastening Elena and then Rebecca from their booster seats, he placed the twins on the ground, took their hands, and headed out of the restaurant.

After exiting the front door, which again stuck, Francisco walked around the building toward the back where they'd parked. From the distance, he could see the Audi, but Derek wasn't there. *What now?* he thought. He started toward the car but was stopped by the roar of a motorcycle as it sped away.

"Seriously?" he quietly said to himself.

Taking the twins' hands firmly, Francisco walked around the Audi before noticing that the rear wheel on the passenger's side was flat. Then he saw Derek, lying on the asphalt between the Audi and the trash bin. Near him was a growing pool of blood. After stepping in front of the twins to shield their view, Francisco reached for his phone to dial 911 while desperately probing Derek's neck for a pulse. But when he saw Derek's crushed skull, he knew that his efforts were pointless. Derek was dead.

Francisco returned his focus to the waves of the Pacific Ocean below his home in Sayulita. Those years had passed, day by day, year after year, but the images of the moment remained emblazoned in his mind. As far as he knew, the police never caught the motorcycle couple. Francisco assumed that Derek had confronted the couple when he saw the punctured tire. It was a fatal choice.

How is it that a moment can define a life? he thought. *And why all the hate? Over a table at Denny's?* After considering the questions for over two decades, he had no answers, and he knew he never would. Francisco again looked down at the letter he held with the lab report from the medical clinic in Mexico City. He knew he couldn't avoid Consuela's concern over it much longer. But he didn't need to read it to know what it said. He'd felt the words bearing its results in his body for months: cancer.

As he refocused his attention on the letter, he caught Consuela's gaze through the mirror. He read it quickly and then shook his head negatively. He wasn't surprised. The results were confirmatory and entirely consistent with his prior tests. So when she started to object, he turned and spoke directly to her.

"There's nothing more to be done, Consuela."

"But Francisco . . ." she pleaded.

"I'll tell the twins when they come," he said. "I promise."

In the meantime, there were fences to mend, and as he could no longer deny, the time to mend them was now. Like the distance between them, the holes in his family had been growing for a decade, maybe even for a lifetime. So he knew the mending wouldn't be easy, particularly given his short window of time. But he was determined to try.

After Consuela reluctantly walked back to her room, he picked up his iPhone and texted the twins: *Hey, girls, it's Dad. Can you come home together for Xmas this year? It's important to me.*

Chapter 2

Elena stared blankly at the PowerPoint presentation on her office computer and then down at the time on the left of the screen. It was 1:00 a.m. The board presentation, called "Project Flintstone," wasn't finished. To prevent leaks of inside information from their mergers and acquisitions transactions, all of the projects were assigned a code name. Their client, the buyer, was *Fred*, and the seller was *Barney*. Elena didn't know who'd come up with these code names. She did know that both companies had objected to being named *Wilma*, a woman's name. Since a merger was a marriage of sorts, she wondered what was worse: being marginalized as a woman in a pending marriage, or marrying another man in a gay wedding. She grimaced, thinking of Francisco, her gay, Latino dad in Mexico. Then she smiled as she warmly thought further about him. He'd never survive a place like this, and at times, she felt like she couldn't, either. But she knew she would anyway.

As a financial analyst at Goldman Sachs, Elena had worked and reworked the Flintstone financial models on the Excel spreadsheet for weeks so that all she had to do was drop in the closing price of the target company's common stock and let the software application update all of the numbers. But for some reason, the spreadsheet showed an error in the bottom of column XY-178.

Obviously, something was wrong with the roll-up, but she couldn't ascertain what it was. The problem was that the cell in question pulled data from various calculations that were embedded in some forty-eight separate pages that covered over twenty-five other transactions.

She clicked through each embedded cell, painstakingly checking each formula, one by one, to no avail. *Christ*, she thought. Once completed, she still had to input the data into their PowerPoint and reorder the summary bullets for the board presentation at 10:00 a.m. To make matters worse, Richard, her boss, had insisted that she switch the colors from green and gold to red, white, and blue. Apparently, several of the board members were traditional conservatives with strong ties to the Republican party. Richard's theory, she presumed, was that changing the colors would help neutralize objections, thereby ensuring the signing of the acquisition and the collection of Goldman's fee. She shrugged while rolling her eyes.

Elena pushed the computer screen aside. She knew she needed a break, but there wasn't any more time. She stood and looked out the window of her shared office on the thirty-ninth floor at 200 West Street in the Goldman Sachs global headquarters in lower Manhattan. From her window, she could see out over the Hudson River to the glimmering lights of New Jersey. When she heard a knock on her door, she turned to see Eric, her supervisor.

"How's it going?" he asked.

"Not so good," she answered. "Still some bugs in the spreadsheet. Do you know who used this model for the last transaction?"

"Maybe Weisel," Eric answered. "Shall I call him?"

"At this hour?"

"Sure. He's just a grunt analyst."

"Like me?" she said with a smile.

"Exactly," Eric answered. "Cannon fodder."

When Eric reached over and picked up her phone to make the call, she gently put her hand on the receiver. "I'll get there," she said. "Just give me a little more time."

He nodded reluctantly.

"It's the wrong time for this question, Eric," she said, changing the subject, "but doesn't this exercise strike you as somewhat metaphysical?"

"What do you mean?"

"I mean, the board's not going to see this spreadsheet with the underlying data. And even if they did, it wouldn't matter. They've already decided to buy the company."

"Maybe, but maybe not," he answered. "You never know."

She nodded, as if in agreement. It was only a $2 billion acquisition, which while big by any standard, wasn't anything special for Goldman.

"The deal isn't a sure thing," he said. "To be honest, the premium's too high. Our client's paying too much."

"A forty-five percent premium is on the high side, but it's supported by the projection," she answered.

Eric smirked. "Yeah, once you've removed every conceivable synergy out of the pro forma and rolled it forward on a static basis."

Elena understood. She'd been an analyst at Goldman for well over a year since graduating from Boston College and had learned most of the lingo. Perhaps most interesting to her was the concept of *pro forma*: a decrease in the historical expenses, or *synergies*, of two companies on a combined basis in order to increase their combined profitability and, therefore, justify an acquisition. Similarly, a *projection* took that pro forma model and ran it into the future, thereby increasing the forward profitability of the combined companies severalfold. The concepts themselves were perfectly sound. The question, as Eric had noted, was how much synergy was reasonable.

"Okay," she said, "but back to the question. Richard said all I needed to do was change the colors for their board and move the 'projection' bullet below the 'strategic compulsion' bullet."

"Richard said that?" he asked.

"Yup," she answered.

"Well, he'd know," Eric said. She could see that he was puzzled, probably by her direct interaction with Richard, Eric's boss, and realized she'd said too much.

"Like I said," she reiterated, "metaphysical."

"In terms of the deal, yes," he said. "In terms of your career, no."

"Got it," she answered.

She wanted to touch the base of her nose, indicating to Eric that she could still see the white of what looked like his last coke line, but decided against it. There wasn't anyone else around to see it, and letting him know she had his number wasn't going to advance her career. *Career*, she thought, as she redirected her attention back to the spreadsheet. Was that all that mattered to her? *Apparently*. Why else would she be crunching numbers in the middle of the night?

Elena sat back at her desk and again turned her attention to the screen. She clicked through each of the embedded formulas one by one. An hour later, she ascertained where the error was in an iterative loop. She made the correction and transferred the revised data into the PowerPoint presentation before turning her attention to its colors. She thought changing the colors at 4:00 a.m. was nothing but ridiculous. She played with the formatting for a while and then did a search online for instructions. The answer she pulled up looked easy enough to step through, and when completed, the new colors quickly rippled throughout the presentation. She thought that the revised slides looked like a Republican convention from the '80s. All that was needed to complete it was an audio of a large woman singing "God Bless America" with too much vibrato. As a Mexican woman, the presentation certainly didn't resonate with her. Would it work for a traditional male board? She doubted it. But then again, Richard was always right, and everyone at Goldman knew it.

Having finished the presentation, she wanted to head over to Richard's place. Only three blocks away, it was just a short walk and would be the fastest path to sleep. Plus, it was so much nicer than her dumpy little apartment on the Lower East Side. She knew he wouldn't mind but quickly realized that climbing in bed with him could just turn him on, and then she'd never get any sleep. Besides, there was always the risk that someone from the firm would see her, and their relationship would be outed. She was perfectly fine with that, but Richard wasn't. When she'd wanted to disclose the budding relationship to human resources and confirm that it was completely consensual, Richard had objected. "Premature," he'd said. "Besides, they'll only transfer you out of my group." She knew she didn't want that, and at the time, they'd been together only a month or so, anyway.

Elena picked up her phone and clicked on the firm's Uber account. It wouldn't take her that much longer to get to her own apartment, and then she could have her choice of what to wear to the board meeting the next day. "Five minutes," the application indicated. She picked up her overcoat and headed to the elevator bank.

After a short night at home, Elena returned to the Goldman office the next morning feeling tired but grateful for the sleep she'd had. She was a little late, but she still had plenty of time to complete her work. She turned on her computer and pulled up the presentation. To finalize it, she removed all of the code names, changing *Fred* to the actual name of the buyer and *Barney* to the actual name of the seller. Then she carefully proofed each of the slides and ran the presentation as a slideshow for an additional check. She corrected some of the bullets that didn't fly in the way the others did and resaved it. Then she noticed that she hadn't reordered the summary bullets, as Richard had specifically asked. She quickly moved the bullet in the second summary slide on "strategic compulsion" to the top and moved the "projection" bullet to the bottom, as he'd directed. Then she ran the slideshow one more time to confirm the correction and resaved the file. As instructed, she then sent a copy by email to Richard and to the copy center, where they'd create hard copies to be distributed to the board. To be safe, she retained a final copy on her laptop. Then she walked around the corner to Richard's office to make sure he had downloaded the presentation to his laptop.

"Beatrice, have you seen Richard?" she asked. Beatrice, a younger Black woman, was his executive assistant.

"He's in a meeting," she answered without looking up.

"He's got Flintstone at ten, right?"

Beatrice pulled up his calendar on her computer. "Right," she said.

"Shall we get the presentation onto his laptop?" Elena asked rhetorically.

Beatrice looked nervous. "He doesn't like anyone using his laptop, but you're right. I think we'd better." She retrieved it from his office and clicked on the email icon, turning the computer away from Elena so that she couldn't see the screen.

"Something's top secret?" Elena asked.

Beatrice started typing on his computer but didn't immediately answer. "Tell him it's on his desktop under Flintstone."

"Got it," Elena said.

Beatrice shut the laptop. "I know I shouldn't ask, but are the two of you still an item?" she said, making eye contact with Elena for the first time.

Elena didn't respond. She knew Richard hadn't told Beatrice about them and presumed she was snooping. "Item?" Elena asked, feigning ignorance.

Beatrice smiled. "Just don't say I didn't warn you," she said, raising an eyebrow but ending her eye contact. "And you didn't hear it from me."

"Excuse me?" Elena said. But Beatrice had already left her station to return the laptop to Richard's office.

Elena then went to the copy room to get the presentation books, which were already printed, copied, and spiral-bound. She picked them up from the tray labeled "Outbox" and put them in her briefcase before heading to the restroom for a final appearance check. She'd worn a maroon designer suit with a tight-fitting blazer and a skirt that was just long enough to be professional but short enough to reveal her long legs and lean figure. She fluffed her hair in the restroom mirror and reapplied a sharp red lipstick. A careful inspection of her eyes revealed the brunt of the short night, but their deep brown color against her long black hair remained striking. Sometimes she wondered how other people saw her. Possibly as Italian, she guessed, particularly with her first name. She'd always felt 100 percent Latina on the inside, but on the outside, she technically was only half. She knew that they liked having a Latina woman for their numbers at Goldman. That was clear. Less clear was how they felt about their professionals looking too Latino—or so she suspected.

After a ride in the firm's limousine service, she, Eric, and Richard entered the clients' offices in Midtown, where they were directed to the boardroom on the forty-second floor. When they entered, the room was empty. Richard took a seat to the right of the head of the board table, and Eric and Elena sat on the seats against the wall, illustrating their subordinate roles. After a while, the chief executive officer and the chief financial officer entered.

"Hello, Richard," the CEO said. "Thanks for all of your work getting us to this point."

"My pleasure," Richard said. "Phillip, these are my colleagues, Eric and Elena."

Phillip shook their hands and introduced them to the CFO. "Have some coffee and food," he said, pointing to the spread at the back of the room. "The board will be here shortly."

The board arrived after another ten minutes. Elena noticed that all of the board members were men, save for one, and all of them were White, including the lone woman. She crossed her legs and tugged at her skirt, seeking to lengthen it. Following brief introductions, the CEO announced that they had a quorum and called the meeting to order.

The CEO made a general presentation to the board about the acquisition, and the CFO discussed the financial impact, describing the transaction as modestly dilutive to earnings for a year, possibly two, but moving into targeted accretion on a projected basis by year three. Elena didn't think the financial presentation was compelling, and several board members mumbled quietly. She couldn't hear exactly what they were saying, but it sounded as if they believed the buyer was paying too much for the target. Elena looked over at Richard, who had noticed them as well, but he simply smiled back at her.

When the CFO finished, Richard introduced himself again and expressed his appreciation for the board's selection of Goldman as their adviser for the transaction. As always, Richard dominated the room with his mere presence. He was strikingly handsome, and his stature put him just a little bit taller than the CEO. His broad shoulders filled his Armani suit, and his emerald green eyes, accented by his shirt and tie, could pierce an onlooker as if they were lasers.

Richard opened the presentation, which flashed on the screen to the left of his head. Knowing what it contained, Elena instead watched three older board members as Richard spoke. She tried not to roll her eyes when one smiled as the colors of the first slide projected onto the large screen.

"As you know," Richard continued, "we had to pay a hefty price for this asset. We'd like to see a projection with accretion at year one. While we're hopeful, as previously mentioned, that might not happen." Elena tried not to smile at his choice of words. He'd intentionally started with the phrase *had to pay* in the past tense, rather than *will have to pay* in the future tense, suggesting that the transaction was already done and that this approval process was a mere formality. And while it was true that the forward accretion "might not happen in year one," it was truer to say that it wouldn't happen in year one or year two; year three was a possibility but questionable as well. More importantly, while Richard was talking about the problematic "projection" bullet she'd moved down, he kept the "strategic compulsion" bullet on the screen. In other words, he was focusing them visually on the strategy of the transaction (its strength), while talking to the projection bullet (its issue), thereby minimizing its effect.

"That's why," Richard continued, "we're going to focus you again on the 'strategic compulsion' for this deal." Now he spoke directly to that bullet, which he kept on the top of the screen. Elena watched as the board members continued to look directly at the bullet she'd thankfully remembered to move up.

"The bottom line is this," Richard said. "Either we accept this dilution, or we accept that this asset will be purchased by a competitor. In that case, we lose the topline growth and end up at the same EPS without the deal—a decrease anyway." The board members listened without reaction or comment. "So, the question is really this: Do you want to have a competitor going forward or not? We at Goldman think the answer is 'not.'" Elena noticed that he still hadn't let the projection bullet fly onto the screen. It was as if he were a magician, focusing their attention on the stone under one cup while cleverly moving it under another cup. She looked over at the board members, who now nodded in agreement.

"I don't want to bore you with the rest of these slides; I know you each have the hard copy that my colleague distributed," he continued. "So I'm going to thumb through them quickly because they illustrate that the price is still reasonable, and I'm here to confirm that Goldman will be opining that the transaction is fair, from a financial point of view, to your shareholders notwithstanding."

Richard then quickly went through the "projection" bullet before continuing through the balance of the slides without interruption. When he finished, there were no questions, and when the CEO asked for a vote on the merger, the board unanimously approved it. Thereafter, the CEO stated that the business of the meeting was complete and that the board meeting was adjourned.

After some congratulatory handshakes and thanks, the board members left the boardroom. The CEO again thanked Richard without readdressing the rest of the team and excused himself. Richard, Eric, and Elena then left and headed to the elevators that led to the lobby.

"Nice," Eric said to Richard.

Richard grinned with his perfectly white teeth. He hadn't lied to the board. And he'd given them copies of the data. But he'd persuaded them, maybe even manipulated them, by playing to their desires and biases. Richard's strong intellect was compelling. It wasn't so much his command of the numbers as his ability to read his audience, give them what they wanted, and encourage them to do what he wanted. That, she felt, plus his incredible quarterback good looks made it all work. It was easy to see why she too was drawn to him. Everything about Richard was compelling.

"What'd we get on the deal?" Eric asked, opening the door to the car for Richard, leaving Elena to walk around to the other side on her own.

"One and a quarter," Richard said.

"Nice," Eric answered. "So, about twenty-five million to us? Citi would have done it for half that."

"Yes," Richard said. "But would Citi have recommended that price for the target and got the deal through the board? That's what the CEO wanted, and we delivered."

Elena could see he was pleased with himself. She knew she was too junior to add much to the conversation, so she remained silent, as expected.

When they reached the Goldman offices, Eric got out of the front seat of the car, and Richard turned to Elena while they both remained in the back.

"So, celebrate tonight?" he said quietly.

"Sure," she answered.

"Dinner at eight? Ruminate?"

"Yes," she said and smiled, following him as he left the car.

Later that evening, Elena arrived at Ruminate a little before 8:00 p.m. Ruminate was a popular bar with upscale dining in Tribeca just across the highway from the Goldman offices. It was always busy after work, but like the rest of downtown, the place tended to clear out earlier than similar bars located farther uptown.

Richard wasn't in the waiting area when Elena arrived, so she headed over to the far end of the bar. The patrons were the same predictable crowd: professional men, mostly White, in their expensive "business casual" sport coats, all having a drink before heading back up to their offices to complete another long night at work. While walking, she could feel heads turn as she passed. The maroon cocktail dress she wore was arguably on the short side, and the heels of her shoes were just a bit taller than was customary in the United States. The fullness of her breasts against her long dark hair completed the look. She knew there was a power associated with her appearance, but she didn't mind that. Besides, they couldn't go dancing after dinner if she'd worn a traditional business pantsuit.

When the bartender approached her, she ordered a soda; if it was to be a long night, she didn't want to flame out too early. After almost an hour of casual conversation with two men at the bar, she saw Richard arrive. He was still wearing his dark Armani suit from the board meeting, and when he hugged her to say hello, she could smell the alcohol on his breath.

"Sorry I'm late," he said, glancing down at his Rolex.

"All good," she answered. "You've got a head start on me?"

"A couple," he said. "Some of us snuck out for a quickie."

She felt a little disappointed but decided to let it pass.

"No worries," he said, as they headed back to the hostess. "We'll catch you up quickly."

Once seated at a secluded table toward the back of the restaurant, Richard ordered a negroni on the rocks for each of them. She preferred margaritas, but she'd learned that they raised eyebrows in the professional world of Manhattan. She watched Richard engage with the waiter about the various wines on the list before ordering a Bordeaux, usually four to six years old, as he always did anyway.

"You look great," he said, reaching over to discreetly kiss her after the waiter left.

"Thanks," she said. "Quite a day."

"Quite," he said.

"I saw the deal's already been announced?"

"Yes," he said. "Stock's down eighteen percent in after-hours trading."

"You knew it would be," she answered.

He smiled silently, while chewing on the bread.

They ordered a pâté appetizer, salads, and their main course. He selected the duck, and she opted for the short ribs.

"Pot roast," he said. "Again?"

"Comfort food," she said. "Again!"

He smiled and toasted her. "To my favorite Mexican analyst." They raised their glasses and drank.

She didn't really like the *Mexican* reference but didn't know exactly why. "You know," she said, "I'm not really Mexican."

"Really?" he asked.

"I was born in California. San Francisco, to be exact. And my mother's Scandinavian." While the information was accurate, the negative inference drawn from it was not. She was Mexican, and she'd always been proud of it.

"I didn't realize that," he said without following up further.

Elena wondered how much he actually did know about her. Did he care? She knew a lot about him, either as a result of their conversations or because of his standing in the office. More importantly, she'd taken a genuine interest in him and wanted to know everything about him.

"We've been dating what, maybe two or three months now?" she asked.

"Yeah, that's about right."

"So, what do you know about me?" she asked. "Besides my being Mexican." The question had a bit of an edge, but after working through the negroni, she was just tipsy enough to assert it.

"What do you mean?" he answered.

"You're ducking the question," she said.

"No, I'm eating duck!" he answered with a grin as he continued to chew.

She didn't respond, keeping him on the hook.

"Okay," he said while taking another bite. "Let me see: You went to Boston College and graduated at the top of your class in economics and math. You've been at Goldman a year and a half. You're an analyst in tech banking, mergers and acquisitions. You grew up in Mexico City, though you're apparently a US citizen. You have a sister in San Francisco, and let me think . . ." He paused before continuing. "You have sexy long legs, perfectly shaped breasts, and you love to give head." He grinned. "How'd I do?"

"Not bad," she said, feeling the rub of his leg against hers under the table. What she thought, however, differed. He'd gotten the professional information right—the stuff from her résumé. But the rest was at least half wrong and more so with respect to the sex. He really knew nothing about her dad or Rebecca—did he even know their names? More importantly, he mentioned nothing about the person she was: her ambition, her sensitivity, her insecurity, or her kind heart. Was she keeping her background private on purpose? Or had he just failed to take an interest in it? Perhaps the better question was whether or not she'd lost the traits that used to identify her—the sensitivity, the kindness, the empathy—in her desire to prove herself professionally. She hoped not. But it didn't seem to matter; kindness and empathy weren't the traits they respected at Goldman.

"But," she added, "you really do have a lot to learn."

He smiled. "Sex stuff, I hope?"

She chuckled back. "And more," she said with a raised eyebrow. She felt the brush of his leg again under the table, which this time remained firmly against her calf.

Her phone then beeped softly, and she felt its vibration in her handbag. "Do you mind?" she asked. "I'm just an analyst; I should check it."

He nodded as she checked the phone. It was a text from her father. "It's my father," she said, while reading it. "He wants me to come home for Christmas." Her father always wanted her to come home for Christmas, and he knew she would if work permitted. But this request seemed more significant; she wondered why.

"Then you should go," Richard said. "Why not?"

Elena thought about his response. It was a *you* and not a *we*. It bothered her just a little, because going together didn't seem to even cross his mind. Was that because he had no interest? Or was it because she hadn't invited him? She didn't know.

"Why don't you come too?" she asked.

He squinted. "To Mexico?" The tone of his question answered her question. Richard had zero desire to go to Mexico, even if it was to see her family.

"I could make it worth your while," she added. She disliked her words, but once spoken, they couldn't be retrieved.

He nodded as if considering the question while evading a clear response. So she decided to let it go. She wasn't sure she wanted to go home for Christmas, anyway, let alone bring him with her. Still, his dismissal made her feel a bit insecure.

"Why don't we go dancing?" she asked. "We have every reason to celebrate."

He retracted his foot before responding this time. "I'm bushed," he said. "How about you teach me more about sex?"

It wasn't the answer she'd hoped for, but she'd clearly opened the door. Besides, it was Wednesday, and she too was exhausted. Furthermore, the last thing she needed was to run into some of his friends at a club, which usually resulted in her pretending she wasn't with Richard and then watching his friends do lines together.

"Honestly, I'd just rather be with you tonight," he added.

"Okay," she said.

Richard caught the waiter's eye and motioned for the check. It was always understood that he would pay. While she'd initially opposed this, the fact was that his salary dwarfed hers. He never seemed to mind, anyway. More importantly, she couldn't begin to afford the fancy restaurants and fine wines that were a necessary part of his lifestyle. When the check was delivered, Richard signed the receipt, and they headed for the door.

After a short cab ride, Elena and Richard arrived at his place in Tribeca. The condo was about a quarter of the twenty-third floor in a new residential tower. The place had walls of glass that spanned from the floor to the ceiling, with views looking out over the Hudson River and then north into the heart of Midtown Manhattan. The furniture was all modern, in iron and black leather, and the floors were made of dark marble. The kitchen cabinets looked as if they were made of plastic laminate, but Richard had made clear they were custom-made by an Italian designer. When they'd started dating, she'd pulled up the purchase price on Zillow: $16 million. The amount had astounded her, but she knew that as a managing director at Goldman, he could easily afford it. She'd later learned that he didn't carry a mortgage on the place.

As they walked to his bedroom, she felt Richard removing her dress, so she kicked off her heels. Her head was still spinning, but she'd sobered up a bit in the cab on the way back. While the lights in the bedroom were off, the room resonated with light from the moon and the glare of the city lights. He removed his clothes and stood gazing at her while she lay on the bed. His arms had the same blond hair, just enough to be masculine. His body was naturally lean and tight; his biceps were muscular, and his calves and thighs were full. Light hair covered the top of his chest, trailing from his pecs to his groin, which was already growing thick and hard. Most compelling to Elena, though, were his translucent green eyes that dominated her with merely a gaze.

"Mexico. It's important to you, right?" he asked.

His question surprised her. "I dunno. Maybe," she answered. She walked over to the bed and sat next to him on it.

"Just the way you reacted before. I noticed it."

She nodded.

"You matter to me, you know?" he said. "Sometimes, I don't think you see that." He smiled. "So I'll go—if you want me to."

She hugged him. "Yes," she answered. "I want you to."

"And you'll make it worth my while?" He winked.

"If you're good." She winked back.

He kissed her gently at first and then more firmly. After a while, she felt him rolling on top of her. The strength of his body was quickly on her, around her, and then inside her. When she recovered enough to again look at him, she felt the power of his green eyes penetrate her being. She thought he was incredible in every way. Within moments, she felt her body convulse with pleasure, and then, always the gentleman, he followed.

He was good, she thought. *Very good*. And meeting her family? He was taking the next step. Was she falling for him? She wasn't sure. *Maybe*, she thought. *Probably. Yes.* When he reached over, she snuggled up against his body before falling asleep.

Chapter 3

Rebecca left her flat in San Francisco and headed south toward her grandparents' country club in Atherton. She loved the tall skyscrapers and vibrant life of San Francisco's densely populated streets. The urban lifestyle stood in stark contrast to that of Atherton, which had no commercial buildings or even sidewalks and was instead comprised entirely of single-family homes on large lots of an acre or more. She'd heard that suburban Atherton was the wealthiest town in the United States; having lived there, she didn't doubt it.

Rebecca continued on the freeway for about thirty minutes before taking the Atherton exit. Then she proceeded for another couple of miles before turning into the tree-lined entrance of the Menlo Circus Club. She drove through its white gates and followed the Kentucky fencing that lined each side of the driveway before continuing past the polo fields on the left and the stables on the right. She saw the valet at the porte cochere in front of the club's entrance, waiting for guests to arrive, but she elected instead to self-park her car in the back of the lot. She understood why many elderly club members liked the valet but couldn't for the life of her understand why anyone else would bother with them. After all, the grounds were perfectly level, and the parking lot wasn't any larger than that of the neighborhood Safeway store.

Rebecca checked the clock before turning off the ignition of her white BMW 5 Series. She was a little early; the drive hadn't taken as long as she'd expected. She shut the car door, not bothering to lock it, and started toward the country club before reconsidering. Maybe she'd stretch her legs and take a walk around the block first. She felt a little bit anxious, and the prospect of some fresh air seemed inviting before the dinner with her grandparents.

She walked back through the same gated entrance of the club and headed across the street to her old high school, Sacred Heart. She knew the grounds would be locked, as they always were on Sundays, necessitating a long walk or drive to the other side of their sixty-acre campus to pass through their gated entrance after getting clearance from the security guard. She wondered if, by chance, the hole in the fence behind a bush near the soccer field was still there—the one she and her friends had used from time to time to escape undetected from school. She quickly found the right spot. The bushes were larger than she remembered from high school, but the covert entrance was still getting plenty of use. She pulled a bush back and entered the soccer field through the hole in the fence.

The school grounds were as beautifully kept as she remembered. The cross at the top of the third story on the red-brick main building towered over the campus below. The windows were surrounded by ornate wooden detailing, all painted white and capped by the dark slate tile of the French-style roof. The Olympic-size pool and spectator seating were on one side, and the football stadium was on the other side. Between them were the numerous tennis courts, additional soccer fields, the baseball diamond, and the lower and middle school facilities. All were newly built or recently renovated.

Rebecca remembered the fundraising activities conducted for some of the new construction. They'd built a new performing arts and academic center with a price tag of $90 million when she'd been a student there. That building now bore the name of her grandparents: *Stimpson*. Ironically, most of the students, like the Stimpsons, weren't Catholic. But what they all had in common was wealth. The school's impressive architecture, grounds, and athletic facilities looked more like a university than a high school; it made the American School of Puerto Vallarta she'd also attended as a child look like a joke. These places of wealth—Menlo Circus Club, Sacred Heart, and Stanford University, located only a couple of blocks away—seemed so foreign and removed from the life she'd lived as a child in Mexico. *Is that my life anymore?* she wondered. *Apparently not.*

Rebecca's cell phone rang, so she pulled it from her bag to check the caller. "Elena," it read. A call from her sister wasn't unusual, but it wasn't common, either. While they certainly weren't estranged, they hadn't been as close as they used to be for some time. She loved her twin; she was certain of that. And she knew Elena felt the same way about her. But since she'd left Sayulita, a distance had grown between them—a resentment, maybe even an unspoken anger. She suspected Elena was calling her about their dad's text; she was curious about it as well. So she pressed "Answer," hoping not to have missed the call by delaying to pick it up.

"Hey, girl," she said. "What's up?"

"Sister!" Elena answered. "I'm just heading back from the office."

"On Sunday? Again?"

"Right. You don't need to say it; I already know I'm a loser."

"Uh, yeah!"

"So," Elena continued, directing the conversation, "did you get the text from Dad?"

"Yes," Rebecca answered. "I'd just been thinking about Mexico, actually."

"And?"

"I think I'm going," Rebecca said. "I haven't been there for a while, so why not? What about you? Please say yes! It's always weird going home without you."

Rebecca thought about what she'd said. It *was* weird going home when Elena wasn't there, but it wouldn't necessarily be easy going home with her, either. Simply put, their history was complicated, and in many ways, their differences remained unresolved. The fact of the matter was that Elena could be unpredictable, and sometimes that made Rebecca anxious. As she waited for a response, she wondered if Elena had similar concerns.

"I'm in," Elena slowly answered. "It'll be tough to get away from work, but whatever."

Rebecca knew that was true, but she wondered if her sister also might be hedging. Rebecca didn't want to talk about that, so she changed the subject. "Hey, it seems like Dad really wants us to come," she said. "Do you know why? I mean, is there a backstory here?"

"That was my reaction, too; that's part of why I called."

"You know him better," Rebecca said. "You two are the close ones." She regretted her words once she'd spoken them. She wondered if they had a bit of an edge—maybe even an implied accusation?

"I wouldn't say *that*," Elena replied. "Maybe we talk more."

"Did you ask?"

"Kind of. He evaded the questions. But it was pretty clear he wanted us to come home. Together."

"*Hmm*," Rebecca said.

"Exactly," Elena answered. "I don't know." She paused before continuing. "Follow-up question?"

"I'm listening," Rebecca said.

"What do you think about my bringing Richard along?"

"To Mexico? *Hmm*," Rebecca said.

"Yeah, risky, right?" Elena responded.

"Not so much risky," Rebecca answered, "as surprising. Are you that serious? You know, bringing him to meet the parents?"

"It's just Dad!" Elena answered. "We don't have a mom!"

"News flash—not," Rebecca responded. "But it's still a big step, don't you think?"

"I'm not worried about that. I just don't want you or Dad to feel left out or weird."

"Well, I won't," Rebecca said. "I'd like to meet him, actually."

"Just don't wear anything too sexy," Elena said.

Rebecca knew the comment was supposed to be flattering. On one level, it was, but on another, it was not. Sometimes Elena didn't seem to understand what she was saying—or so it seemed. Rebecca decided to just ignore it.

"I'm sure Dad'll deal," she answered. "He might actually like Richard, you know, if you're happy and all."

"Right," Elena said.

Rebecca didn't think Elena sounded convinced. "So, then, you'll go the whole time?" she asked. "What was it, seven days?"

"Yes, I think so," Elena said. "It did seem important to him—coming, the dates, all of it."

"Okay," Rebecca responded. "I just have to tell the grandparents now that I'm not going to be here for Christmas."

"You're meeting them for the regular Sunday dinner at the country club?"

"Yup."

"Good luck with that one. I mean, they're so understanding and flexible, right?" she said with obvious irony.

"Right," Rebecca said.

She knew that Elena disliked her grandparents. Sometimes she wondered if that was because Elena didn't have grandparents of her own. Still, she'd asked Elena more than once not to criticize them and was tired of hearing it. So she decided to ignore this comment as well.

"Hey, send me your flight information when you book it, and I'll coordinate around it."

"Okay," Elena said. "Bye."

"Bye," she replied.

Rebecca put her phone back in her bag and hurried toward the club, hoping she wouldn't be late because of the call and her detour. When she arrived at the entrance to the club's dining room, the valet opened the door and greeted her.

"Good evening, Ms. Stimpson."

"Good evening," she said.

While she appreciated the way the staff remembered each member's name, she found it irritating that they continued to address her by her grandparents' name, Stimpson, rather than her own last name, Montoya. She presumed it was a logical mistake and a harmless error, but she wondered if it was a result of her grandparents' instructions.

Rebecca passed through the dining area, which was populated almost entirely by elderly White people, and continued until she saw her grandparents toward the back at a window table overlooking the polo fields. When she reached them, they stood to greet her, kissing her on the cheek and forehead.

"Hi, honey," her grandmother, Beverly, said.

Her grandfather, Ben, smiled. "Thanks for coming down."

She took one of the two empty seats and opened the menu on her place setting. As always, the table had a white tablecloth, and the decor for the Sunday dinner was formal.

"Sorry I'm late," she said.

Rebecca noticed that her grandparents were well on their way through their first martinis. Their drinks looked good, and she considered partaking, but then she thought better of the idea. While they could manage driving back to their nearby home easily enough, getting back to San Francisco for her was another matter.

When the waiter returned, he took their orders for dinner and then left again as their conversation started.

"So," Ben started, "how's McKenzie?"

"Work's fine," she answered. "More of the same, you know, management consulting and all."

"Is there anything catching your interest? A new project?"

"Yes, actually," she started. "I found this incredible art class just a couple blocks away, and the teacher seems really good. I just sneak out of work around five on Tuesdays and Thursdays, paint with them for an hour or so, and get back to work by seven, grabbing a bite to eat on the way back."

"Sounds risky," her grandfather said.

"I don't want to be scandalous," she continued, "but last week, they brought in nudes for us to practice with: a man on Tuesday and a woman on Thursday. The woman had an absolutely perfect body—toned but feminine. She was pretty easy to paint. The man was a little older and kinda fat. It was much harder to paint him."

"That's great, dear," her grandmother responded, "but I think your grandfather's asking you about your job."

"Right," she answered, muzzling her enthusiasm. "We have a new project for a life sciences company."

She started to explain when the waiter returned. After serving their salads, he opened a bottle of wine and waited for her grandfather to taste and approve it before pouring each of them a glass.

"I never understood that stuff," Ben responded. "At Chevron, we're—what do you call it?"

"Brick and mortar," she said. "Low tech."

"Right," he answered. "You know, there's a lot of money in low tech, too. When I was there running the Alaska division, we made a fortune cutting production for just a week or so each month to keep prices up. The profit ran right to the bottom line and ultimately resulted in my promotion to CEO of the company."

Rebecca nodded respectfully. She'd heard the story a number of times and suspected she was going to hear it again. It was a common theme, particularly after her grandfather was well into his martini. But she didn't mind. She knew his intentions were good, and now that he was retired, he relied on the stories of prior times to participate in the conversation or to provide her with appropriate guidance. She wondered if her grandmother tired of the repetition but didn't notice any reaction, one way or the other. Instead, Beverly watched her husband intently, as if listening to the story for the first time. Like her grandmother, Rebecca listened patiently as he spoke. After a while, the staff cleared their plates and served the main course.

Rebecca wasn't entirely sure what bored her more: Ben's job or her own. After a couple of years as a consultant at McKenzie, she knew she could do the work, but she seldom found it interesting. Many of her assignments revolved around running synergy numbers to justify the premiums paid for mergers and acquisitions. In the life science industry in which she specialized, that meant either removing excess "bodies" via a merger or a "RIF" (reduction in force) that was realized through a corporate restructuring. In either case, company management looked to McKenzie to assess and justify taking the necessary action.

Rebecca didn't like the idea of facilitating the termination of employees. But after studying economics at Stanford for years, she knew that business inefficiencies usually had to be eliminated, or the business would likely fail anyway. After running synergy numbers for almost two years, however, the exercise had become tougher for her. As the long days had passed, her experience had grown and her insight had become more respected. But she increasingly found herself gazing out the windows of her office tower at the Golden Gate Bridge, Alcatraz, and the bay below, wondering if this career was the right one for her. And while the art classes had at first seemed like a welcome recess, she'd recently noticed that it was getting harder and harder to return to the office when the class ended.

She returned her attention to her grandparents and listened patiently as they spoke about the various things going on with their friends' grandkids, waiting for the right time to broach the issue of Christmas vacation. When dessert was served, she considered her words carefully before tackling the topic.

"Are you going to Hawaii again for Christmas this year?" she asked. "It looks like I'm going to go down to see Dad in Mexico."

"Why on Earth would you do that?" her grandmother asked. "You know, Hawaii is so much nicer."

"And safer," her grandfather added. "I feel so sorry for those people down there, living with all of those drugs, gangs, and violence."

"You know," her grandmother continued, "that's why they all want to leave."

Rebecca nodded without responding. It was tiresome listening to Ben tell the same stories about his success, but it was much worse having them speak about her childhood home as if it were a drug den. Besides, the only place in Mexico they'd visited was their beloved Four Seasons in Punta Mita, so how would they know?

"Well," she started, preparing herself, "he is my father, and I want to see him."

Beverly looked at her husband before responding. "I'm not sure what he is, sweetheart, but our son, Derek, is your father, and he always will be."

"Right," Rebecca acknowledged. Why did they need to go over this time and time again? She knew Derek was her father, but Francisco was, too. She was tired of their belittling him and her sister. "Well, I do love him and want to see him anyway," she continued.

"More than us?" her grandmother persisted. "We always spend Christmas together! We're counting on your coming—the whole family is!"

"Why don't you visit him some other time?" her grandfather asked.

"I'd love to go to Hawaii, but I've been with you every Christmas since I moved here," she said.

Her grandparents continued to look at her but stayed silent.

"This one's important to Dad," she added, intentionally again referring to Francisco as her father, "and I don't want to let him down this time."

Rebecca watched as her grandmother pursed her lips and her grandfather terminated his eye contact, looking down again at the dessert menu, despite having ordered before the conversation had begun.

"Well, I guess she's gotta do what she's gotta do," he said to his wife. "That's just the way kids are these days."

Rebecca thought the remark was condescending. She wasn't a kid, a child, or a girl. She was a woman and an adult at that. She appreciated that they wanted her to be with them for Christmas. They loved her. But that didn't mean Francisco wasn't her father, or that she shouldn't spend Christmas with him now and then.

After finishing the apple cobbler that the waiter had brought, they slowly sipped an after-dinner port wine in awkward silence. When they'd finished, Rebecca rose to leave. "I'm sorry I can't go with you this year," she said. "But maybe next year." She kissed her grandmother on the cheek and her grandfather on the forehead.

"Thanks for coming down, dear," her grandmother said.

"We'll see you next week?" her grandfather asked.

"Yes," Rebecca answered. After gathering her jacket and bag, she headed for the exit.

Rebecca thought about the conversation as she walked back to her car. She appreciated everything her grandparents had done for her—taking her in, paying for high school, paying for college, and supplementing her income so that she could live in a nice apartment in San Francisco. But their guidance and demands were becoming tiring. She missed her family—Francisco and Elena—and she missed the life she'd known with them in Mexico. She knew that her time living with them in Sayulita had ended. Still, they remained her family. So, if her father wanted her to come home for Christmas, she would be there—period. Her grandparents would just have to adjust.

Chapter 4

THE MONTHS BEFORE CHRISTMAS PASSED QUICKLY FOR FRANCISCO. In Mexico, there was almost always a fiesta of one type or another, but with its strong Catholic heritage, none was as special or sacred as Christmas. Francisco wanted his family to be together during the holiday, and he wanted them to again feel happy being together. So he was pleased that his twins had agreed to come home to Sayulita for the week, and he wanted to make sure everything went well for their dinner that night on Christmas Eve.

As was always the case, his home and his restaurant, the Vista Linda, were fully decorated with Christmas cheer: A tall pine, covered with red and green ornaments, streamers of silver and gold, and bright white lights rested peacefully in the living room of their home, and another tree, elaborately decorated, stood in the entrance of the restaurant. Similarly, the bamboo railings of the decks throughout the home and the restaurant were wrapped with garland and strung with the same white lights.

Francisco walked over to the Christmas tree and looked down at the presents beneath it. With little difficulty, he remembered the gifts his girls had enjoyed year after year under similar Christmas trees: the red, yellow, and blue plastic beach toys, comprised of two shovels, two buckets, and the forms to make castles and sea shells of sand; the My Little Pony toy collection, of which

Rainbow Dash was the clear favorite; the matching blue and red bodysuits he'd used to block out the sun, which were lifesavers; the purple and pink princess costumes, complete with tiaras and wands; the boogie boards, and a couple years later, the surfboards, which Rebecca had quickly mastered but Elena never did; and the leather boots, tube tops, and spiky heels, which they'd both loved but relentlessly fought over. The memories filled him with feelings of satisfaction and love.

Francisco left the home and walked into the adjacent office of the restaurant he owned. He'd been running it since his girls were just toddlers, now well over twenty years. The weeks before and after Christmas were always the busiest nights; that Tuesday night would be no exception. His preference had been to close down the restaurant completely for the week his girls were back. He didn't need the distraction, and the lost income was irrelevant to him. But the sales from these key weeks were critical for the staff, and the tips over Christmas helped compensate for the slow times during the summer rains. So he knew he'd just have to juggle.

Francisco looked down at the screen of his office computer and worked through the profit and loss on the Excel spreadsheet one more time. The year had been a good one, but he had concerns looking forward. He turned to the restaurant's balance sheet. There was cash there. *Enough*, he thought, *but not a lot*. He remembered what it had been like when he was a waiter at the very same restaurant. He added 25 percent to the bonus column, saved the file, and shut down the computer. That would take care of the staff for the next several months. After that, who knew? He wondered if the business would be sold; he wondered if it should be. His daughters certainly didn't need to deal with a restaurant in Mexico. Regardless, there wasn't anything more he could do about it, and he didn't want to worry about it further—at least not now.

Francisco left the small office and walked up to the rooftop deck, located directly above the restaurant's main floor, to check on the arrangements for his family's dinner. As anticipated, there were place settings for four. He couldn't help feeling a little bit disappointed. He'd invited Consuela and Guillermo to join them, but they had declined, preferring instead to host the event. He wasn't surprised.

As anticipated, Rebecca had come to Sayulita alone, but Elena had brought a new boyfriend. So Francisco presumed it was serious. Richard had seemed nice enough when they'd met briefly earlier that day after checking into their hotel in Punta Mita. Francisco had wanted them to just stay with him at the house, but Richard had been reluctant. Richard seemed to dote on Elena, and he'd seemed skillfully charming with him. But was it too much? He doubted that his girls would ever bring home a boyfriend that he considered to be a truly worthy companion. Did all fathers feel that way? *Probably*, he thought. *But probably not as much.*

The bigger question for Francisco was how his girls would interact. They hadn't been physically together at the house since the time Rebecca had left almost a decade ago. That hadn't been good, and as far as he knew, the baggage remained. As twins, the two had always been inseparably close and completely interdependent in their youth. But they'd also seemed compelled to measure themselves through comparison: their appearance, their academics, their boyfriends, and unfortunately, their race. He knew all siblings did this. He also knew that with twins, it was worse, particularly with twins of the same gender, and arguably even more so with girls. Over the years, they'd seemed to work through a lot of that. But the difference of ethnicity and race, compounded now by their enormous disparity in wealth, had become too much—or so it seemed.

"What do you think, Consuela?" he asked.

"*Perfecto*," she answered.

"I want it to be perfect," he said.

"*Sí, patrón*, I know." She smiled. "It will be."

The tablecloth was white, and the flowers were fresh orchids. The setting was traditional Mexican pottery, with vibrantly painted yellow and blue plates. The glassware was all a deep blue, and the napkins all matched. The wineglasses were crystal, but the margarita glasses were thick Mexican glass, wide rimmed with a matching blue trim. Beyond the bamboo railing of the rooftop deck was the same panoramic view that the restaurant below held.

"How are you doing on the food—all good?" he asked.

"*Sí, patrón,*" Consuela said sarcastically. "I've prepared this same meal for the twins a thousand times—since they were babies. They will love it."

Francisco enjoyed the way Consuela called him *patrón*, meaning boss. It was her way of showing him that he wasn't her boss. He wished she would have consented to letting their restaurant chef prepare the meal rather than preparing it herself. He knew that the chef would have created a more impressive dinner, and Consuela's cooking was nothing special, with the risk of being kind of bad. This time he really wanted his girls to enjoy the meal. He also wanted to impress Elena's new boyfriend. But Consuela had insisted that she cook, so he'd reluctantly agreed.

"What about the heat?" he asked. "Should we get the umbrellas out until the sun sets?"

"*Sí,*" she answered, indicating with her tone that the right answer actually was no. "I'll get Guillermo to bring them."

"*Gracias,*" he said.

He turned to head back to the home, but she stepped in front of him, almost blocking his passage.

"So, Francisco, when are you going to tell them?" she asked. Her voice was unusually stern and direct.

Francisco knew he was stalling. But he wanted the time they had together to be fun, not dismal, and more importantly, he wanted his twins to have the time to start to reconcile their differences before it was too late. It all seemed silly, as he thought about it—maybe even just a rationalization. But he remained determined to try.

"It's Christmas Eve," he answered. "Give me a couple more days?"

Consuela shook her head. Having made her point, she picked up the extra linens and headed back down to the kitchen area. When Francisco was certain she'd left, he walked to the edge of the rooftop and lit up a joint, hoping to relax. After taking a deep pull, he gazed across the rooftop and paused to reflect. So much had changed in the thirty-some years since he'd first arrived in his youth. Then he was just an employee, a dish boy. Now, he was the owner.

Back then, the rooftop deck was nothing more than wooden slats nestled haphazardly over the gravel roof of the restaurant below and accessed by a wooden ladder that was nailed to the side of the building. Now, the floors were covered with the same beige marble that was found throughout the restaurant and home. The improvements created the perfect ambience for an upscale, private event. But the roof had lost its romantic charm and no longer provided the staff with the hidden getaway it once had. He took another draw of the joint and smiled as he remembered.

Francisco was only twentysomething when he first arrived at the restaurant with its rooftop deck. He saw the job advertisement posted in the local paper in Puerto Vallarta, called the owner, Jose, and took the bus from town out to Sayulita for an interview. In fact, there was no interview; instead, Jose put an apron on him and handed him a broom.

"The problem," Jose explained, "is the sand. Everyone wants to walk on the beach, but no one wants sand in the restaurant. That, and the rats. If you help me with those, you've got a job."

Francisco nodded. He'd do anything; he needed the money and a place to stay. He was overqualified, no doubt, but he didn't have many options. Having completed high school at an exclusive Catholic school in Mexico City, he'd started college, studying law at a prestigious university reserved for the children of the wealthy and elite. Those students regularly were the children of the traditional governmental party (PRI), as was the case for Francisco, or they were the children of wealthy businessmen, usually tied to the nationalized oil industry that generated much of Mexico's wealth. That preordained path had ended for Francisco when his parents cut him off. At the time, he presumed it was a temporary tool they'd used to redirect him. When over time they called less and less, he realized he was wrong.

Noticing that Francisco was riding the bus several hours from town each day to work, Jose offered him the in-law unit in the adjacent house. Jose was good to him, but Francisco lasted only a week as the sweeper in a restaurant. When Jose realized he could speak English fluently, and that his dashing looks were a natural draw for the women from abroad, he quickly promoted Francisco to headwaiter, reserving for him the best-tipping clients, typically Americans. But it wasn't the women who held Francisco's attention. Jose quickly figured that out but didn't mind, as long as Francisco kept his personal business personal. And that was how he met Derek.

Francisco noticed the group of gay men when they arrived for dinner at the restaurant. The guys in the group were all handsome, and they'd come without dates. They didn't get a lot of gay groups in Sayulita; most of that clientele remained in Puerto Vallarta proper. But Jose had been in the business long enough to know that gay men drank a lot and gave generous tips. So Francisco wasn't at all surprised when Jose had assigned him to wait on their table. The hostess took the men to the best table overlooking the bay, and after they'd settled in, Francisco went to the table to take their drink order.

"*Buenas noches*," he said. "My name is Francisco, and I'll be your waiter tonight. *Algo para tomar?*" When they didn't immediately respond, as he'd anticipated, he repeated the question in English. "Can I get you something to drink?"

Francisco focused on an older man, Miles, who seemed to be leading the group, but he couldn't help noticing the much younger blond man they called Derek, or "the doctor," sitting at the end of the table. He was older than Francisco and a little bigger and taller. His hair was light, somewhat longer, and he had a day's growth in his blond beard. While several of his friends wore more upscale designer clothing, Derek wore a simple tan button-down shirt with khaki shorts and leather sandals—the type that could be purchased from local vendors in Sayulita. When he caught Francisco looking in his direction, he smiled, causing Francisco to quickly avert his eyes.

"A fresh margarita with lime or papaya?" Francisco suggested.

"That's great," Miles answered. "Everyone else?" They all nodded, save the younger man. "What about the doctor?" Miles asked. Derek nodded while watching Francisco more intently.

"*Herradura Reposado?*" Francisco asked. When they didn't respond, he reiterated the question. "With our house tequila, or if you prefer, with Herradura?"

"We'll take whatever you're offering from the house," the older man said to Francisco with a wink that made him mildly anxious. He didn't mind a little attention from the doctor, but he really didn't want to deal with it coming from Miles.

"No," another guest said. "We're going with the Herradura. Make them doubles." The group nodded in agreement.

"Yeah, Miles, get with the program," one said. "You never buy, anyway."

"I'll be right back," Francisco said, smiling.

Francisco headed for the bar but turned quickly to reassess the table once he'd reached it. Derek was watching him again and smiled. It was a full smile, and his perfectly white teeth glistened. Francisco turned to see if the doctor was looking at something behind him. It seemed like he wasn't. But when Francisco looked back, the doctor had reengaged in the group's conversation.

When Francisco returned with the drinks, the group was engrossed in a lively conversation. As anticipated, they were all staying at the Four Seasons across the Sayulita inlet in the upscale resort area called Punta Mita. While he wasn't able to draw a complete picture, they seemed to be at some type of medical conference. Some of them were sales representatives, others were hospital administrators, and the remainder were medical doctors of one type or another. More interesting, however, was that he'd been right: All of them were gay and quite comfortable about it. After they finished their drinks, Francisco took their dinner orders and left, unable to reestablish eye contact with the doctor, who had apparently lost interest.

"How are they doing?" Jose asked.

"Good," Francisco answered.

"Lots of drinks; that's good."

Francisco nodded.

"Hopefully, the tips will flow, too," Jose added with a grin.

"Hopefully," Francisco responded, before leaving to check on the preparation of the meal.

When the order was ready, he returned to the table with plates of food for the first course, which was received with enthusiastic delight. The dishes they'd ordered were some of the restaurant's finest: freshly caught *hauchinango a la Veracruzana (Veracruz-style red snapper)* with a fresh fruit salsa as an appetizer; a lobster bisque intermediary; three enormous steaks, served rare on salt blocks, family style for everyone, accompanied by asparagus and roasted peppers (both spicy and not); and an apple tart or chocolate lava cake for dessert. For wine, they'd chosen an expensive Chilean malbec.

With each course, the conversation grew louder as the group became more intoxicated. As the evening progressed, the other restaurant guests slowly departed, and eventually, the band started packing up to leave as well. But the group of gay men remained, fully enjoying the evening and each other, not in a romantic way but as friends with a simple commonality.

"Francisco," Miles said, gesturing for him to come to the table.

"Yes," he answered after arriving.

"We'd like more music."

"Of course," Francisco said. "The band will stay as long as you like." He wasn't sure *band* was the right word, since it consisted of a karaoke machine, a string bass, and a singer. But he assumed that's what was intended.

"I mean," the man continued, "we'd like to sing."

Francisco looked at him, puzzled.

"Actually, what we'd like is for the doctor to sing." The group of men then roared with drunken delight.

"Forget it," the doctor said. "I'm not nearly drunk enough. Why don't we get Evan to dance? He's totally drunk."

"Evan did his *Chorus Line* gig last night, and it sucked. It's your turn tonight."

"I don't think so," the doctor responded.

"Unless you're buying, you've gotta earn your board," Miles said. "So, are you singing or buying?"

Derek shook his head no, triggering an immediate response.

"*She works hard for the money*," Evan started, singing one of their favorite

Donna Summer songs. Hearing their cue, the rest of the group immediately chimed in on the instrumental backup while raising their arms and snapping their fingers, "*dun-dun, dun-dun—dun-dun, dun-dun.*"

"I'm not buying you any more margaritas, that's for sure," the doctor answered.

Evan ignored him and continued singing, "*. . . so you bet-ter treat her right,*" as the rest of the group jumped in again, "*dun-dun, dun-dun—dun-dun, dun-dun.*"

The group of men then repeated the verse together, *fortissimo*. They were a mess, but Francisco was intrigued. He wondered if the doctor would actually sing. At any rate, they weren't going to give up on him. Francisco looked around the restaurant and noticed that all of the other guests had left.

"I'm sure we can make that work," he said.

"A torch song," Miles said. "We want a torch song."

"Torch song, torch song, torch song," the group chanted in unison. "We wanna torch song from the sexy doctor; we wanna torch song from the sexy doctor!"

The doctor took a deep breath, recognizing that he didn't really have an option. "Okay," he said.

Francisco led him to the band area and started talking to the leader in Spanish. He handed the doctor the menu of songs available on the karaoke machine.

"I need to find something good," he said to Francisco. He finished paging through the book before returning to the middle and pointed. "*Beaches*. We're on the beach, right? It'll be perfect."

Francisco showed the selection to the band member running the karaoke machine. "He wants to know what key?" Francisco asked.

"Baritone range," the doctor answered. "But as drunk as those guys are, I'm pretty sure it won't matter."

Francisco smiled and explained the answer in Spanish to the operator, who input the selection and handed the portable microphone to the doctor.

"By the way, my name's Derek," the doctor said to Francisco. "Thanks for putting up with all of us tonight." He extended his hand, and Francisco shook it.

"My pleasure," Francisco answered.

"Hey, do you have a dish towel?" Derek asked.

"Sure." Francisco looked at him, puzzled.

He left for the kitchen to get one as the group started up again with the torch song chant. When he returned with the dish towel, Derek turned his back to the group. Then he put the towel over his head, as if it were long hair, and nodded to the karaoke operator to start the song.

When the musical introduction began, Derek turned, slowly, feigning sensuality by running his hand along his hairy chest and now unbuttoned shirt before stopping at his groin and comically cupping it.

"I want it," Evan said. "How much?"

Derek blew the guys in his group an affected kiss as they howled.

"Make it stop!" one yelled.

"Who sprayed her with ugly?"

"Nice hair!"

Francisco laughed. The guy wasn't delicate or feminine, and he certainly wasn't ugly. He was tall, blond, hairy, built, and handsome. Francisco could tell that Derek didn't care about their comments; he was confident to the very core—secure in who and what he was. *That's what makes him so attractive: gay and self-confident*, he thought. It was an uncommon combination. *Okay, maybe the deep blue eyes matter, too*, Francisco admitted to himself.

When the lyrics came onto the screen, Derek started to sing in a hushed voice while looking down dramatically. Francisco thought that the melody was inviting and the words were warm. He didn't know the piece, but he liked it.

"It's 'The Wind Beneath My Wings' from *Beaches*," one said. "Bette Midler!"

As Derek sang the first lines of the song, Francisco realized that he was acting out the words, as if mimicking them, while exaggerating a traditional singer's affectation for comic effect. So, when he sang about the *sunlight*, he pointed and looked to the sky. When he sang about *love*, he touched his heart. And when he sang about *strength*, he flexed his fairly impressive bicep—all while entertaining the group and keeping a watchful eye on the karaoke screen. The men loved it and burst into laughter.

"Oh, dear," the older man shouted. "Shoot me! Shoot *him*!"

Derek missed a line because of the interruption but was unfazed. He continued with a brush of the towel "hair" nestled uncomfortably on his head. Francisco couldn't help but grin while suppressing a laugh. Derek was funny, and he seemed pretty good. Despite the act, he had a deep, robust voice, and his pitch seemed accurate.

"Go, girl, get 'em!" one hooted.

"Make him stop, please!" another yelled.

But Derek didn't miss a beat, singing the lines of the piece in character while the group laughed and taunted him. Then he walked directly over to Francisco and looked him in the eyes. Francisco felt his face flush when he realized that Derek was singing about a previously unknown but handsome *hero* going *unnoticed* while he took Francisco's hand.

"Uh, that's not gonna happen," Miles said.

"Way outta your league, Derek," another added.

Scowling back, Derek missed a couple of lines again but then quickly caught up with the words as they came across the screen of the karaoke machine. Obviously, the performance hadn't been rehearsed. But he really did seem pretty talented. The music was delightful, and Francisco had to admit that he'd liked it when Derek held his hand. When the chorus ended, the group interrupted Derek with applause, and Francisco couldn't stop grinning as he listened while wondering if Derek would approach him again.

Derek then continued with the second verse, this time walking seductively around the dining table to each of the guests, rustling their hair and touching their cheeks as he sang. While some of the men in the group went wild with feigned erotic excitement, Evan pretended instead to hurl into his napkin. Hearing the commotion, Jose and the staff from the restaurant started coming out from the kitchen; they, too, couldn't help but chuckle at the spectacle.

Derek then walked over to Miles and sat seductively on his lap. But this time, when he sang about his *heart*, he instead placed his hand over his stomach. Then he made a pained facial expression. And when he sang again about the *wind beneath his wings*, he gently lifted himself off Miles's lap and looked around, as if embarrassed, before again moving on to the chorus.

"A fart?" Evan asked. "Did Derek just fart on Miles?"

When the lines repeated a third time, he almost jumped off Miles's lap, as if propelled forward by an invisible force.

"Oh—my—God," Miles said. "He's so crude!"

As the music climaxed, Derek started flapping his arms like wings, as if then rising in flight while circling the table for liftoff. Then, while singing the word *sky*, he dramatically reached into the air, pointing first, and then clutching, as if grasping it. And when the music eventually slowed, Derek fanned his behind one more time vigorously before nestling down in the old man's lap and hugging him. In response, Miles plugged his nose.

When the music ended, the group leaped to their feet in applause, and the restaurant staff enthusiastically joined them. Francisco realized he hadn't stopped grinning while applauding the performance. *The guy's hysterical*, he thought, *and so very sexy*. When the clapping stopped, Francisco realized that his thumb was gently rubbing the inside of his palm where Derek had held it. He smiled. Yeah, he liked the sexy doctor. *Who wouldn't?*

"Bravo," they shouted. "Encore!"

Derek politely bowed before taking off the towel wig and walking back to the table to take his credits. "Autographs are five dollars," he said. "Leave your napkins here for signing."

The men then enjoyed another drink, maybe two, and the volume of their voices increased as their inebriation took over. After a while, Miles motioned for Francisco to bring them the check. When he did, Francisco noticed a disagreement over who would pay it. He watched as they each tossed a credit card into a hat. Then Miles drew one out.

"*Ohhh!*" they yelled, as Miles read Derek's name.

As directed, Francisco handed the tray with the bill to Derek, who took out a pen but instead paid it in cash.

"Keep the change," Derek said, smiling directly at him.

"They made you pay, even after your award-winning performance?" Francisco asked.

"After being gassed?" Miles protested. "He should pay us!"

Francisco wanted to ask them why they didn't think the doctor had "worked hard for the money," but he knew better than to insert himself further into the customers' conversation. Anyway, there was a lot of cash on the bill tray, all of it American, so Francisco hoped the tip would be a good one.

Before handing the money to the cashier at her station, he looked back at the men to see if they needed anything further. Rather than getting up to leave, he noticed that they were all looking at him while whispering quietly among themselves. He didn't understand. Derek had told him to keep the change, hadn't he? He didn't appear to be seeking Francisco's attention, so he handed the tray to the cashier. After a moment, she returned the change to him.

"That's a good tip," she said. "Maybe you can retire?"

Francisco smiled. "Right. But you don't need to keep the check?" he asked, handing it back to her.

"I think you'll want that one." She smiled before turning the check over so Francisco could read it: *Join me for a nightcap? Derek.*

Francisco looked at the note. Was this for him? Francisco read the note again before looking back at the men, all of whom were watching him inquisitively. One guy questioningly gave Francisco a thumbs-up with a smile, and when he didn't immediately respond, changed it to a thumbs-down with a frown. Had the doctor just asked him on a date? Did Derek think he was gay? How would he know? It wasn't unusual for guests to try to pick up on the staff, especially when they were drunk. Francisco looked for Derek, but he was no longer at the table.

While at first these types of overtures were flattering, after a while, Francisco, like the other members of the staff, understood them to be what they were: demeaning—a onetime sexual fling for the foreigners with the locals. If you thought you might actually like the person, well, that would only make it all worse. After a night of sex, maybe two, it always ended abruptly. Francisco looked at the note again before putting it in his pocket. But when he looked up, he saw Derek standing right in front of him. Then the drunken men started their chorus again. "*Sí, sí, sí, sí,*" they chanted in unison.

Recognizing there was no saying no, Francisco gave the group a thumbs-up, and they all started hooting, "Der-rek, Der-rek, Der-rek." He smiled charmingly at Francisco.

"Okay, okay," Francisco said to the group, motioning for them to settle down. He then turned to Derek. "I'll be back in a minute."

Francisco finished clearing the table and headed to the restaurant office to check out. At least the tip had been good—and the entertainment. But when he got back to the bar, he realized he'd changed his mind.

"I appreciate the offer," Francisco said.

Derek touched his arm warmly, cutting him off. "Just one drink," Derek said. "I can't be that bad, right?"

When Francisco didn't answer, Derek added, "We'll have it right here."

Francisco watched him, gauging his intent. The guy was unusually handsome and a doctor, for Christ's sake. He could have anyone. Did he just like Latinos? Or maybe, as a wealthy American, the guy liked the power of "having the help." Francisco hated that. No, he *really* hated that.

Derek seemed to understand his reluctance. "Just a drink," Derek repeated. "*Uno.*"

Francisco smiled. "Well, ya gotta admit, it was confusing."

"Confusing?" Derek asked.

"Metaphors. Particularly in a foreign language."

Derek looked puzzled.

"Yeah, I mean, am I your *hero* or your *fart*?" Francisco asked.

Derek laughed. "Touché." He looked into Francisco's eyes and touched his arm again. "But I don't get the feeling you have any trouble with English," he said. "Or metaphors."

Francisco didn't answer.

"You don't really belong here, do you?" Derek asked, changing the subject. "I noticed it as soon as I came in."

"Me?"

"Something about how you look," Derek said, "but that's not what I'm talking about now."

"Most guys go for my butt," Francisco said.

"Okay, that, too!" Derek smiled. "What's your story? I'm curious."

"My story?" Francisco asked. "Is long and troubling. Maybe another time."

"Or maybe tonight," Derek said. "Why not?"

Francisco nodded to the bartender for a drink. "What do you want?" Francisco asked. "On me."

"What do you suggest?" Derek answered.

Francisco looked at the bartender and then at Derek. "A joint."

"Okay. Here?"

"I know a better place," Francisco offered. "Just upstairs."

Derek paused.

"The roof deck," Francisco said. "No, I'm not inviting you to my room."

He watched Derek's eyes; for a moment, he seemed disappointed. Francisco led him out of the restaurant to the back and to a simple ladder that led to the roof deck. Derek followed him through the restaurant and then up the ladder.

"I see what they mean," Derek said, "about your butt."

Francisco turned around and smiled. "Be careful, or I'll kick you off!"

When they reached the top, Francisco took him to the front edge of the deck, where the view was unobstructed.

"Wow," Derek said. "The view up here's even better."

Francisco nodded as Derek peeked over the edge of the roof. "But don't get too close, especially if you're drunk."

"I'm pretty tipsy but not drunk," Derek said while scanning the panoramic view. The ocean was peaceful that night, with the almost full moon reflecting on the waves as they gently lapped against the sand of the beach. "You're really lucky to live here."

"I know," Francisco said. "Maybe I don't belong here, but I do like it here." He pulled a joint from his pocket, lit it, and inhaled deeply before handing it to Derek. "Sit here on the edge, but don't lean over."

"So," Derek continued after releasing his own drag, "what's your story?"

Derek put his hand on Francisco's and listened. Francisco thought it was aggressive, but he quickly started to relax as the calming effects of the pot kicked in. Francisco told him about growing up in Mexico City as the son of a district governor, going to private schools during the school year, spending summers in San Diego with an uncle to work on his English, and starting college to become a lawyer.

"So, what happened?" Derek asked.

"My dad found out about a boyfriend and offered me a choice: Drop him or drop out."

"You left?"

"Apparently," Francisco said. "I didn't think he was serious, but I was wrong. After the semester ended, my tuition check for the next year never came. Eventually, I moved out of the dorm and found my way here."

Francisco wondered if his dropping out of college would cause Derek to lose interest. It didn't make much sense for a doctor from the States to take an interest in a college dropout in Mexico. But then again, Derek knew he was just a waiter. Derek continued his questions between tugs of the joint.

"With your boyfriend?" Derek asked.

"No. He stayed."

"I'm sorry," Derek said. "Still together?"

"No," Francisco answered, looking in the other direction while taking another tug on the joint. He appreciated the genuine interest but was starting to feel like he needed a break from the questions. "What about you?" Francisco asked, before turning back to meet Derek's gaze.

"Well, I'm here at a medical convention. We have one every year."

"With gay guys?"

"No, not really," Derek answered. "A bunch of us have been going to these for four or five years now. We've become pretty good friends."

Francisco nodded. "You're really a doctor?"

"Yes. Pediatrics," Derek said. As he spoke, he moved his hand from Francisco's and put it around his waist.

"And a musician?"

"No, but I studied music as a kid and always got the lead in high school musicals."

"For your voice or looks?" Francisco teased.

Derek just smiled, enjoying the compliment. "Probably because I was the only guy who'd do it."

"A kids' doctor who's gay," Francisco continued. "Does that work up there? That'd be tough here."

"In the United States? It's still not easy—definitely on the down-low. You know, some still think gays are pedophiles, so pediatrics isn't a natural—at least not for now. But I enjoy helping kids. It works well enough."

"Boyfriend back home?" Francisco asked.

"No."

Francisco mustered his courage and put his hand on Derek's leg. He could feel Derek's strength through his shorts. Derek pulled him closer in response.

"Family?" Francisco asked.

"Yes."

"That's it? Just a *yes*?" Francisco said.

"However bad it is with your parents, it's probably worse with mine."

"How so?"

"Tough to explain," Derek said. "My parents are pretty wealthy, and they have everything that goes with it: They went to the right schools, Stanford, and they live on the right side of town, Atherton. My father works in the right type of job, as a CEO. And their friends are all the right type of people—you know, White, rich, and so on."

"You probably went to Stanford, too?" Francisco asked.

Derek nodded.

"But you don't fit into their picture?" Francisco asked.

"I try." He took another drag on the joint and looked Francisco in the eyes. "They're family."

Francisco wasn't sure what that meant. Was Derek telling him that he wasn't really out? From his own experience, Francisco understood the need to balance things with family. But dating a closet case was a clear no for him.

"Look, Derek," Francisco started, withdrawing slightly. "I like talking to you. But I don't do the traveling-tourist thing—even for a handsome American doctor who sings."

Derek laughed. "But I like you."

"And I like you," Francisco said without moving. "But you don't know me, and we don't even live in the same country."

Derek nodded. "You know, the story only ends when someone chooses to finish it. I'm still reading." Derek kissed him quickly but warmly before getting up. "Are you working tomorrow?" he asked, changing the subject.

Francisco was surprised by the persistence, particularly since he'd made clear that the night had come to an end. "In the evening," he answered.

"Then you're free all day. Let's go fishing," Derek said. "I've always wanted to."

Francisco felt the penetration of Derek's blue eyes and the warmth of his hand as he again took Francisco's. He didn't really want to go fishing, but he had to admit that he did want to see Derek again.

"Okay," Francisco answered.

He kissed Derek softly before heading to the ladder and showing him out. *Yes*, he thought, while grinning to himself. *That'd be very okay.*

And so it happened, so many years ago, Francisco remembered. The next day, he and Derek were on Guillermo's boat, drinking beer and catching nothing. That night they ate fish tacos on the beach, drank margaritas, and then enjoyed a joint on the same rooftop deck after Francisco got off work. Afterward, they'd gone to Francisco's lackluster apartment—now Guillermo and Consuela's. Francisco smiled. It'd been wonderful. And Derek had been right, as the story didn't end: A year later, he'd moved to the United States with Derek, where they were married—at least in their minds.

Francisco took another drag of his joint and looked across the rooftop deck, down at the palapa, and then across the glimmering waves of the sea. He thought it was all pretty much the same. But it had never been the same without Derek. He felt his thumb rub against the wedding ring he still wore. It'd been twenty-three years since Derek's death, but he still missed him. He missed him a lot.

Francisco looked back at the festive table Consuela had put together. She'd gone to a lot of trouble. Whether she agreed or not, excluding her and Guillermo from the meal wasn't acceptable. He pulled another table from the stock room and pushed it next to the one she'd already arranged. Then he set it the same way and added two more chairs. He knew she'd protest. But he knew she'd like it, too.

Chapter 5

Rebecca checked her cell phone for the time: 6:45 p.m. She had fifteen minutes before her father's dinner at their family home. She opened her suitcase and looked through the clothes she'd brought to Mexico. She wanted to wear something nice. She wasn't sure why this particular week was so important to her father, but she didn't want to let him down her first night home. She pulled out a black light-knit cocktail dress. It was a little dark for Sayulita, but with the short sleeves and higher cut midway down her thighs, she thought it would work. She pulled it over her head and returned to the bathroom for a final check in the mirror. It clung nicely to her firm body and accentuated her full breasts. She liked it. With her strong jaw, blonde hair (cut short now), and blue eyes against her delicate White skin, she looked attractive, and with the dress, sexy. She added some light lipstick, fluffed her hair, and sat down on the wicker chair of her childhood bedroom to reflect.

The bedroom was largely the same as when she'd lived in it. The "matrimonial" bed—a queen in Mexico but a double in the United States—remained covered with the same brightly colored quilt over the tan comforter of her childhood. The pillows were splashed with matching tropical fluorescents. The walls were white, save for the one behind the bed, which was a deep maroon. Above the door was a cross—her father's doing. On the opposite wall were several paintings by Lento, a local artist. The first, "Puerco Pistola," was of oversized pigs wearing sombreros while slinging guns. The second, entitled "El Centro," depicted a festival in the town center, with *folklórico* dancers in traditional dresses and mariachi musicians in their customary black suits, playing a Mexican bass, viola, violin, and trumpet. Painted in festive colors, the pictures combined a cartoonlike freedom with realistic elements. She loved them.

She left her bedroom but paused for a moment in the central palapa of the living room and looked out across the beach and the ocean. The wind had picked up, and the surfers were heading in. The beachgoers were also packing up, but the beach vendors were still walking from person to person in their all-white clothes, trying to make one last sale of a blanket, bracelet, or similar wares. It had been a good place to grow up, she thought, but it was not a good place to work and live as an adult. She felt lucky to have been able to leave.

Rebecca continued through the covered walkway from their home to the entrance of her father's restaurant and paused once inside. On the far wall beyond the hostess area was a large painting, illuminated with soft down lighting, and framed in a festive blue wooden frame.

"What do you think?" her father asked, noticing that she'd arrived.

"I like it." She smiled. She approached the work she'd painted to look at it more closely. The work depicted two young girls of the same age: One was a blonde with lighter skin, and the other was a brunette with darker skin. Behind them were two men: One was Latino, and the other was White. The girls played with a shovel and bucket on the beach while the men behind them drank beer and ate shrimp on a stick from a beach vendor. They all laughed happily. While realistic in portrayal, the modern work was painted in vibrant, festive colors.

"I think of it as a happy Diego Rivera," he said.

"You framed it," she said. "Do you like it, or did you just hang it for me?"

"I love it," he said. "Did you see the note on the bottom?"

She bent down and looked more closely. "You sold it?"

"That's what you wanted, right?" he answered.

"For fifteen thousand dollars?" she asked.

"They offered me ten. I told them I'd need to check with the artist, but yes, I sold it!"

"I don't know," she answered. "I painted it for you and didn't think it would actually sell."

"Shall I keep it?" he asked.

She paused. As he well knew, the painting portrayed their family, but she'd taken the artistic liberty of including Derek, her other father, as if he were alive then, enjoying the beach with all of them. In effect, she'd written him back into the family—an artistic pro forma of sorts—so as to share a wonderful day with them on the beach.

"I'm going to have to think on that for a bit."

The restaurant door opened again, and Elena and Richard entered. "*Buenas noches*," Elena said, hugging each of them.

"*Buenas noches*," she and her father responded.

Richard shook each of their hands with a firm, professional grip. "Thanks again for including me, Francisco," he said.

Rebecca had seen photos of her sister's boyfriend but hadn't met him until earlier that day. He was handsome in the photos but even more so in person. He was tall, with a light complexion, light brown-to-blond hair, cut short, and emerald-green eyes that were mesmerizing. He wore a lightweight tropical shirt; tan, tropical pants, and some type of designer sandals. She could tell that his clothes were expensive, but they also were tastefully understated.

"Did you bring your bags back?" Francisco asked hopefully.

"We decided to stay at the Four Seasons after all," Richard said. "They wouldn't refund the reservation, and it seemed like that would be easier on you anyway."

"All good," her father answered.

While the words were right, Rebecca could hear the disappointment in his voice. She knew that in Mexico, having the family home for Christmas was a big deal. Attendance wasn't optional; it was mandatory. Admittedly, she hadn't been home for Christmas since she'd left Sayulita years earlier. She knew her father hadn't liked that, but he hadn't really objected, either. While occasionally, each of them had separately returned from the States, they'd come at the same time this year, as he'd requested. Apparently, he'd also wanted them all in their old rooms during the visit. Perhaps his patience with them had reached its limit; perhaps the loneliness of the empty nest was catching up. She wasn't sure, and he wasn't offering explanations.

"Shall we head up?" Francisco asked.

They nodded and started following him until Richard stopped. "Excuse me," he said when his phone beeped. He read the message and then dialed a call. "It'll just take a sec."

As they waited, Elena noticed the painting. "It's yours, isn't it?" she asked.

Rebecca smiled. "Do you like it?"

Elena looked at it more carefully. She approached the painting and then stepped away. "When did you do it? I mean, when did you have time to do it?"

"Last year. For Dad."

Elena continued studying it. "I love it, Rebecca. I really do. It kind of has a Rivera feel to it, absent the anger—don't you think?"

Rebecca looked at her father, and they laughed. "Yes," she said. "We do."

Richard finished his call, and Francisco directed them up the stairs to the rooftop deck.

"Wow," Richard said. "The views here are incredible. And the warm but fresh air? I can see how you'd like it here."

Consuela and Guillermo then approached them. Rebecca had enjoyed catching up with them earlier that day and was pleased they were joining them for dinner. While they looked older than she'd remembered, it was the decrease in their energy, maybe their spark, that she'd immediately noticed, particularly with Consuela. She hugged Consuela, who firmly hugged her back but seemed unable to sustain eye contact. Rebecca knew that she couldn't just drop in after being away for years and expect everything to be the same. But she sensed on some level there was something more going on.

"Richard, this is Consuela, and that's her husband, Guillermo," Francisco said. "While they prepared most of the meal, they are part of the family and will be joining us for dinner."

"*Mucho gusto,*" Guillermo said, extending his hand while walking over. *(Pleased to meet you.)*

"*El gusto es mio,*" Richard responded. *(The pleasure is mine.)*

"Impressive," Rebecca said to Elena. "Did you teach him that on the way over?"

Elena laughed. "On the plane, actually."

After a moment, a waitress appeared to take their drink orders. Noticing her arrival, Francisco formally welcomed them. "*Feliz Navidad y Próspero Año Nuevo,*" he said. "A round of margaritas for everyone to start?"

"Richard and I'll take a negroni," Elena said.

"I'll take one of those, too," Rebecca said.

After the rest of the group ordered margaritas, the waitress left to prepare the drinks.

"What's with that?" Francisco asked. "The two of you used to love your frozen margaritas."

"The sugary vodka's popular these days," Rebecca answered. "Sweet tooth?"

Elena nodded, raising her hands in mock guilt.

"As long as you're here with me, I'll forgive you this time," Francisco said. "But understand you're going to have to transition back to Mexico—at least for a week."

The waitress returned shortly with the cocktails, and they started their drinks on the deck overlooking the bay. After a while, Francisco directed them into the dining area.

"Richard, you sit there next to Elena," he said. "Rebecca, why don't you sit opposite Richard? We'll put the two of you at the heads on each end," he continued, pointing to Consuela and Guillermo, "and I'll sit here next to Rebecca."

Francisco took his seat before continuing. "What wine would you like to drink?"

"Can I see the wine list?" Richard asked.

Rebecca watched Richard peruse the wine list, seemingly unimpressed. "Do you have a Bordeaux?" he asked. "Something about five years out?"

"No, señor," the waitress responded. "Just what's on the menu."

"I'm at a loss," Richard said. "Francisco, why don't you choose?"

"We'll go with the Argentina malbec, the grand reserve," he said to the waitress.

The waitress returned and poured the wine. After a while, the first course, bacon-wrapped shrimp, was served.

"I loved this stuff as a kid," Elena said.

"And I still do," Rebecca added, after taking a bite. "You remembered, Dad?"

Francisco smiled. "That's all Consuela."

Richard apprehensively tasted his. "I've never seen anything quite like that before," he said. "Interesting."

They spoke about a variety of topics before their appetizer plates were cleared. Rebecca noticed that while leading the conversation, her father wasn't really speaking much about himself.

"What about you, Dad?" she asked. "What're you up to these days?"

Rebecca watched as his gaze darted to Consuela before he answered.

"Well, you know what it's like here," he said. "Does anything really change?"

While he smiled the way he always did, she thought it seemed just a bit forced. She started to ask him another question but was interrupted when the staff approached the table with serving dishes.

"Our next course should be a real treat," Francisco said. "Consuela prepared the dorado Guillermo caught this morning. It doesn't get fresher than that."

The waitress served the fish, which was traditionally prepared with olive oil and garlic in the Mexican style, along with rice and mixed steamed vegetables.

"It's delicious, Consuela," Rebecca said. "Light, flaky, just the way I remember you making it for us as kids."

Consuela grimaced. "I should be the one actually cooking it tonight," she said. "Then it would be done right."

"Where did you catch it?" Elena asked, turning to Guillermo.

"About five miles north," Guillermo said, looking down.

Consuela rolled her eyes. "Did they move the fish market?" she asked. "That fish is fresh, but it didn't come from the *Esperanza*."

Rebecca laughed.

"The *Esperanza*?" Richard asked.

"That's Guillermo's boat," Elena explained. "She's teasing her husband for *not* catching the fish."

"Ah," Richard said. "Well, it's excellent nonetheless."

Rebecca enjoyed the conversation that followed. They talked about their current lives, their memories, their struggles, their successes—all of it. To Rebecca, it seemed as if she'd never left. But she again noticed that her father seemed off. His color wasn't how she remembered it, and at times, he seemed to squirm in his chair. Clearly, he was getting older. As with Consuela, she couldn't expect him to look as he did in their youth. But his aging seemed more severe than Consuela's or Guillermo's.

"My compliments," Richard said to Consuela. "The food is exquisite—perfectly prepared and deliciously unique."

"*Gracias*," Consuela answered.

Rebecca wondered if the compliment was disingenuous. Was he trying to impress them? Or was this just his personality? She'd noticed that he hadn't eaten a lot of the meal or drunk much of the wine. The fish was tasty, and the meal was nice, but it wasn't anything special. She presumed that her father had asked Consuela to prepare the dinner for them for old times' sake. Of course, Richard had no way of understanding this.

"How long have you had the place?" Richard asked.

"Well, you girls are what, twenty-five?" Francisco said. "So, over twenty years. We moved here after my husband died. And I bought it from the prior owner a couple of years after that when he retired."

"That must have cost a bundle," Richard said.

"It did," Francisco answered.

Rebecca noticed that Richard had made no mention of Derek's death. Instead, his interest was the cost of their house. Nor did he have much to say about himself. Perhaps he was wise enough to realize that the evening was about the family, not him. But at times, it seemed as if he wasn't really listening or didn't really care. She wondered what her sister saw in him, other than his looks.

"So, tell us about you, Richard," Francisco said. "We know you're at Goldman with Elena, but that's about it."

When Richard adjusted himself in his seat, Rebecca felt his leg brush against her own.

"I'm the head of tech M and A," he said.

"Elena's division. What does that mean?" Francisco asked.

"Well, we are an investment bank. We help one company buy another company if we're representing the buyer, or we help a company find a buyer if we're representing the seller." Francisco didn't respond, so he continued, "You can think of us as being like a real estate broker: One broker represents the person buying the house, and the other represents the person selling the house."

"How big are your transactions?" Rebecca asked.

"Big," Richard said. "We usually won't do anything less than a billion."

"Impressive," she said.

Richard didn't respond but instead started typing on his phone. "Shit. They can't do that!" he muttered. "Just a minute," he added, as he continued typing into the phone.

The conversation at the table stopped, as they waited for him to reengage. "Sorry," he said, turning his attention back to the group.

Rebecca could see that Francisco was thinking about the discussion. He knew what Elena did at Goldman, so she was puzzled by his question. When he continued, she understood his concern.

"Then you're Elena's boss?" Francisco asked.

"Well, I guess so," Richard said. "She reports to someone else who's between us, though."

Francisco's brow tightened. Rebecca could sense that Richard was sidestepping what he knew was an issue. The fact of the matter was that Elena shouldn't be dating her boss; apparently, they both knew it. When she looked over at Elena, she again felt the rub of Richard's leg against hers and sensed it lingering for a moment.

"Excuse me," Richard said, while checking his phone again. "I gotta respond to this one." After another moment, he looked up and continued, "What about you, Rebecca? What do you do—I mean, besides paint?"

"I'm a consultant at McKenzie," she answered. "I work in San Francisco in the health care vertical."

"And I heard you went to Stanford?" he asked. "Impressive."

"That's right," she answered, noticing his lingering gaze and the sweep of his leg, which was now touching her bare leg. Then he looked down at his phone again.

"Sorry. This always happens," he said.

He was making her uncomfortable, so she decided to take a break. "Excuse me," Rebecca said. "I'm going to take a quick run to the restroom."

Rebecca walked down from the restaurant's roof level to the main floor. After using the restroom, she noticed that Richard was in front of her painting, speaking on the phone. As she neared, he hung up.

"I like it," he said. "You've obviously got talent."

She wasn't sure he was serious. Regardless, she felt that he was standing a little bit too close, and it was making her uncomfortable. "Thanks," she answered, taking a step back. "It's just a hobby."

"Should it be more?" He smiled, stepping forward again, ostensibly to look more carefully at the painting while again entering her personal space.

"Probably not," she answered, turning toward the painting, as if examining it while reestablishing some distance. "But I'm not sure I'd mind if it were."

"You know, the two of you don't look at all alike," Richard continued. "Are you really sisters?"

"I guess it's a matter of perspective," she answered.

"I mean, you're both beautiful," he continued, smiling and looking directly into her eyes.

"I guess," she responded with a mildly forced smile, again feeling uncomfortable. "We're just different and always have been."

He nodded.

"Shall we head back up?" Rebecca asked.

Richard motioned for her to lead the way and followed behind her. When they arrived at the dining table, coffee and dessert were being served. They ate the soufflé and finished the last of another bottle of the malbec. After a while, the dishes were cleared, and the conversation wound down.

"Shall we call it a night?" her father suggested. "We've got plenty more planned for the balance of the week."

They nodded, and he led them down the stairs to the entrance of the restaurant.

"Thanks for a wonderful evening, Dad," Elena said.

"Thanks, Consuela," Rebecca said, "for making our favorites. And to you, Guillermo, for buying that fresh fish." She hugged them both.

"Thanks, Francisco," Richard added. "I had a delightful time."

When a taxi arrived, Elena and Richard left for their hotel, promising to return early the next morning for a day of fishing in Guillermo's boat. Rebecca followed her father back to their bedrooms in their adjacent home.

"Night, Dad," she said.

She again searched his eyes with the hope of better connecting with him. But when he smiled without comment, she instead gave him a quick kiss and a hug, holding him just a little longer than usual.

"Night, love," he said. "Thanks for coming. It means the world to me."

Chapter 6

AFTER THE FAMILY'S ROOFTOP DINNER HAD ENDED, FRANCISCO SAT on his bed, reflecting on the evening. He felt happy. Both of his daughters had found success in the States. They'd both graduated from prestigious universities and were successfully working in high-paying, professional jobs there. He was both satisfied and proud. Still, he missed them enormously. While they called and wrote regularly, they were so far away. It wasn't the Mexican family he'd imagined.

The meal had gone about as well as expected. He was glad Consuela and Guillermo had joined them at the table—even if it was somewhat uncomfortable for them, and they hadn't said much. Consuela's food was nothing special, as expected. But it did foster warm memories for the girls, and he could tell that they'd enjoyed it. However, Richard had not. That didn't surprise him. Richard was handsome, and he could certainly turn on the charm when he felt like it. But did Richard actually care about his daughter and her family? He wasn't interested in staying with them at the house, but that wasn't particularly surprising. However, the employee/boss relationship was surprising. The fact of the matter was that Elena lived in a world that he didn't understand and never really would. She was intelligent and beautiful, but she was also young and naive. And she lived a long way from home in a foreign country. But he trusted her judgment; she'd figure it out.

Francisco could tell that Rebecca had enjoyed seeing her painting. He hoped that she'd keep up with her art. He knew she was talented. He also knew she was perceptive. More than once, he'd felt the inquisitive reach of her gaze and the unasked question on her lips. Was that just him, or could she sense him hiding something? He wasn't sure. He knew he couldn't avoid her questions for long, particularly with Consuela looking vulnerable. Still, he had a plan. It was a good plan, and he remained determined to execute it.

He knew his twins needed this week together to start processing the years of distance that had arisen—a distance he'd caused by bringing them to Mexico, a distance caused by Derek's death. And he was determined to give the week to them. He well understood that he'd have to tell them about his illness soon, and he would. But telling them now, he reasoned, would change the week from one with the potential for reconciliation, kindness, and love into one of certain hopelessness and death—his death. He'd thought about it a thousand times, and he still wasn't sure what made the most sense. But for him, a reunion week of despair over Christmas just didn't work. Instead, he'd use these precious moments for what would matter most: enjoying their last week together as a family with him and preparing for their future together as a family without him.

He went to the deck of his bedroom and lit up a joint, checking the direction of the wind to make sure it was blowing toward Consuela's apartment and away from Rebecca's bedroom. It wouldn't do much for this anxiety, but he knew it would help with the pain. He took a quick drag and started to reflect. He thought it was ironic that, after sneaking his girls out of the States, they'd both ultimately chosen to live there. Rebecca had returned to the States with Derek's parents when she was only sixteen, and Elena had returned for college when she was only eighteen.

Twenty-three years ago, he thought, as he inhaled deeply. Francisco remembered returning to his flat in San Francisco with his infant twins a little less than an hour after Derek's funeral services in Atherton. He'd known that the funeral would be tough; he just hadn't imagined how tough. But it had proven to be enlightening. Because at the services, he'd learned he had a choice: return to Mexico or give up one of his girls. He'd chosen to return.

Francisco pressed the garage door button and then drove down into the parking garage of the San Francisco flat he and Derek had shared. They lived in the bottom of a two-unit building located on a quiet street in the part of the city known as the Haight. The home was an Edwardian that was built sometime after the turn of the century. The facade was made of wooden shingles that were painted in a grayish mud color. The trim for the door and windows was blue, as were the matching shutters. The place had been perfect for a young family just getting started. There were two bedrooms and two bathrooms, with an entrance just a half flight of stairs from street level. The apartment was within walking access to a number of shops and stores, and it was just a short distance to the medical center where Derek had worked. Francisco pulled the twins from their car seats and headed up the internal staircase to their flat. After quickly feeding them both, he set them in their playpens, hoping they would take their afternoon nap so he could think.

Francisco felt his thumb twirling the silver platinum ring Derek had given him when they were married. They'd exchanged vows in a simple and informal ceremony before a handful of friends only a few years earlier. It had been wonderful, loving, and, as Francisco well knew, entirely illegal—it was the '90s. He glanced down at the ring, wondering if he should take it off now that Derek had passed. *No*, he thought. *Not now—maybe never.*

Francisco opened the metal filing cabinet in the makeshift office they'd set up in the master bedroom. He scanned the green hanging files until he found the one labeled "Twins." Inside were various documents relating to the girls' surrogacy and birth. He rifled through them until he found their birth certificates. They were both issued by the State of California. Elena's certificate listed Elizabeth, their surrogate, as the birth mother and Francisco as the birth father. *All good*, he thought. But as he'd expected, Rebecca's certificate listed Derek as the birth father along with Elizabeth as the birth mother. Since they couldn't list themselves as both the father and mother, they'd decided to just "split the babies."

They'd met Elizabeth through one of their gay friends. She's already had two children of her own but wanted to help another family get started. She was a tall, beautiful Scandinavian woman, with blonde hair and light blue eyes. She was a progressive, and she loved children. For a fee, she'd carried their babies to birth, and thereafter, they'd intended to jointly adopt the twins. But it wasn't the money that really motivated her. It was helping someone else build a family. Admittedly, having twins instead of a singleton had been a bit of a shock for everyone.

Francisco dug further through the file folders and found the adoption paperwork. They'd filled it out and filed it, but the process had never been completed. Elizabeth had moved back to Sweden, making it more difficult to coordinate with her, and Derek, always on call as a doctor, had never focused on it. The reality was that with newborn twins, it was all they could do to keep up with their responsibilities as parents while Derek kept his job. But the excuses didn't change the reality he'd been confronted with at Derek's funeral: On paper, Rebecca was Derek's, and Elena was his. And because gay marriage was illegal, he was only a friend or guardian to Rebecca. So, as a legal matter, Derek's parents, the Stimpsons, were right: Rebecca was theirs, not his. And, as they'd made clear at the funeral, with Derek out of the picture, they expected to raise her.

It would be difficult and time-consuming to finish the adoption process on his own. In the meantime, would Rebecca have to live with the Stimpsons, as they'd proposed at the funeral? It would be financially impossible for him to litigate custody of Rebecca against the Stimpsons, particularly as an undocumented, unmarried immigrant, subject to deportation at any moment. Francisco hadn't been able to think clearly at the funeral. It had been too much, coming all at once. But when he carefully considered what Beverly, Derek's mother, had said to him then, he remembered that the Stimpsons hadn't proposed taking Rebecca from him; they'd insisted upon it.

Francisco looked at the pile of unopened mail and sorted through it, looking for their last joint bank account statement. There was about $4,000 in the main account—not much. He had no family in the United States, and his family in Mexico had quite clearly disowned him. He was sure he could find a job, but as an undocumented foreigner, his earning potential would be limited. Regardless, he'd always been the stay-at-home "mom." So who would take care of the twins if he started to work? And, without citizenship or a green card, how would he earn enough to pay them?

He and Derek had been meaning to set up a will, but that, too, hadn't seemed like a priority. He knew Derek had an investment account somewhere, though. He looked through the various papers in Derek's file folders. As he suspected, Derek was more focused on practicing medicine than keeping financial records. He did find one green hanging file labeled "Investments." Inside were statements from a fund called Franklin. It appeared that, at least as of last year, there were over $500,000 in stocks in the account. It was a long shot, but he picked up the phone and dialed the number. When the attendant answered, Francisco read the account number from the statement and asked her if there was currently an account balance.

"I'm happy to give you that information," she said, "but first, I need to verify your identity. What is your name?"

Francisco wondered if he should give her Derek's name but, without time to think, decided against it. "Francisco Montoya," he said, hoping that his obvious Spanish accent wouldn't raise any flags.

"I see this is an investment account for Derek Stimpson," she said. "But you do have signing authority."

"That's right," Francisco answered, as if he'd known that all along.

"The aggregate balance is currently five hundred fifty-seven thousand thirty-one dollars. Would you like to effect a transaction?"

Effect a transaction? What did that mean? When he didn't answer, she continued, "Buy or sell some of the stock?"

"Yes," he answered. "We need to sell all of it." He could feel his hand tremble and could hear in his voice his attempt to mask his accent.

"One moment, please," she said, as she continued typing into her computer. She reminded him that the conversation was being recorded before asking him for additional identifying information, which he quickly provided. After a pause, she continued, "I can confirm that transaction, effective as of today. You will receive a statement in three to five business days with the actual sale price and net proceeds."

"Net proceeds?"

"Yes, the amount that's left over after the deduction of our commission," she said. "A check will be mailed to your address of record then as well."

"Great," Francisco said. "But can you wire the funds?"

"Just a moment, sir," she said as she continued typing. "Yes, I think we can. Can you give me the last four digits of your joint checking account along with the name and address of the bank?"

"Just a minute," he said. Francisco pulled their bank statement from the pile of documents and read the information off to her.

"That's consistent with our records and your preauthorization," she said. "The funds will also be wired within two business days."

"Thanks," Francisco said. It wasn't as fast as he would have liked, but it would help. He knew he could access the funds once they were in their joint bank account.

Francisco put the phone down and watched his hand tremble as he considered what to do next. Had he just stolen half a million dollars? He wasn't sure. But he knew he couldn't stay in the States; he had to leave. It would be easy enough to take the twins to Mexico if he had passports for them, but he didn't. That process would take weeks and probably wouldn't be possible without Derek's consent—or now, the Stimpsons'.

He picked up the phone again. This time, he dialed the Vista Linda restaurant in Mexico. Perhaps Jose, his old boss, could use his Latino connections to help him. Realistically, he didn't have any better options.

The phone rang twice before someone picked up. *"Buenos días,"* a woman said.

"Buenos días," he answered. *"Jose, por favor?"*

"*Momento,*" she responded, putting him on hold.

After a moment, Jose picked up the phone. "*Hola,*" he said.

"*Hola,* Jose," Francisco responded. "Francisco Montoya *aquí.*"

"Francisco," he said with surprise. "It's great to hear your voice. How are you?"

"Not good," Francisco said. He explained how Derek had died; how his resident status in the United States and his marriage were illegal. And how Derek's parents wanted to take one of the twins. "I need to get out with my girls right now. Can you help? I wouldn't bother you, but it's an emergency."

"That's a lot. Maybe." He paused. "I'll call you back later today."

The twins woke up shortly after the call, so Francisco put them in the double stroller and took them for an evening walk. As usual, the windy summer fog of San Francisco made it cold and unpleasant. On the way, he stopped by the local grocery store and picked up a meal to go for himself and additional toddler food and diapers for the girls. He quickly realized, however, that if they were going to be traveling, it wouldn't be enough. He doubled and then tripled the supplies, pushing the shopping cart while pulling the twins behind him in the double stroller. After he returned home, the phone rang again.

"Hello?" he said.

"It's Jose. You know," he continued, "you may be the first Mexican seeking to illegally cross the border *from* the United States?"

"Probably." Francisco chuckled. "What do you think?"

"Can you be in San Diego tomorrow by eight in the morning?"

"Yes," Francisco said. "I think so."

"Go to the Dana Landing Marina and ask for Javier. He will take you to Mexico by boat, and Guillermo will pick you up there and bring you here."

"San Diego, Dana Landing. Ask for Javier," Francisco repeated.

"That's right," Jose answered. "Pay him five hundred dollars."

"Five hundred dollars," he repeated.

"Good luck, Francisco. You're always welcome here with your girls—we'll see you soon."

"*Gracias,* Jose," he said. "*Muchas gracias.*"

Francisco put down the phone and looked around the flat one more time. What would he take? What did they need? He'd loved living here—it was like living a dream life. But Derek was dead, and that life was quite clearly over. The phone rang again, and he picked it up.

"Jose?" he asked.

"Hi, Francisco, it's Ben Stimpson."

"Hi, Ben," Francisco responded.

"Hey, we missed you at the burial. Are you and the girls doing okay?"

"Yeah, we're okay," Francisco answered. "They were getting tired, and I'd had as much as I could handle."

"I know. It was tough on all of us." When Francisco didn't respond, Ben continued. "Hey, I wondered if maybe Beverly upset you with the talk about transitioning Rebecca."

Francisco felt as if he were going to explode but quickly gathered his composure. "Yeah, that was hard to hear."

"I'm not sure what your plans are," Ben continued, "but I wanted you to know that you'll always be welcome to visit her here. You know that, right?"

"I appreciate that," Francisco said. "Thanks."

"Would it make sense for us to come up tomorrow morning and pick her up?"

Were they serious? Francisco felt stunned. "Why don't you give us through the weekend?" he responded. "Let's let the dust settle before we work on the . . . *transition*." He regretted his sarcasm and tried to refocus.

"Beverly won't be happy; she's already so attached to the girl," Ben said.

"Make it four o'clock on Sunday, after her nap?" Francisco continued, not backing down.

"Fine. Remind me of your address?"

Francisco politely gave him the information before hanging up.

Fucking asshole, he thought. They didn't even know their son's address. And now, they were just going to swing by this weekend and take his kid? *No way*, he thought. *Forget it.*

He glanced over at the girls to see how they were doing. Elena was pulling on Rebecca's foot, and Rebecca started to cry. Francisco picked her up and rocked her while looking into her blue eyes. She was White, there was no doubt about it, and these were her people. If she stayed in the States, she would live a life of privilege in a country with boundless opportunity. If he took her, she would grow up as a White child with a Latino father who didn't have a job in Mexico—a country that was poor. He wondered if taking her was just plain selfish. Still, he didn't think Derek would have wanted her left with his parents. "With my parents, less is more," he'd often told Francisco.

No, he thought. Leaving his daughter—with the Stimpsons, or anyone else for that matter—wasn't an option. *So now it's time to pack*, he concluded.

Francisco started with the diaper bag, filling it with everything possible. Then he pulled out his suitcase and filled it with the twins' belongings. He pulled out Derek's suitcase next and stuffed it with his own belongings as well as the bank information and the file containing the twins' birth information. He packed as much as he could into the car, and when the girls fell asleep, he fastened them into their car seats and left.

Chapter 7

Feeling restless after the family dinner, Rebecca left her bedroom at her father's home in Sayulita and started walking back to the restaurant. She hoped it would still be open and thought a nightcap might help her sleep. She guessed it was the cappuccino she'd had with the dessert that was bothering her. Even with the alcohol, one coffee could keep her up for hours. But she knew it was more than that. Her father's dinner earlier that evening had surprised her. She hadn't realized how much she'd missed her childhood: eating the meals Consuela had prepared for them as children, burying Elena in the sand of the beach, taking their family trips to the pyramids, sleeping in her childhood bed, and living with the security only a loving family can provide. While she'd been back in Sayulita only a day with her sister, it instantly seemed like her childhood home again: happy, inclusive, and safe. But she still couldn't shake the feeling that her dad wasn't telling her something. She hadn't missed the concern in Consuela's eyes when she'd looked at him, either. She dismissed her thoughts. Whatever it was, if anything, he'd tell her when he was ready.

When she arrived at the restaurant, the Vista Linda bar was empty, but the bartender was still there, preparing to close.

"Too late?" she asked.

"It's never too late," he said. She took a seat, and he handed her a bar menu.

"What can I get you?" he asked.

"Just a glass of the house malbec?" she answered.

He poured her a glass and started stacking the glasses. "You're Francisco's girl, right?" He spoke in perfect English.

"Yes," she answered. "You're new?"

"I've been here about nine years now. It's a living." He smiled.

"That'd be right about the time I left," she answered. "That must be why I don't recognize you."

"Well, you're back now," he said. "I hope you're enjoying being home."

"I am," she answered. "Very much so."

As she watched him tidy up the bar, her gaze returned again to her painting behind the bar and to his right. She wanted the money. Ten thousand dollars was a lot. More importantly, the sale validated her as an artist, so she wanted to tell her grandparents about it. But as she considered that further, she realized it didn't make sense. The Stimpsons had millions, so a couple thousand dollars wasn't going to persuade them of anything. Besides, she liked having the painting where it was. It validated her view of their family. She had two dads, and she wanted Francisco to remember her as being a present part of the family here on the beach in Sayulita—not absent. As she scanned the dining room again, she remembered why. At age sixteen, nine years earlier, she'd been dragged into a fight—someone else's fight. She hadn't realized it at the time, but she was starting to fully understand it now.

Rebecca walked up the stairs for the regular Sunday dinner with Elena and their father in the family restaurant. As she waited in the lobby entrance for the restroom to open, she saw two couples, Americans, coming up the stairs and then stopping to wait for their table. She could tell they were Americans because they looked like her, and they spoke English. They were older. The men had gray hair, but the women did not. She could also tell that they were rich by the type of clothes they were wearing: formal evening gowns with jewelry for the women and sports coats for the men. She watched them as they tried to use their poor and limited Spanish to ask for their table.

"*Numbree ester . . .*" the woman with the blonde hair said, pronouncing the Spanish incorrectly, "Stimpson. S-T-I-M-P-S-O-N." She spelled it, but she pronounced the letters in English, not Spanish, making the exercise pointless. "The Four Seasons made a reservation for us earlier this afternoon."

Rebecca hadn't ever met anyone with her middle name. She tried to listen to the conversation without being noticed.

"Welcome," the hostess said. She nodded graciously before checking them into the reservation system and picking up the menus. "Please follow me."

"Thank God," the other woman said, rolling her eyes. "She can speak English."

Of course they speak English, Rebecca thought. *They work in a restaurant in a tourist town visited by Americans.* The more interesting question, by contrast, was why none of the Americans could speak a word of Spanish. Rebecca watched as the hostess led the group to a table overlooking the bay. After using the bathroom, she headed to the other end of the dining room to rejoin her father and sister, and they continued their regular Sunday dinner.

"More gringos," she said to Francisco, knowing that the word would annoy him.

"Like you?" Elena said to her.

"Enough, Elena," her father said. "It's just enough." He scolded her further with his eyes before turning to see the patrons entering their restaurant. Then Rebecca noticed him abruptly turn away.

"What?" she asked.

"It's nothing," he answered. "Let's finish up and go."

Rebecca watched him as he continued to look away. "Do you know them, Dad?"

He didn't respond, nor did he change the direction of his glaze.

"What's going on?" Elena asked, appearing to also notice his unusual behavior.

"Dad, they have our middle name," Rebecca said.

"Come on, girls. Let's get going." He started to rise, but they didn't move. Instead, Rebecca and her sister curiously watched the two American couples, whose presence was obviously troubling their father.

Francisco hesitated before sitting back down. Then he looked his girls in the eye before slowly starting to speak. "I guess at sixteen, you're old enough to know," he started. "And this is as safe a place as any." He paused. "Two of them are your grandparents." He raised his eyebrows in a kind of smirk. When Elena looked puzzled, he continued. "They're Derek's parents."

Rebecca and her twin immediately turned their heads and again looked directly at the tourist couples.

"Girls, stop staring," he said.

"Which ones?" Elena asked.

"The blonde woman and the man to her right near the rail," Rebecca said.

They continued to stare, despite his instructions.

"Stop it," her father said more firmly.

"I thought we didn't have grandparents," Elena said.

"We've never seen them," Rebecca added.

"They are Poppy's parents from America," Francisco continued. "You've just never met them before—at least, not when you were old enough to remember."

"Can we talk to them?" Elena asked.

"Not a good idea," Francisco answered. Apparently sensing their frustration, he added, "But I will tell you all about them after we leave the dining room."

Rebecca and Elena couldn't stop staring, and one of the women at the table noticed. She said something to the other woman and nodded toward Francisco's table. Rebecca watched the blonde woman turn toward their table and then stare back. She nudged her husband, and then, without waiting for a response, started walking over to Francisco. Her husband followed several steps behind her.

"Hello, Francisco," she said. "It's been a while."

Francisco got up and formally shook their hands. "Hello, Beverly," he said. "Ben." He continued to stand but said no more.

"And who do we have here?" Beverly continued, looking directly at Rebecca.

"These are my daughters, Elena and Rebecca," he said.

"Ben, she's stunning," Beverly said. The woman beamed before hugging Rebecca as she sat in the chair next to her. "Rebecca, I'm your grandmother. I've missed you so much!"

Rebecca smiled somewhat tentatively.

"You know, we've been looking everywhere for you—for years!" She looked sternly at Francisco.

"Oh," Rebecca said. "I'm pleased to meet you."

"You can speak English! That's great!" She hugged her again.

Francisco's face tightened.

"And how are you, Francisco?" she asked, while continuing to look at Rebecca.

"Fine," he answered. "Just fine."

"We have so much to catch up on—will you join us at our table?" she asked.

Francisco looked at her, searching for a response. "No, Beverly. I don't think that's a good idea."

"Nonsense," she responded.

"Maybe some other time," he added.

"Francisco," she started. "My son dies, and you sweep my granddaughter away to Mexico without even saying goodbye? And here, of all places. Now, I can't even see her? For a minute?" The look on the woman's face was as incredulous as her rhetorical questions.

Rebecca watched her father search for an answer. It was strange that they wanted to talk to her and not to her father and sister. Clearly, her father didn't want her to engage with them, either.

"Sure," he said. "Is that all right with you, Rebecca?"

Beverly smiled, holding her arms out for her granddaughter to accept.

"Yes," Rebecca answered before hugging her grandmother.

"Fifteen minutes," Francisco said before taking Elena's arm and leaving. "I'll be right back."

Rebecca watched him approach the manager before leaving. She knew he was directing the manager to watch her. That's what her father always did with his employees; he used them as spies. Why shouldn't she spend time with her grandmother? She felt the tug of her arm and redirected her attention to her new grandmother. Beverly walked Rebecca back to the other table and introduced her to the other couple with them. After joining the group at the table, her grandmother started the conversation.

"So," her grandmother said, "tell me all about you!" She smiled broadly.

"Well, we live here in the restaurant. My dad owns it," she proudly added.

"Oh," the woman answered, seemingly surprised. "You live in a restaurant?"

"Yes," Rebecca answered. "There." She nodded to the adjacent wall.

Beverly followed the line but didn't seem to understand. "Ben," she said softly to him, "I think she's saying they actually live in this restaurant..."

"Really?" he answered.

Beverly shrugged her shoulders, questioningly.

"Right there," Rebecca pointed to the wall, noticing their confusion.

"Well," Beverly said, looking at her husband, "that's fun, right?" Her tone was not convincing. "What else?"

"You know, I'm a twin," Rebecca said.

"Yes, I know," her grandmother said, clearing her throat.

Rebecca paused before continuing. "So Elena's your granddaughter, too."

Beverly cleared her throat again while looking over to her husband for guidance. His brow furrowed slightly, making him look both old and irritated.

"Kind of, honey, but no, she's not. Not really, anyway," Ben said.

Rebecca looked at the man more carefully. She understood her grandfather's words, but she wasn't sure what he meant by them.

"But we're twins!" Rebecca said.

"That's right," her grandmother said. "She's not our granddaughter, but *you* are!" She extended her White arm and placed it gently next to Rebecca's. "See?"

Rebecca looked at her arm, confused. The woman's arm was old and wrinkled. Hers was soft and smooth. They were not the same.

"Your dad was, well, friends, with our son, Derek," she started to explain.

"You mean Poppy," Rebecca said. "I never really knew him."

"That's right," she continued. "You are our granddaughter, and Elena is Francisco's daughter."

"But we're one family: Dad, Elena, and me," Rebecca said.

Beverly's face tightened, and this time Ben stepped in. "That's because Francisco took you after your dad died."

"Took me?"

"That's right," Beverly said. "We're your real family."

"That's enough, Beverly," Ben said. "She's just a child, for heaven's sake."

As Rebecca listened to what they were saying, she felt afraid but also curious. She'd always been an equal part of her family, but she really didn't look like Francisco and Elena. They looked Mexican, and she looked American. Francisco and Elena loved her; she knew that. But she was different—or so it seemed. She looked again at the woman's lily-white arm before quickly glancing down again at her own.

"What do you mean, 'took' me?" Rebecca asked again.

Ben looked at his wife sternly, but she seemed unfazed.

"Well, Francisco and our son, Derek, were roommates who lived together. When you and your sister—what's her name?—were born, you lived with both of them. Of course, Francisco came to love you very much. So, when Derek, your dad, died, Francisco took you down here with him."

Rebecca tried to understand what the woman was saying. She knew her dad loved her. She knew she didn't look like him. But she'd never considered him not to be her real father. Were these people her real family?

"We tried to stop him," Beverly continued. "But he lied to us and snuck you away."

"He took all of Derek's money, too," Ben added. "Just plain stole it."

Rebecca didn't understand. It didn't make sense, but it did as well.

"We love you, too," her grandmother continued. "Very much." Ben nodded. She paused before adding, this time without checking with Ben, "And we'd like you to come and visit us in America."

"Visit you?"

"If you want," her grandmother said. "You can stay as long as you want."

Rebecca considered the offer. She wanted to know her family, and she wanted to visit them in the United States. Her father had been angry with her for the past couple of weeks—ever since she'd been rushed to the hospital after her procedure. And Elena still wasn't really talking to her. She wondered if they'd be happier if she just left for a while. "I'd like to visit you in America sometime."

"Just a minute, honey," Beverly said.

Rebecca watched as her grandmother turned and whispered to her husband. After conversing for a while, he nodded in agreement.

"Why don't you come back with us?" Ben asked.

"When?"

"Tomorrow," her grandmother said. "We are going back on a yacht—a big, fancy boat!"

"Will you bring me back home on the boat after the visit?"

Beverly looked again at Ben. "A plane," he said. "That's faster."

Rebecca didn't answer.

"How about we come and get you tomorrow around eight a.m.?" she said. "Just pack a few things. We'll go shopping and get you whatever you want when we get home."

"Okay," Rebecca said. "But I need to check with my dad."

Beverly bit her lip. "Rebecca, I don't think he'll let you go if you do. It's your decision, but he will say you're too young." Rebecca guessed that her grandmother was right. When Rebecca didn't respond, Beverly continued. "We're your family, Rebecca. We'll take care of you and bring you back after the visit. Promise."

Rebecca thought about what her grandmother was saying. She didn't want to lie to her dad, but she did want to go. She'd heard all about the United States but had been there only as a baby. Now, it sounded like her father wouldn't let her go. She turned away when she saw him coming back to the table to get her.

"Tomorrow morning at eight," Beverly said. "Go to the beach."

Rebecca didn't respond.

"Rebecca, it's time to go," Francisco said, once he'd reached their table. "Ready?"

"I'd like to stay a little longer," she said.

"No, Rebecca," he answered.

Rebecca nodded slowly; she could tell that he meant it. "Thanks, Grandma and Grandpa," she said. She extended her hand, but they both hugged her instead.

"We love you, Rebecca," they said. Then her grandmother started to cry.

Rebecca smiled. It felt good to meet her grandparents and to know that they loved her.

"I'm glad she got to meet you," Francisco said to the Stimpsons. "Perhaps we can keep better in touch."

"We'd like that," Ben said, shaking her father's hand.

"Thanks, Francisco," her grandmother said.

Rebecca turned with her father and started walking back to their home. Francisco took her hand firmly, as if she were a small child. It annoyed her.

"Why didn't you tell me?" she asked her father.

Francisco didn't answer but just continued walking.

"You never told me I had grandparents that *wanted* me!"

He still didn't respond but tightened his grip on her hand, pulling her as she resisted.

"They invited me to visit them," she said. "Can I go?"

"We'll talk about it later."

"No, now," Rebecca said, stopping in the living room of their home.

Francisco looked into her eyes. "No, Rebecca, you can't."

"Why?" she asked. "Because I'm too young? I'm already sixteen!"

"Well, yes," her father answered, "but that's not the only reason."

"Then why?" she demanded.

"Because, Rebecca, they're not nice people, and I don't trust them."

Rebecca shook her hand free. "Well, they don't trust you, either. They told me how you stole me and the money."

"You're *my* daughter, Rebecca," he added, ignoring her last comment.

Rebecca felt the warm tears start to well up on her face. "Am I, Dad?" she said. "I mean, are you really my dad, or are you just my dad's boyfriend?"

She held out her freckled White arm, placing it next to the dark brown color of his own. When her father didn't answer, Rebecca abruptly left for her bedroom, slamming the door after entering.

Rebecca took another sip of her wine at the bar of the Vista Linda and looked toward the entrance of their adjacent home. It was hard to believe that nine years had passed since the time she'd left Sayulita with the Stimpsons. She chuckled while thinking back on all of it, trying to dismiss its significance. But she couldn't. That evening had changed everything—and all because of a fluke. While the Stimpsons were vacationing in Punta de Mita, the Four Seasons concierge had recommended that they try the Vista Linda for an authentic local meal. It happened all the time. That time, it just happened to them.

That conversation with her father, she remembered, was the last time she'd seen him and Elena for several years. The next morning, she'd met her grandparents on the beach, as they'd proposed, and she'd left with them. They'd climbed into a motorboat that took them to a yacht anchored a couple of miles from the Sayulita inlet. From there, they'd traveled for several days to San Diego, where a man with a manila envelope met them at the US immigration office. When questioned by the immigration officer, Ben showed the officer in the uniform a birth certificate, apparently hers, as well as a death certificate, apparently Derek's. Her grandparents spoke for quite a while with the officer, but eventually, they were allowed to proceed into the country. Then they boarded a private jet, which took them from San Diego to San Francisco.

Rebeca had known for some time that the Stimpsons had tricked her into returning with them to the United States back then. But hadn't her father also tricked the Stimpsons by taking her in the first place? She remembered at the time feeling overwhelmed and amazed when she'd arrived at her grandparents' home in Atherton. She also remembered feeling relieved about leaving the problems of her youth back in Sayulita. But what had made her satisfied then left her feeling deeply disappointed now. She finished her glass of wine before leaving the restaurant and heading down to her bedroom.

Chapter 8

"Four Seasons, please," Elena said to the taxi driver, who picked her and Richard up in front of her father's restaurant after their family dinner. Their hotel was in Punta de Mita, about twenty minutes from Sayulita. Elena thought they'd had a lovely meal with her father that evening, but it was late, and she was exhausted. Richard had been interrupted several times with work, but that was inevitable. And Rebecca had looked incredible. She was pleased that Richard had liked Rebecca, even though at times she'd felt a bit upstaged. She'd noticed that her father had looked annoyed more than once with Richard. But he'd managed to hold his own, so she was glad she'd brought him.

"Thanks so much for coming," she said to Richard. "It meant a lot to me."

Richard kissed her. "Welcome." He paused. "It was . . . interesting. Kind of a rustic, native meal, would you say?"

Elena thought about explaining but thought better of it.

"And the wine list—are you kidding? There was nothing French on it!"

"It's Mexico," she said. "They draw their wines primarily from South America, and they're delicious."

Richard nodded without responding. "So, do they actually live there in the restaurant, too?" he asked.

"Yes," she answered. "We'll go back again tomorrow. The house is pretty incredible."

"I'll bet," he said, with a hint of sarcasm.

Elena looked at him, trying to assess his meaning. Richard noticed, and responded, "What?"

She looked away. It had never occurred to her that their home was inadequate in any way. But as she thought about it, she realized that it was odd living adjacent to a business. And while she'd always considered the home to be wonderful, she recognized that relative to the country club estates and Park Avenue flats Richard was used to, it was not. The realization made her sad. Rather than feeling proud of her home and her family, as she always had, she saw them for the first time from the perspective of someone wealthy and accomplished in the United States. What she felt was inadequate.

"I mean it. What?" he continued. "I really hate it when you do that, hon. You know, silently pick at me."

"But I didn't say anything," she answered.

"Yeah, that's the silent part."

Elena didn't respond.

The small, old yellow taxi passed by the tiny shops of the town along the cobblestone street before turning right at a green sign that marked the way to PUNTA DE MITA. Within moments, the quaint Sayulita shops ended, and a canopy of trees covered the now-paved road that traversed the seemingly endless forest. With the windows of the taxi open, the dry warmth of the evening filled the car with the nurturing scent of the tropical jungle. Elena took a deep breath of the oxygen-rich air, as if capturing it now would allow its transport back to her urban life in New York City. As their taxi climbed along the winding coastal road, the expansive views of the ocean emerged below, gleaming in the moonlight and sparkling with the light of the waves before disappearing again into the dark blanket of the tropical forest. Though she'd driven the road hundreds of times in her youth, Elena felt overwhelmed with the beauty of its panoramic intrigue. She reached over to take Richard's hand, hoping to share the moment with him, but he remained preoccupied with the messages on his phone.

After a while, he briefly looked up from his phone. "You know, your sister's quite the looker," he said. "But what's with her painting? That's really bad stuff!"

"Why do you say that?" she asked.

"Well, it looks like paint by numbers, don't you think? Totally amateur."

"I didn't ask you *why*," she responded. "I asked you why you'd say *that*?"

Richard continued typing on his phone. Was he even listening?

"Actually, she studied art in high school and at Stanford," Elena added. She regretted her words even as she'd spoken them. She didn't need to justify her sister's talents to her boyfriend. Rebecca was wonderful, whether or not she'd studied at an elite college. Why didn't Richard see that?

"I mean, I liked her and everything—and she's definitely hot. But, well, she really shouldn't quit her day job at McKenzie," he said.

His condescending attitude started irritating her, but she knew there was no point in calling him out on it.

"Did you like Dad?" she asked hopefully.

"Yeah, sure," he answered. "Seemed like a great guy. Not educated, right?"

"I guess not," she said. She wanted to point out that her father had attended a prestigious university, but she realized that the university in Mexico that he'd dropped out of would not count in Richard's mind. Her own degree from Boston College barely did.

"So he just hangs out there twenty-four seven? For what, twenty years? I'd go crazy bored." He continued scrolling through his phone as he spoke.

"Actually, you might like it. At least you'd get away from the phone," she added sarcastically.

"Look," he said, raising the volume of his voice while putting down his phone. "I told you I was busy, but I'd come down here anyway. So enough already." After making his point, he looked down at his phone again and continued scrolling.

Elena carefully considered her words before responding. The right answer was, "Thanks, honey." She knew that. But that felt like giving in.

"Well, you seemed to enjoy my sister, anyway," she said.

Richard put his phone down and again looked directly at her with a furrowed brow. "What?"

Elena could tell he was getting pissed off, but she was unwilling to back off. "My sister. You liked her. I could see it. She could, too."

"Honestly, Elena, she's a sweet kid. But if you're going to drag me into the middle of some sister drama, I'm going to take a hard pass."

She thought he was probably right. She felt her cheeks redden and was relieved it was too dark for him to see them. Rebecca looked great, as always, but that had nothing to do with Richard. Why was she picking a fight with him now? She'd made a mistake.

"I'm sorry," she said. "It's just been a long day. You'll have more fun tomorrow. We're going fishing with Guillermo."

Richard took a deep breath. "Can't wait for that."

They sat silently in the taxi for the rest of the drive. When they arrived at the hotel, the doorman opened the car for her while Richard paid the taxi driver. Another doorman held the door to the hotel's entrance as they passed.

"I'm going to stop by the gift store," Elena said. "See you up at the room?"

"Sure," he answered, before heading to the elevator bank.

Elena found the shop and scanned the mini pharmacy shelf for some antacids. Her stomach was off, and she wanted to settle it quickly. She knew that the water at her father's restaurant was both clean and purified, but apparently, she was no longer accustomed to it.

"Here you go," the shopkeeper said. "Bill it to your room?"

"No, I got it," Elena answered, pushing a bill onto the counter. "Keep the change."

When she arrived back at the hotel room, she saw Richard watching the television.

"Champagne?" he asked, popping the cork.

Richard already had his shirt off and was pouring her a glass without waiting for her answer. He stood in his bathrobe, a white one with the Four Seasons logo, which was open and hanging loosely from his broad shoulders. The blond hair of his chest covered his pecs and trailed down his tight stomach. Within the robe, she could see that he was already firm and quickly getting firmer. He looked as sexy as he always did, and the way he grinned made him even sexier. She felt that the romantic moment for her with him had been during the incredible drive back from the restaurant, but apparently, the moment for him with her was now.

"I'm bushed," she said. "Tomorrow, okay?" She could see that familiar disgust quickly overpower the smile on his face.

"Not really," he said. He started stroking himself while ignoring her.

Elena could tell that her choice was to comply or have a fight. But she was too tired for a fight. So she reached down and gently touched him. She could hear the pace of his breath quicken, so she decelerated, forcing him to wait before she started again. She knew he loved that. After a while, he turned and started to remove her clothes as well.

"No," she said. "Not tonight. My stomach's off."

He frowned.

She continued, glancing up at his eyes quickly to see if his reaction had improved. He was irritated; this wasn't his sex of choice. But after a moment, he closed his eyes again, and within seconds, she felt the ripples in his abdomen convulse before relaxing again.

"Thanks," he said. He got up and retied his robe. "But I thought we came down here to have sex on the beach."

Elena put on her own robe and fastened it firmly about her waist, as if voicing her frustration. "And I thought we came down here so that you could meet my family," she answered.

"Yeah, that was it," he said with mild sarcasm. He opened his suitcase, which was mostly still packed, and put on some clean underwear. "I'm going to head down to the bar for a nightcap."

Elena wasn't sure if he was being crummy, or if she was just feeling off. She waited, expecting him to invite her to join him. When she realized that he wasn't going to, she responded, "Sure." But the words were silenced by the sound of the door, shutting firmly behind him.

Why was he being so difficult? He hadn't enjoyed the evening; then he'd seemed so judgmental. Now, he was mad about the sex. She knew it had been hard for him to get away. And she appreciated his taking the time to come with her. Maybe the stress of the vacation was just a little too much for her. But as she considered that question, another one lurked in the back of her mind: What did her father think? She'd noticed his concern from the time she'd introduced Richard, and then again when he asked about Richard's role as her boss. Her father didn't understand how significant Richard was, but she trusted his judgment. She wasn't sure what Rebecca thought of Richard, either, but it didn't feel entirely good.

Elena wanted to call her sister, her twin. She was pretty sure she could convince Rebecca of Richard's merits, and she wanted to compare notes about their dad. She picked up her cell phone but then paused. The fact of the matter was that she didn't feel entirely safe with her twin, and she hadn't since the time Rebecca had left Sayulita in high school. What had started as a silly high school crush nine years earlier quickly had gotten a lot worse. And then it was too late.

Elena's bedroom was similar to her sister's. The bed was a matrimonial queen with a wicker backboard that rested against a wall in a softer, lime-green color. Against the opposite wall were several Lento paintings that were similar to those in Rebecca's room. Above the door was a wooden cross. When she heard a soft knock on her bedroom door, Elena put down her book.

"What's up?" she asked.

When Rebecca entered, Elena could see that her sister was fidgeting. She sat up when Rebecca didn't immediately answer.

"What's wrong?" she asked.

"I need your help," Rebecca said.

"Tell me," Elena said, moving to the side of the bed to make room for her sister.

Rebecca sat down and before she could speak, the tears started. "I messed up," she said, handing her sister a pregnancy test stick that illuminated a green plus sign for positive.

Elena felt shocked. "You're pregnant?!"

"Apparently," Rebecca answered.

"Who's the father? Does he know?"

Rebecca took a minute to respond. "Promise me you won't get angry or tell Dad."

"Okay," Elena said, reluctantly.

"It's Miguel," she said. "I'm sorry."

Elena felt her body flash with anger. Miguel was the most popular senior boy in their high school and the son of a prominent family in Puerto Vallarta. His father managed a large hotel in town. He was tall and athletic. And for weeks, he'd been talking to her while leaving romantic notes in her locker. She'd never had that kind of attention from a boy, and she'd liked it. More importantly, she liked him, and Rebecca knew it. It hadn't been all that long since she'd explained to Rebecca that she'd decided that Miguel would be her boyfriend—maybe even her first. Apparently, Rebecca had beaten her to him.

"You're mad, aren't you?" Rebecca asked, before looking down at her hands as she knotted them in her lap

"Yes," Elena answered.

"It's not like you were actually dating," Rebecca said. "You weren't a couple."

Elena didn't answer.

"I know, and I'm sorry," Rebecca said. "He told me it was over with you—that it never really started."

"Why didn't *you* tell me? You knew I liked him!"

"I dunno. I knew you'd be mad. Maybe I was embarrassed."

"Do you love him? Does he know?"

"No. Kind of. I did like him . . . I was confused."

Elena felt sorry for her sister, but she also felt angry. She didn't know what to say, so she said nothing.

"Maybe I was jealous," Rebecca added.

"Of what? Me?"

"You have everything—I have nothing," Rebecca said.

Elena wanted to tell her sister that her comment was silly if not stupid. But instead, she again didn't answer. Miguel was popular, but Rebecca could have had anyone. As one of a handful of White girls at the school, Rebecca stood out. The fact that she was tall and blue-eyed with long blonde hair made her particularly unique there. It wasn't the same for Elena, as one of many Latina girls in the high school, and Rebecca knew it. Elena watched Rebecca's hand tremble with the pregnancy stick in it.

"You gotta tell him," Elena said. "And Dad."

"No," Rebecca answered. "No way." Elena didn't respond.

"I've got it figured out, anyway."

"How's that?" Elena watched her sister, waiting for her to continue.

"There's a clinic in Pitillal," Rebecca said. "I've already checked it out."

Elena frowned once she realized what her sister meant. "That's against the law, Rebecca."

Elena didn't know much about abortions, but she knew that they were illegal—at least where they lived. Pitillal was a small local *colonia* adjacent to Puerto Vallarta. So they couldn't be legal there, either. Besides, the hospitals were all in Puerto Vallarta or the marina area where they went to school. She wondered if there even was a hospital in Pitillal.

"Are you going to help me or not?"

"What can *I* do?" Elena asked. "*You're* the one who stole my boyfriend."

Rebecca started to cry again, but Elena didn't respond. She didn't care. Her sister needed to learn that there were limits. She couldn't have every boy at the school, let alone her sister's boyfriend—even if they'd just started to like each other. More importantly, why did Rebecca feel that she needed him? She couldn't believe Rebecca would have sex with someone she barely knew as her first. But since she had, why him?

"No," Elena said. "This is your problem, not mine. You gotta tell Dad and leave me out of it."

Rebecca got up from the bed and slowly started toward the bedroom door, leaving the pregnancy stick on the bed.

"Take this with you," Elena said, tossing the stick to Rebecca as she left.

Elena watched her sister pick up the stick off the floor and leave the bedroom. She heard her sister walk quietly back to her room and close the door behind her. Elena felt so angry and hurt. She'd told Rebecca all about Miguel in confidence. But for what? To create a new prize for her sister to steal? It was crazy. And now, she was just going to run to some clinic in Pitillal to fix it? That was even crazier.

Elena got up from the bed and started for the door. Rebecca needed to tell Dad. If she wasn't going to do it, then Elena would. She left the bedroom and headed down the hallway toward their father's room. But when she passed Rebecca's door, she heard her sister softly crying inside. Elena paused, listening. She loved her sister, but this time Rebecca had gone too far. Still, she couldn't bring herself to continue on to their father's bedroom. Instead, she softly knocked on her sister's door and opened it slowly when Rebecca didn't respond.

"I'm sorry," Elena said. "I'm just really, really angry."

"I know," Rebecca said. "You should be."

She sat next to her sister, who was lying on her stomach on the bed. "So, what do you want me to do?" Elena asked.

Rebecca looked up. "I want you to go with me."

Elena swallowed. "When?"

"Tomorrow. During school." She dropped her head back down and started uncomfortably picking at the fabric of the bedcover.

Elena thought about what her sister wanted. It seemed like a mistake, but she didn't see another option. "Okay," Elena said. "I will."

Rebecca hugged her. "Thanks," she said.

Elena reached out to smooth Rebecca's hair in order to comfort her. But from the tears she saw on her sister's damp pillow, she knew there would be no comfort for her sister that night.

The next morning on their way to school, Elena still felt disappointed and angry, but she could see that her sister was desperate. What choice did she have? So when the public bus they rode each day stopped at the marina in front of the American School, Rebecca and Elena got off. But instead of following the other high school kids past the security guard and into the school facility, they walked several more blocks past the Walmart and boarded another bus heading into the center of Pitillal.

Pitillal was a small town next to Puerto Vallarta. While the tourists—American, Canadian, and Mexican—always went to Puerto Vallarta, they never went to Pitillal. Pitillal was not on the beach but instead was located on the hills a couple of miles above the ocean. Pitillal was clean, with water, plumbing, and electricity in both the constructed and makeshift houses, but it didn't have hotels, condominiums, skyscrapers, or swimming pools. Instead, it was where the local people lived—the gardeners, cleaners, waiters, hotel clerks, and other Mexicans who provided the services to Puerto Vallarta proper. As the bus proceeded, Elena realized that they'd been to that town only once, despite having lived in the area their entire lives and having gone to school only a couple of miles from it.

Elena's emotions vacillated. She was still angry, frustrated, and afraid to skip school. But mostly, she felt rejected and hurt—by Miguel but much more so by Rebecca. How could her sister do this to her? And why was it now her problem? But as the sporadic tears continued to appear on Rebecca's cheeks, she knew there was nothing she could do but help her. She reached over and took her twin's hand, trying to reassure her.

Elena watched the building addresses as the bus passed central Pitillal, heading up toward the mountains. After another five minutes or so, Rebecca abruptly got up. "*Espera, por favor.*" *(Stop, please.)* The bus driver noticed her through the rearview mirror and gestured for her to wait a moment longer. After the bus passed through an intersection, the driver pulled the bus to the side of the road and opened the rear door for them to exit.

After walking a couple of blocks, the twins arrived at a small nondescript building that looked fairly run-down. It appeared to be a house, or at least it used to be one. After passing through a gate, there was a doorbell with a yellow sticky note saying in Spanish, "*Toca el timbre.*" Elena rang the bell, and they waited. When an older woman opened it, they entered.

"Do you have an appointment?" the woman asked.

"No," Elena answered. Rebecca just looked down at the floor.

"You'll need to wait as a walk-in, then," she said, pointing them to a couple of empty chairs as she wrote the number three on a piece of paper and handed it to Rebecca.

Elena saw several other women waiting in the small room. They were sitting around the perimeter on plastic folding chairs that were designed to be easily moved. The women were of various ages, but most of them looked young. All of them were Latina except for Rebecca. Many of them bore the signs of poverty. Their skin was dark, probably from living outdoors without sun protection, and their teeth were crooked in the case of the younger girls and missing or encased in metal frames for the older women. Most all of them looked short in stature, possibly suggesting indigenous roots. As they whispered quietly among themselves, Elena could tell from their informal Spanish and more rural grammar that many of them weren't from the Puerto Vallarta area at all.

"I don't like it here," Elena said. "Let's go."

Rebecca's red eyes widened. "No," she said. "You can leave if you want to, but I'm staying." She took a seat on one of the folding chairs. Elena hesitated before taking an empty seat next to her sister.

One by one, the women were called into an adjoining room about every forty-five minutes, apparently leaving from a separate back door once their appointment was completed. During the wait, some women arrived with appointments, and they were taken next. After several hours, the older woman returned and called, "*Numero tres?*" Elena and Rebecca followed her into a small office, apparently where the business was handled. Another woman met them there.

"You're here for an examination?" she asked. "Or a removal?"

"A removal," Elena answered. She looked toward her sister. "For her."

"Are you sure you're pregnant?"

"I think so," Rebecca answered.

"The nurse will check you first, then, and we'll proceed afterward if you are. Do you know how far along you are?" she continued.

"Not very far," Rebecca said.

"Okay," the woman answered. "It's five hundred fifty pesos for the checkup and nine thousand five hundred pesos for the removal. You can pay me now, and I'll give you back the extra if you don't need it."

"They told me it was ninety-five total," Rebecca said. She reached into her backpack and pulled out her money. "That's all I have."

The woman looked irritated but quickly took it. "Okay, since you're young."

She left the room for a moment before taking them to an adjoining room, which appeared to have been a bedroom. After a few minutes, a man wearing blue surgical scrubs entered the room.

"I'm Ramon," he said. "I'll help you. Don't be afraid."

Elena looked at him carefully while continuing to scan the room. "Are you a doctor?"

"No," Ramon answered. "Doctors can't do this procedure because it's illegal here. If you want a doctor, you must go to Mexico City, where it's legal."

Elena looked at Rebecca questioningly and then back at the man. "Do you do this all the time?" Elena asked.

"Yes," he answered. "I'm a midwife."

The answer didn't make sense to Elena; she thought midwives delivered babies. She looked at Rebecca, who nodded, indicating that she wanted to proceed. "Okay," she said.

The man instructed Rebecca to take off her clothes, put on the gown hanging on the door, and sit on the medical chair. He said he'd return in a few minutes. Rebecca removed her clothes, and Elena folded them neatly and placed them on the chair. Then Rebecca put on the gown and sat in the examination chair. After but a moment, her face turned red, and her tears started again.

Elena took Rebecca's hand in both of hers. "It'll be okay," she said. "These women seem to be done in less than an hour."

After a while, there was a knock on the door. The man returned, washed his hands, and started to examine Rebecca. He opened her legs and put them in two metal stirrups that looked like they were designed for a woman giving birth. "Yes, you're pregnant, but it's early," he said, after performing a brief examination. "Are you sure you want me to take it out?"

"Yes," Rebecca answered.

He nodded. "If you want a Valium, it's five hundred pesos." Having no more, Rebecca looked to Elena, who reached into her purse and pulled out some money. The man took the money quickly, putting it directly into his pocket.

Rebecca took the pill with a drink from the glass of water that the man's assistant offered her. He returned after about another five minutes with the assistant and started the procedure. Elena again held Rebecca's hand but didn't watch. She could feel Rebecca squirm and jump reflexively as the man worked. Elena heard some type of vacuum noise followed by suction. When the noise stopped, the man's assistant left, apparently with the pregnancy remains. Then the man closed Rebecca's gown and left as well.

When the assistant returned, she led Rebecca into another bedroom and told her to lie down for at least fifteen minutes. "If you see bleeding, then you need to see a doctor immediately. Spots aren't bleeding," she said, as if it were an afterthought. "But if you call the police and tell them about us, you will be arrested, and the nurse won't . . . The police can't help you anyway—only a doctor can."

Sometime after they'd returned home later that night, Rebecca started to cry softly. Elena went into her sister's room and tried to console her, thinking her sister was still feeling overwhelmed. But when the crying got louder after she'd returned to her own room, she woke up her father. When they entered Rebecca's room and he lifted her from her bed, they could see blood on her sheets.

"What's wrong?" Francisco asked, panicked.

"It's just spotting," Rebecca said.

"I don't think so," he answered, and then, "What did you do?" He took her in his arms and started running to his Jeep. "Grab some towels and come with me," he said to Elena. She pulled the towels from her sister's bathroom drawer and followed her father to the garage.

"How could you let her do this?" he asked Elena. "You've always been the responsible one!"

Elena didn't respond. Why was it her fault? Again. She felt angry, but as she watched Rebecca, she mostly felt afraid.

Her father quickly drove them to the on-call physician at the Four Seasons. The doctor at the hotel examined Rebecca quickly and sent her to a hospital in Puerto Vallarta in the hotel's private limousine. When they arrived, another doctor met them in the emergency room and immediately took Rebecca to an operating room. Elena remembered waiting in the hospital with her father for over an hour. Eventually, the same doctor returned.

"She's fine," he said. "Resting."

Elena gathered her thoughts as she blankly stared at the dark wooden bedpost in their room at the Four Seasons almost a decade later. She vividly remembered feeling an overwhelming sense of relief when she'd learned from the doctor that her sister would be all right. Only years later would she learn what the doctor had privately told her father and Rebecca: that, as a result of the reparative surgery, it was unlikely that Rebecca would be able to bear children.

Coming home, seeing Rebecca, her father, and the Four Seasons—the memories seemed like too much. She remembered that it had been only a week or so after the procedure that Rebecca, without warning or notice, got into a boat with the Stimpsons and just left. While it had been almost a decade since then, the sunken, empty feeling she'd felt at the time remained. She looked down at Rebecca's name as it appeared on the contacts list of her phone. Then she turned the phone off. For the time being, at least, she'd need to sort things out on her own.

The electronic lock to her room clicked, and Richard entered. "I'm sorry," he said, kissing the top of her head. "I'm just a little beat."

"I'm sorry, too," Elena answered. "I've been feeling off for a while."

Richard walked over to her and held her to him. "We'll figure it out," he said. "Let's just go to sleep now."

Chapter 9

FRANCISCO TOOK THE LUNCHES CONSUELA HAD MADE AND PLACED them inside the storage compartment of Guillermo's boat, the *Esperanza*. He'd been packing these same lunches for restaurant guests for their fishing day for years. This time, he packed them for his own family. He thought it would be nice to spend the day fishing with his girls. As he reached for the beer, he noticed Consuela running down the boat ramp.

"*Momento, un momento,*" she said.

"*Hola.* What's up?"

"You forgot the guacamole!" She handed him a plastic container and a grocery bag. "Did you get the *totopos*?" she asked, meaning the chips.

"Yes. All good. Hey," he continued, "why don't you come, too?"

"*¿Estás loco?*" she answered. *(Are you crazy?)* "I can't swim. And Guillermo is always drunk on this boat." She looked at her husband judgmentally. "Or stoned."

Realizing there was no persuading her, Francisco took the bags from her and smiled.

"You have a good time today with your girls," she said quietly to him.

"*Gracias,*" he said.

After stowing the remaining food, he looked up to see that the rest of their group was approaching from the beach. Elena and her boyfriend were ahead with Rebecca behind them.

"Hi, Richard," he said. "You remember Consuela and Guillermo?"

"Sure," Richard said. "*Buenos días.*"

"Then come aboard, everyone," Francisco said. He helped Rebecca and Elena onto the boat, but Richard seemed hesitant. Francisco knew that Guillermo's boat was old and somewhat run-down, but it remained fully seaworthy. "Don't worry. Guillermo's been taking guests on this boat forever—it's not going to sink!"

"Are you sure?" Richard asked.

It seemed like he was trying to be funny, but Francisco wasn't entirely sure. "Consuela isn't," Francisco answered. "You noticed she didn't get on the boat?" He looked over at Consuela, who zipped her lips, indicating that they were sealed. Then he steadied the boat as Richard boarded before he winked back at her.

Francisco watched Richard as he found a seat and tried to settle in. It seemed pretty clear that he was out of his element. His hair was neatly combed and looked as if it had been gelled. He was wearing some designer sunglasses and a type of hat that Francisco didn't recognize. His pants were all white—not the best choice for dripping fish bait or oozing fish entrails—and his shirt looked like some type of designer polo in a bright green color. He'd apparently purchased some shoes that appeared to be made for a luxury sailboat, but Francisco couldn't imagine how they would be necessary on an old boat like the *Esperanza*.

"All ready?" Guillermo asked. They nodded, and he tossed the mooring line off the boat and started backing out of the slip.

Within minutes, the boat slowly passed through the marina buoys before heading out to the open sea at full speed. The spray of the ocean invigorated everyone against the heat of the sun, which had already risen well above the Sayulita bluffs surrounding their home. Rebecca sat in the front, speaking with Richard, while Elena sat to his left, also enjoying the vista.

"Something to drink?" Francisco asked. "Anyone?"

"I'll take a beer," Richard said. "It's happy hour somewhere."

"Have you got a mineral water?" Elena asked.

"One beer, one water. You, Rebecca?" he asked.

"I'm good," she said.

Francisco pulled the drinks from the boat's mini fridge, including a beer for himself, and handed them out. He watched as Elena kept her view focused on the horizon while holding to the side of the boat.

"Queasy?" he asked.

"Yeah, a little. Maybe I'm not used to the water here anymore?" she answered.

"Guillermo's probably got a Dramamine," he replied. "Want one?"

"I think I'm good," she said, "but thanks."

As they traveled north along the coastline, Guillermo pointed out the various hotels and other sites. Over the years, the level of new construction had grown substantially. After the boat had proceeded for about ten minutes or so, he nodded ahead to the right. The group turned in the direction he'd indicated. "Dolphins."

"I see them," Rebecca said. "There's a couple, right?"

"I think so," he said. "I'll head over for a closer look." Guillermo redirected the boat and reduced its speed. As they approached, the dolphins swam over. When he picked up the boat's speed just slightly, the dolphins started following them.

"Why do they do that?" Rebecca said.

"Beats me," Francisco said. "Maybe something about the drag of the boat?"

"They're wonderful," Elena said. "So playful."

The dolphins swam alongside the boat for about ten minutes or so before losing interest and swimming away. Guillermo then increased the boat's speed, and they continued north along the coast.

"I think we'll do better another half hour out," Guillermo said.

Francisco nodded.

As they proceeded, the coast became less inhabited and increasingly tropical. However, a number of multicolored tents appeared from time to time along the edge of the jungle on the beach.

"It's getting worse," Francisco said, pointing to the tents on the beach. Rebecca nodded, frowning.

"What *is* that?" Richard asked.

"A homeless town," Guillermo said.

"Do they let them just live there?" Richard asked.

"Not really," Francisco answered. "But where can they go?"

"Anywhere," Richard said. "They're not prisoners, right?"

"Right," Francisco answered. He bit the inside of his cheek to keep from elaborating. Now wasn't the time for this conversation.

"No restrooms," Richard continued. "Do they just use the ocean?"

Francisco silently sighed. "Probably," he said.

"You shouldn't put up with that. You'll end up like us: people living on the streets and peeing in the subways. It's a huge mess now in Manhattan—shit everywhere."

Francisco wanted to assure him that the ocean was much cleaner than the subways in New York City. Instead, he looked again at the designer clothes Richard was wearing. He knew the guy was a senior investment banker in New York, so he presumed Richard was loaded. Regardless, poor people using the ocean for relief wasn't the same as using the sidewalk.

Guillermo slowed the boat down and handed out the poles. "Who's fishing?" he asked, changing the subject.

"I'm in," Rebecca said, heading to the rear of the boat.

"In," Francisco said.

"You, Richard?" Elena asked.

"I'll pass," he said. "I'll take another beer, though."

"Great," Francisco said, reaching into the storage bin before shaking the ice off the bottle.

While Guillermo baited their lines with small sardines, Francisco pulled out the lunches that Consuela had made them. "My rule," he said, "is to make sure we feed the fish *and* the humans. It's only fair."

"Do the fish get to catch us?" Elena asked.

"Not that fair," Francisco answered.

They continued trolling without much success. After a while, Francisco handed out the fish tacos with the chips and guacamole Consuela had made for them.

"It's well after noon," Francisco said. "Anyone for a margarita?"

"I'm in for that," Richard said, having finished his beer.

"Me too," Rebecca added.

"Now we're talking," Francisco said. "Elena?"

She shook her head. "Too early for me," she said.

Francisco chuckled. "That's okay," he said. "The day is young, so there's plenty of time to rediscover your roots."

The fish tacos Consuela had packed came with all of the accoutrements: guacamole, salsa (spicy and mild), Mexican cheese, and *pico de gallo*. Also included in the lunch bags were cucumbers and jicama with paprika and tabasco sauce, a Mexican favorite. A large thermos contained the mixed margaritas. Francisco opened it and poured the contents into salted cups and garnished them with fresh limes, making the drinks cool and refreshing, particularly as the heat of the sun increased and midday arrived.

With the lines again baited and the meal underway, Guillermo started the boat. They trolled along the coast at a modest pace, hoping for a bite. Elena sat comfortably on the bow, enjoying the sun and the meal, while Rebecca and Richard continued their conversation in the cabin.

Francisco turned his attention back to Guillermo's boat. It was hard to imagine that this was the same boat, the *Esperanza*, that had brought them to Mexico from the States over two decades ago. Since then, his girls had grown up and left—their worlds turned upside down. Or was it right side up? But for Guillermo and Consuela, life remained largely the same. Francisco remembered feeling afraid while traveling with Guillermo and his twins back then: afraid the boat wouldn't make it, afraid they'd be caught, and afraid he'd been wrong to take them from their country of birth.

After hastily leaving their home in San Francisco on the night of Derek's funeral, Francisco and his toddler twins arrived at Dana Landing Marina just outside of San Diego on Mission Bay. Once parked, he rolled down the window of his car. The cool ocean breeze smelled of salt and the sea. Francisco checked his watch: 5:00 a.m. The drive from San Francisco had taken about nine hours. There hadn't been much traffic; he'd driven all night. But with twin toddlers, stopping occasionally had been a necessity. Francisco checked the rearview mirror of their Audi before getting out of the car. The twins continued to sleep peacefully—the quiet before the storm? He hoped not.

Francisco felt worried. He got out of the car to briefly stretch his legs. The decision to leave had been a hasty one. Did it make sense? Was he putting his girls in harm's way? Derek would have never gone for that. Would he have wanted his girls raised in Mexico? *Absolutely not*, Francisco thought. But Derek would have wanted them together as a family. He would have wanted them raised in love. After climbing back into the car and getting as comfortable as possible, Francisco closed his eyes and tried to sleep until daybreak.

With the sunrise came the morning cries of one and then both of the twins. Francisco started with Elena, who seemed to be the loudest. First, he moved her car seat to the front; then he pulled the diaper bag out. He unwrapped a toddler cereal bar, her favorite, and tied a little bib around her neck before breaking the snack into bite-size pieces. She ate quickly, oblivious to the changed surroundings. When she was finished, he removed her from the car seat, pulled the changing pad and wipes from the diaper bag, and gave her a quick change. Then he put her back in her car seat with a sippy cup of water and repeated the same tasks for Rebecca.

"Gimme a cookie," Elena asked.

"Okay," he responded. He reopened the bag and dug around for her favorite. He handed one to her and another to Rebecca.

"Now stay quiet," he said, putting his index finger to his mouth.

By 7:30 a.m., the tourists had started to arrive. They waited in front of the small marina store. When it opened, Francisco opened the car windows a bit and secured the girls in their car seats. He didn't like the idea of leaving them unattended, but bringing them into the store would likely increase their being noticed. He increased his pace as he walked into the store with the others.

"Which boat does Javier run?" he asked the woman behind the desk in the store.

"Slip twenty-nine on the right," she said, pointing.

"Thanks," he said. "Do you have baby supplies?"

"Some," she noted, pointing to the back.

Francisco quickly grabbed a couple of things for the twins and him and paid for them in cash at the counter before exiting. After closing the door, he realized his mistake. *More cookies*, he thought. He turned and walked back into the store to buy the "essentials." He didn't like the idea of loading the girls up on junk, but this weekend wasn't the one to focus on a healthy diet. After purchasing a box of Chips Ahoy! and a bag of Doritos, he started back to the car. When he arrived, he unhooked the girls from their car seats, took one in each hand, and headed out to the boat dock.

The slips were fairly close and clearly marked. Twenty-nine was toward the end on the right, as the clerk had noted. When he arrived, he saw a short Latino man preparing the boat for a day of fishing. The vessel was a fairly large motorboat, maybe thirty feet, which had been rigged for tourist fishing.

"Are you Javier?" he asked.

"Yes," the man answered. "You're Guillermo's friend?"

"Francisco," he answered. He released Elena's hand and extended his to Javier.

"Are they coming?" Javier asked, looking down at the young twins. As he spoke, he continued stowing away food supplies and what appeared to be fishing bait.

"Yes," Francisco answered.

Javier stopped packing and looked more closely at the twins. "I didn't realize how young they were. What, two or three?"

"Yes," Francisco answered, deliberately being vague. "How long will it take?" he asked, seeking to divert the man's attention away from the twins.

"They're both yours, right?" Javier asked. "I'm not getting involved with stealing a baby." He looked at Rebecca and then back at Francisco.

"Yes," Francisco answered directly. He was surprised by the conviction in his voice but not by the accuracy of the answer.

Javier nodded. "We'll meet your friend halfway down the Baja Peninsula. That will take a day. Then another day and a night with your friend from there—if the weather permits him to go quickly."

"Okay," Francisco said.

"It's five hundred dollars, paid in advance."

"Right," Francisco said, pulling out his wallet and handing him the money. "Anything important I need?"

"Hats, sunscreen, and maybe more blankets." He nodded to the marina store before looking down at the girls. "You can leave them here in the boat with me for a minute."

Francisco handed him the twins and then headed back to the store to pick up the additional supplies. He found some blankets, water, sunscreen, and snacks. He took the items along with the car seats and their suitcases, one by one, from his car to the boat.

He wasn't taking much. He'd left almost everything behind, knowing that he had no way to move it. It all seemed so sudden—and permanent. A week ago, he was happily married to the man of his dreams, and they were raising their daughters in an incredible flat in San Francisco. Now, he was alone, unemployed, and homeless with two toddlers, trying to sneak over an international border. It was too much and too fast. But what choice was there? He squeezed Rebecca's little hand and watched her squeal with delight. There was no choice. Besides, he'd always wanted to be a father. And he was determined to be a good one. He would be the father Derek's parents never were. He would be the father his parents never were. He may be jobless, but he was determined. Regardless, the truth was quite simple: He loved his daughters—both of them. And he'd never give them up—either of them.

He watched as Javier stowed away the last of their bags, hiding them carefully under a tarp within the boat's storage bins. Francisco realized he hadn't thought about the car. To anyone looking, it provided a clear road map to where he'd been and where he was headed.

"Can I ask for another favor?" he said.

Javier nodded, as he continued packing the boat.

"Can you take my car away when you get back and just leave it someplace else? Anywhere would work, but maybe a train or bus station?"

Javier looked at him with concern. "When will they start looking for you?"

"Tomorrow evening or later," Francisco answered. "Just make sure that you don't keep it."

"One hundred fifty dollars to move it," Javier said.

Francisco handed him the keys with the additional money. Now the car was gone, too. *Yes*, he thought. *Too much, too fast—way too fast.*

Javier started the engine, and the boat slowly proceeded past the marina buoys before accelerating to cruising speed. "We're not far from the border," Javier explained. "So we may see the US Coast Guard, ICE, or the DEA."

"DEA?" Francisco asked.

"The Drug Enforcement Agency," he answered.

"Yes, but why would they come after us?"

"They track all the boats along the border with their radar."

"Have you been stopped before?"

Javier smiled. "Yup. It's the drugs they're looking to stop. No one will be so interested in Americans headed south, assuming an alert hasn't been issued for you."

Francisco nodded again.

"If they stop us, remember, you're just here on a day trip, fishing. Think of some reason why you have two babies and not a wife. They might look around the boat for money or drugs. But we're not doing anything illegal, so just don't panic."

Francisco nodded again.

Javier kept the boat running at a fast and consistent speed. While the San Diego Bay had been fairly choppy, the water of the open ocean was relatively smooth. The fresh air and occasional gentle bouncing of the boat quickly put the girls back to sleep. Francisco rested his head on the seat cushion panel and quickly fell asleep, too.

He awoke sometime later to the cries of Rebecca, which, of course, then woke Elena as well. The sun was midway up, and the Baja coast extended along to their left as far as he could see. While the boat continued at a fairly quick clip, the bow started bouncing as the afternoon wind picked up. He removed Rebecca from her car seat. As expected, she needed a change. He pulled the ever-faithful diaper bag out from the storage bin and changed her before doing the same with Elena. Then he fed them both in their car seats, this time with bananas and some of the cooked rice and peas he'd brought from home.

"Are you ready for a break?" Javier asked.

"I'd rather just get there," Francisco said.

"Yeah, but I've got to earn a living." Javier smiled. "We'll troll for a bit up ahead and see if they're biting." He slowed down the boat, pulled out three or four fishing poles, and baited each with a small fish. "Sardines," he said. "They love them."

Francisco didn't want to fish but realized he had no choice. Javier handed him one of the poles and then started making lunch.

"Fish tacos," he said. "My wife makes them." He prepared several on a small interior table, spreading the fish over the small tortillas before filling them with fresh salsa, lettuce, and guacamole.

"Here," he said, handing Francisco two of the tacos and a bottle of water. "*Servicio completo.*" *(Full service.)*

Francisco took a bite of a taco. It was delicious, and the water was icy cold and refreshing. "*Gracias,*" he said.

It wasn't long before a fishing pole bent with the tug of a bite. Javier walked over to the line and picked it up, pulling gently. "You ready?" he asked.

"Sure," Francisco said.

Javier handed him the pole and told him to reel it in slowly. Francisco did as he was instructed. The fish's pull was solid but manageable, so he reeled it slowly but firmly. After a few minutes, he heard the splash of a fish in the water below. Javier pulled a long net from the back and scooped it up.

"Not bad," he said. "Dorado."

Francisco smiled. "They call it *mahi-mahi* in the United States, right?"

"Yes, it's the same."

The fish had a large head and fin. Its striking fluorescent and dark green colors ran the length of its body. Javier clubbed it on its big head, taking it out quickly, before laying it in a panel on the side of the boat that was filled with ice.

"How many do you usually catch?" Francisco asked.

"Sometimes nothing," Javier answered. "Sometimes five or even more."

"Dorado?"

"That or red snapper are the most common. Maybe a tuna."

"How much do you sell one for?"

"A lot," he answered, avoiding the question.

Javier handed Francisco back the now-baited pole along with another taco. The sun was warm, but the sea air was still fresh with a mild breeze. Francisco took another drink of the icy water, finished his second taco, and then leaned back into his seat. They quickly caught several more fish before Javier pulled up the lines and stored them away in the boat.

"That'll do," he said. "Ready to move on?"

"Ready," Francisco answered.

Javier then pushed the throttle forward, increasing the boat to full speed, and they continued along the Mexican coast of the Baja Peninsula. As the afternoon wind increased, the surf became choppier, bouncing the boat haphazardly. Francisco was afraid the girls would start to cry, but they managed for the most part. Javier ignored the waves and kept the boat moving forward.

Francisco wondered if the Stimpsons had figured out that he'd left with the twins. They weren't to arrive at the house for another day to pick up Rebecca, but it wouldn't surprise him if they'd checked in early or at least called. He looked down at Rebecca's pudgy cheeks as she slept soundly in the car seat he'd fastened to the seat of the boat. All she had now was him. Was that enough? He didn't have a job or a place to live. He didn't have a college education. His girls, both American citizens, were entering Mexico with him illegally and leaving the United States illegally—at least that's how the Stimpsons would present it to the authorities. And if he were arrested, Elena would have no one. He'd have to be careful to cover his tracks and then stay off the grid—at least for a while. As he considered that possibility, he realized that it wouldn't be all that tough. His parents had no idea where he lived and hadn't for years. But returning to the States was going to be impossible for the foreseeable future. He again looked down at Rebecca, who peacefully slept.

It was all so confusing. No, it was all just plain crazy. But he knew that he'd made up his mind, and it was too late to go back. He looked out at the vast horizon of the empty sea and took a deep breath. It was hard to comprehend, but this was his new reality. Derek was gone forever, and now he was alone. He'd just have to get used to it—quickly. But the realization didn't stop the tears from forming in the corners of his eyes.

They continued in the boat for the balance of the day. The hum of the boat's engine and its consistent bounce on the ocean waves quickly lulled the twins to sleep. When they woke from time to time, he walked the boat with them, fed them, and then securely placed them back into their car seats. He was surprised at how calm the girls remained and how easy it all seemed. After the afternoon hours passed, Javier pointed to a small white boat in the distance.

"That's him," Javier said, squinting into his binoculars.

"How do you know? Did you call him?"

"The name." Javier handed the binoculars to Francisco.

Francisco scanned the boat. On its side was painted in script, the *Esperanza*. Francisco instantly felt relieved.

Javier headed to Guillermo's boat, which slowed to meet them. When they arrived, Guillermo tossed a rope over, and the two captains tied their boats together to facilitate the transfer.

"*Hola,* Guillermo," Francisco said. "Thanks for helping us."

"No time," Guillermo responded. "Risky here. Hand me your stuff—the girls first."

Francisco quickly handed him Rebecca, and Javier passed Elena across the side of the boats. Javier then started pulling out Francisco's suitcases, handing them to Francisco, who in turn passed them to Guillermo. Within minutes, the transfer was complete, and Francisco was aboard as well.

"*Gracias*, Javier," Francisco said.

"No problem," he responded, waiting.

Guillermo laughed. "He wants a tip," he said.

"Of course," Francisco said, handing him another fifty dollars.

"*Gracias. Buenos suerte*," Javier added, waving good luck to them as he unleashed the boats before speeding away.

Guillermo fired up his engine as well, and they continued heading south down the Baja Peninsula toward Puerto Vallarta.

Francisco wondered if Javier would actually move the car or just keep the money. The guy seemed decent enough, but why would he assume the risk? Francisco realized that Javier probably wouldn't. He'd have to presume that the car would be left there, despite their agreement. If the car wasn't moved, then the marina would have it towed, probably tomorrow—the same day the Stimpsons would know for sure that he'd left. If so, the license plates would likely be entered into some registry, and the police would know he was on a boat headed down the Pacific Coast to Mexico. He felt the tightness in his chest start up again.

He nervously scanned the horizon as the sun started to set before turning to Guillermo. "How's Consuela?" he asked, seeking to break some of the tension.

"Great," Guillermo said.

"She's still helping Jose?"

"Yes."

"And you?"

"I'm still managing the restaurant facilities and running the tourist fishing trips," he said.

"And smoking pot?" Francisco grinned.

"Well, maybe a little. Do you want some?"

"For sure," Francisco said.

Guillermo reached into a pocket under his seat and pulled out his pipe. He filled and lit it before passing the pipe to Francisco for a turn. Within minutes, Francisco felt relaxed.

"Great stuff," Francisco said.

"Welcome back to Mexico," Guillermo answered.

They passed several boats as they continued along the Mexican coast in the darkness of the evening. Some were fishing boats, some were sailboats, and one was a large cruise ship. The boats were heading both north and south, and the cruise ship seemed to be heading out to sea.

After traveling in darkness well into the evening, Guillermo pulled the boat to a small inlet near the shore and dropped anchor. "We'll get a little sleep here tonight," he said.

Chapter 10

Francisco returned his attention to his adult girls and watched as they fished from Guillermo's boat on their day trip from Sayulita. The boat was the same, the sea line was the same, and Guillermo was the same—more or less. But his daughters, once toddlers strapped to the very same boat seats, now sat comfortably next to him as women. They'd grown up, and that had changed everything. And, of course, he was dying. *How did it all happen, seemingly overnight?*

Francisco wondered what it would be like once he was gone. He knew his girls would return to Sayulita from time to time, but it wouldn't be the same. How could it be? Simply put, their journey together was ending. The sadness of moving on without them weighed heavily upon his heart. But the twins' journey, together—the closeness, the connectedness, the bonding, and the love—didn't need to end. Nor should it. But he felt, no, he knew, that if something didn't change, the distance would only grow as their paths continued to separate. How could he help them see it? How could he help them care? He could try, and he would. But ultimately, it would be up to them. At least they had a few more days together before he'd have to tell them about his illness.

Rebecca's line went taut. "I've got one," she said. "It's huge—I can tell!"

Guillermo cut the engine and walked over to where she and Richard were standing.

"You do," he said. "Now reel it in, but slowly. Don't fight it."

"Ah!" she hollered. "It's pulling—it's getting away!"

"Help her, Richard," Francisco said. "Just hold the pole so she doesn't lose it in the ocean."

Richard reached around both sides of Rebecca and held the pole with her between him and it, pressing his body against hers. That wasn't what Francisco had expected, but it was what he'd asked. Rebecca reeled the line slowly, little by little.

"It's huge," she said again. "I can feel it."

Guillermo laughed without correcting her.

"Richard, you look exhausted," Francisco joked. "Have another margarita." He took Richard's cup and refilled it.

"Gladly," Richard said. "Just hold it for a minute."

Francisco had hoped to separate Richard from Rebecca. But Richard wasn't letting go of the pole—or Rebecca. After some vigorous reeling, the fish appeared, flapping randomly, as it breached the safety of the ocean before heading down again.

"Just keep reeling," Guillermo said, searching for the net, as Richard continued to hold Rebecca. When the fish reached the side of the boat, Guillermo swept it up in the net and dropped it on the floor of the boat, where it fluttered with spasms against Elena's feet.

"It's just a baby," Rebecca said. "So disappointing!"

Guillermo nodded. "Shall we throw it back?"

"Yes," Rebecca said. "Let it live, please."

"What?" Richard said. "You caught it!"

The fish continued to gasp for air, flapping frantically between Elena's legs, leaving the wet slime of its body on her calves. She sidestepped and danced to avoid it.

"Are you okay?" Francisco asked.

She started to nod but then couldn't stop herself. Vomit sprayed on her legs as well as the fish, which continued flopping in it. Elena stepped up on the bench to get away from it while shaking her hand over the side of the boat.

"Gross," Richard said, as the rest of them laughed.

Francisco took her hand to stabilize her before placing it on the side of the boat, where she clung.

Elena wiped her face with her free hand, and Francisco handed her a towel. "It's better now," she said, laughing at herself.

Guillermo took the line just above the fish's head and grabbed it around the center of its body. He then effortlessly removed the hook from the fish's mouth, even as it squirmed. He offered it to Richard, who declined, and then to Rebecca, who took the fish and tossed it back into the sea.

"That's a shame," Richard said.

"It's just a baby, Richard," Elena said. "Why not let it live?"

Richard smirked back at her.

Francisco pulled some water from the canteen along with a towel and used them to wipe Elena's mouth. "I'm sorry, honey. Are you okay?"

She nodded.

"When did you start getting seasickness?"

"Who knows?" she answered, as he started wiping her dress in a pointless effort to clean it.

Guillermo offered her a blanket. "Take this," he said. Then he looked at the rest of the group. "Shall we head back?" he asked.

"Yes," Rebecca said. "She's not feeling well."

"No," Richard said. "Not if we still have margaritas." He reached around Rebecca for the rail of the boat and gently brushed his arm against hers. Rebecca laughed and stepped away, but Richard again moved closer to her. "We can't leave now. Rebecca and I need to catch a grown-up fish—one we can eat without Elena barfing on it." He grinned at his joke.

Did he think that was funny? Francisco wondered. He reached into his day bag and pulled out a sweatshirt and swim trunks. "Put these on," he said to Elena. "You'll feel better—or at least cleaner."

Elena smiled. "Thanks, Dad," she said.

After she'd changed her clothes, Francisco started to rub her back. "Are you sure you don't want to head home?" he asked her. Elena shook her head. He watched her return to the front of the boat, away from the rest of the group, and again take hold of the boat railing.

"It happens to someone every time," Guillermo said. "Don't worry about it."

Guillermo rebaited the lines, and Francisco refilled the margarita glasses. He could see, however, that his daughter really was not feeling well. He wondered, too, if she was uncomfortable with the attention her boyfriend was giving Rebecca while ignoring her. But when Richard walked back to Elena and pulled her close, he dismissed the thoughts. Apparently, they were all in his head.

"That's about where the coast guard stopped us—what was that, twenty years ago?" Guillermo said to Francisco. "Remember?"

Francisco looked in the direction Guillermo pointed. "*Sí*," he said. *To be exact, twenty-three years ago*, he thought.

After the long journey from San Francisco by car and then from San Diego by boat, Francisco remembered waking the next morning with his twin toddlers on the deck of the *Esperanza* even before the first rays of the sun breached the darkness over the ocean along the Baja Peninsula. Guillermo was already up, preparing for the long day's journey down the Mexican coast to Sayulita. Francisco pulled his toiletries from his bag. He washed his face with the washcloth and the soap Guillermo had given him before brushing his teeth and then repacking.

"Here," Guillermo said, handing him a coffee.

"Thanks," Francisco said. "For picking us up at the border and bringing us back home."

Guillermo smiled.

Home, Francisco thought. *Was that where they were going?* It felt like it. He hoped so. The *Esperanza*, the name of Guillermo's boat, meant *hope*, and at the moment, hope was pretty much all they had. He looked again at Guillermo and felt a deep sense of gratitude.

Noticing Elena stirring in her car seat, he took her out and opened the diaper bag. He placed her on the portable plastic changing table and quickly replaced her dirty diaper with a new one. She squirmed when he tried to put her back into the car seat, but he didn't want her toddling around in the dirty boat.

"Just a minute, sweet pea," he said. "I'll help your sister, and then you can stretch your legs."

When he finished changing Rebecca, he noticed that Guillermo had already pulled up the anchor. "Ready to head out?" he said.

"Yes," Francisco answered.

"Here," Guillermo said. "Try this." He handed Francisco a large bowl of yogurt with diced peaches in it.

"Consuela?" Francisco asked.

"*Sí*," he said. "She made it for you and the girls; she's really excited to see them."

Francisco smiled. He missed her. Consuela would help them. He was sure of it.

After walking each of the girls around the boat, Francisco refastened the twins into their car seats and secured them against the seats of the boat. Then he alternated spooning the yogurt into their mouths while occasionally sneaking a bite for himself. As the boat's speed increased, he could see that the twins were getting cold when goose bumps started to appear on their chubby little arms. He pulled a blanket for each of them from the diaper bag, pressed them over their little bodies, and tucked them into the sides of their car seats.

"They look like burritos," Guillermo said.

Francisco smiled. "How long do you think we've got?"

"About a day," Guillermo said. "If the weather's good."

They continued heading south for several hours with little interruption or change. Francisco felt a sense of relief as they sped along the dry, unchanging coastline. As the distance from San Francisco increased, so did his comfort. *We'll be fine*, he thought.

He picked up Rebecca first and started playing with her. "Pat-a-cake, pat-a-cake, baker's man. Bake me a cake as fast as you can." He clapped her little hands as she giggled. "Pat it and prick it and mark it with *B*." They wrote the letter *B* in the air. "And pop it in the oven for baby and me!" He tossed the make-believe cake into the oven, swinging open her little arms, as she squealed with delight. They sang the song several times before he repeated the nursery rhyme with Elena.

"That's got to get tiring," Guillermo said. "You think you're done, but you're only halfway there."

"Exactly," Francisco said. "And they'll do peekaboo for hours . . ."

He remembered Derek's words for it: *marginal exhaustion*. Taking care of the twins had been tough for both of them. Exhaustion didn't begin to capture the feeling in the middle of the night when changing one, then the other; then feeding one, then the other; then rocking one to sleep, then the other— all before finally getting to go to sleep yourself, only to be awaken seemingly immediately to start the process all over again. They'd both thought it was about as close to torture as one could imagine. Now, he'd give anything to have those moments back. He walked with Elena in the boat, helping her stretch her little legs, before securing her in the car seat again, hopefully for a nap.

The boat continued at full speed down the Mexican coast. The sun was peaking overhead, and the horizon was blue, vast, and empty. With an afternoon wind, the swell of the waves increased, cresting over the bow of the boat and knocking at its sides with constant thuds. It was already dusk, and they were about an hour outside of Sayulita, Guillermo estimated, when he cut the speed. Francisco looked over the bow of their boat as a wave crashed against it, only to see another boat approaching them. When it neared, Francisco saw the police light above the cabin with the Mexican Coast Guard designation written in large black letters in Spanish on its side.

"*Cuidado*," Guillermo said, advising caution.

"What do they want?"

"I don't know. Just let me do the talking."

Francisco looked down at the girls to make sure they were okay. Then he took the blanket tucked around Rebecca and pulled it gently over the top of her head, covering her White face and blonde hair from view. "Just stay quiet for once," he said to the girls. *"Por favor."*

The officer on the police boat spoke to them in Spanish from a bullhorn. "Cut your engines," he said. "Keep your hands in the air."

Francisco watched as the police boat came alongside them, and the second officer secured the boats together with a rope. He pulled Elena's car seat forward and pushed Rebecca's back, wrapping her firmly under the blanket.

"Your name," the officer said, now speaking without the horn.

Guillermo gave him the information he wanted, including his boat registration and license.

"Who are your passengers?" the officer asked.

"Fishing trip," Guillermo said.

"Who are your passengers?" the officer reiterated.

"This is Francisco Montoya and his girls,"

"ID, please," the officer said.

Francisco opened his day bag and searched for his California driver's license in his wallet before reconsidering.

"Momento," he said. "I'll get my passport." He reached into the side compartment of his bag and pulled out his Mexican passport, handing it to the officer in the adjoining boat.

"¿Eres Mexicano?" the officer asked. *(You're Mexican?)*

"Sí," Francisco answered.

Francisco watched as the officer examined the passport and then went back to his radio. He spoke into the receiver and then waited. Francisco felt the panic start to grip his body. Had the Stimpsons come early? Had someone found his car? Did Amber Alerts work internationally? The questions flooded his mind. He wondered what he'd done wrong—what he'd missed. Derek hadn't told the Stimpsons much about him—just that he was from a wealthy family in Mexico City. Did he also tell them about Sayulita? Francisco didn't think so. But it didn't matter; there was nothing he could do. When the officer didn't immediately return, Francisco sank with despair at the possibility that, in a matter of minutes, they could take away his daughter. He looked down at Rebecca, still covered with the blanket but gurgling happily to herself underneath it.

"Who are the children?" the officer asked when he returned.

"They're mine," Francisco continued in Spanish. He removed Elena's car seat and held her, as if demonstrating her native look to the officer.

"Where is the mother?"

"She died," Francisco lied. "Childbirth."

"Can I see an ID for the children?" he said.

Francisco knew he had the twins' birth certificates, but those had been issued in California. "No," Francisco said. "They are children; I didn't think we needed ID for a fishing trip."

"Why didn't you come back last night?" the officer asked Guillermo. "You didn't check back in yesterday at the marina."

"I did, I did," Guillermo said, feigning innocence. "You can ask them!"

"I did," the officer said. "I just radioed, and they said you didn't."

Guillermo didn't respond.

"If there are drugs on this boat, we're going to have to impound it."

"Check," Guillermo said. "Check everywhere."

"I don't want to check," the officer said. "I'm going to have to impound the boat. I can't believe you'd try to hide drugs with two babies. They should be with their mother."

"They don't . . ." Francisco started before noticing Guillermo cutting him off by shaking his head with a frown.

"You can pay a fine if you'd rather," the officer said.

Guillermo nodded before turning slightly to wink discreetly to Francisco. "I'd rather have you search our boat," he said, "or let me explain it all to the authorities in town."

"Of course, that is your option," the officer said. "Would you like to follow me, then?"

"How much would the fine be?" Guillermo said. "If we just paid you directly."

"Twenty thousand pesos," the officer said.

"We don't have that much," Guillermo said. He opened his wallet to show the officer. "I have five thousand."

Francisco realized that Guillermo was negotiating with the officer now. Was he really being cheap when the lives of the twins were at stake? He started to object—Christ, he'd pay the guy anything—but he remembered Guillermo's instructions.

"What about you?" the officer said to Francisco. "Can you pay the difference?"

Francisco knew that he had much more than that in his bags. He thought about getting some before realizing that the amount he had was in US dollars and that transporting large amounts of money across the border was illegal. Guillermo noticed him hesitate and scowled a "no" to him again.

"No," Francisco said. "Only credit cards." He knew he'd just have to trust his friend. When the officer frowned, Francisco added quickly in Spanish, "The fishing trip is all-inclusive."

"Okay, then," the officer said.

Guillermo took all of the money out of his wallet and handed it to the officer. The man took the money quickly and then started to untie the boats. "Make sure you check in at night," he said. "Otherwise, you'll be boarded and inspected for transporting drugs."

Guillermo nodded as the officer started his engine and sped off. When Guillermo did the same, Francisco could see the officers dividing the money between themselves.

"*Bienvenidos a México,*" Guillermo said again, this time with a sarcastic smile. *(Welcome to Mexico.)*

Francisco smirked in agreement. *Mexico,* he thought with frustration. *You wouldn't see that in the United States.* But as he considered the situation further, he realized that Mexico was exactly where they needed to be—at least for now.

The sound of Richard's laugh startled Francisco, refocusing him on the present. He turned his gaze from the Mexican coastline to Rebecca, his adult daughter, who was now soaked. Apparently, the breach of a wave by the boat had showered her with seawater. Rebecca's wet blouse, now molded to her breasts, quickly captured Richard's notice. Richard smiled, as he fully wiped her with a towel from top to bottom. She laughed uncomfortably. While he'd likely intended to be helpful, the attention seemed excessive. Francisco knew that his generation was very different from this younger one, but still, he felt uneasy. Regardless, he couldn't help but believe that his daughters' backstory wasn't helping. Francisco looked aft and saw Elena watching Richard as well from the front of the boat.

"Hey, hon," Elena said to Richard. "Can you bring me some lotion?"

Richard opened the boat's storage bin, pulled out her bag, and started rummaging through it. Unable to find the lotion, he took the whole bag to the front. Elena shut the cabin door after he passed.

"What're you doing?" Elena said quietly to Richard.

"What do you mean?" Richard whispered back.

Francisco presumed they didn't think they could be heard, but the sound of their voices followed the stream of the wind that passed through the boat. He moved to the back of the boat, hoping to offer them some privacy, but he could still hear them speak. He looked over at Rebecca; apparently, she could hear them as well.

"I see you're getting to know my sister," Elena said.

"What?" Richard said. "Are you going there again?"

The rest of the group mingled uncomfortably, now collectively pretending that they couldn't hear the conversation.

"You don't think I notice these things, but I do."

"This is crazy," he said.

"I'm not crazy," she said, "and you know it."

Richard didn't respond, as if challenging her without a clear denial.

"You seem so uncomfortable here," she continued. "What's wrong?"

"This dumpy boat? Seriously?" Richard said. "It's much nicer at the Four Seasons."

"Is Rebecca nicer, too?" she asked.

"Are you kidding me?" he said, exasperated. "Do you really want to do this now?"

"Elena," Rebecca said, walking forward, apparently done pretending. "He's just keeping me company while you're not feeling well."

"I know you're trying to help," she said to Rebecca, "but it's not helpful."

When Rebecca returned to her seat, Elena turned her attention back to Richard. "When your girlfriend is sick, you take care of her, Richard. You don't flirt with her sister."

"You were covered with vomit," Richard said. "What exactly do you want me to do with it?"

"You mean *me*?" she answered.

Francisco wanted to intervene but thought better of it. It was their issue; they needed to work it out.

"You're ruining the day for everyone," Richard said, "and making Rebecca very uncomfortable. I don't know what's going on with you down here, but maybe you should apologize for making such a scene."

Elena paused, as she apparently considered what he'd said while recognizing that everyone was watching them. "I'm sorry," she said. "I don't want to spoil the day for everyone, but I do need to get off this boat."

Francisco looked around at the group. "I think we're all getting tired, Guillermo," he said. "Shall we head back?"

"*Sí, patrón*," Guillermo said, turning the direction of the boat slightly and increasing its speed. "Maybe fifty minutes. Relax, and I'll let you know when we're close."

Chapter 11

After awakening at the Montoya family home the next morning, Rebecca decided to spend the day relaxing. After the fishing trip, Francisco had told them to take a group "skip day," and that seemed like a good idea to her. Rebecca had thought about going into town but decided against it. Since Elena and Richard were going to spend the day working at the hotel, she decided instead to enjoy the day by reading in the morning and painting in the afternoon. As she sat on the couch under the palapa of their living room, the warmth of her morning coffee and the recurring crash of the morning surf left her with a strong sense of comfort and belonging. She opened her novel and settled into the next chapter with the hope of finding a distraction.

Before long, a quiet knock on the front door interrupted her moment. She put down the novel and started toward the door until she heard Consuela's short steps scurrying ahead of her to open it.

"*Hola*," Consuela said.

Rebecca could hear the voice of a woman outside, but she didn't know who it was and couldn't ascertain what was being said. Consuela invited the woman into the entrance hall of the home. The woman was Mexican, shorter in stature, and was wearing the uniform of a cleaning woman from one of the hotels.

She leaned on the heel of her left shoe and nervously twitched the index finger of her right hand. Rebecca presumed the woman was there to apply for a job at the restaurant, so she was surprised when Consuela invited her in rather than directing her to the office.

"*Espera aquí,*" Consuela said to the woman, telling her to wait before walking up to the bedrooms to find Francisco.

After a few minutes, her father came down from his bedroom and greeted the woman. "*Hola,*" he said.

"*Hola,* Señor Montoya," the woman said. She didn't make eye contact but instead looked at the floor.

"Why don't we speak outside?" He directed her back out the front door and closed it behind them.

Rebecca knew that her father had long supplied the local food bank with provisions from the restaurant. Typically, he just donated the food from the restaurant that needed to be consumed before expiring. From time to time when the food bank's supplies were low, he would order food from the restaurant and have it sent directly to them. But for some reason, this interaction seemed different.

"What's that all about?" Rebecca asked Consuela.

"*No sé,*" Consuela said, picking up the bucket she'd just set aside before vigorously mopping the area of the living room she'd already finished.

"Seriously, Consuela, who's that woman?" Rebecca insisted.

"I don't know her," Consuela answered.

"Why is she here then?"

Consuela didn't respond.

"Why don't you want to tell me?" Rebecca insisted, now more emphatically.

"Because your father told me not to. He said it would just upset you." She picked up the bucket before scurrying to another room to continue her work alone.

Realizing that further discussion was pointless, Rebecca tried to turn her attention back to her novel. After several more minutes, her father opened the front door and returned to the living room.

"I'm going to step out for a bit," he said. "I'll be back in an hour or so."

He started to head to his bedroom, but Rebecca lightly grasped his forearm. "What's wrong?" she asked. "Is she okay?"

Her father didn't answer and instead turned away.

"Dad, what is it?"

Her father hesitated again. "She's not feeling well," he said. "I'm going to take her to see a doctor."

"Dad, what's going on?"

He paused a third time. When she didn't move, he continued. "Do you remember how you needed help when you were sixteen? I'm just going to help."

Rebecca didn't know how to respond. Her father turned without further explanation and gathered his wallet and keys. "Back in an hour or so," he said. "No worries."

Noticing that Consuela had returned to the kitchen area, Rebecca looked up at her, seeking some further information or an acknowledgment. Noticing her gaze, Consuela approached her, presumably to answer the unasked question.

"They come once in a while to see your father," she said. "I know it is a sin; I tell him no. But they keep coming." She looked down at the floor as if she'd done something wrong.

"How often?"

"Maybe one—every couple of months."

"Where did Dad go with her?" she asked.

"*No sé*," Consuela answered.

Rebecca was surprised by the information. She knew that the Mexican courts had recently struck down the federal laws criminalizing early abortions. But as far as she knew, these types of services were still problematic in many Mexican states, including Nayarit and Jalisco, where they lived. In any event, her father was right: the memories were a low part of her life—one she didn't ever want to revisit. She returned her attention to her novel and again tried to refocus on it.

After a little more than an hour, Francisco returned, walking directly up to his room rather than engaging with her. "*Hola*," he said quickly.

Obviously, he didn't want to talk about it, but she felt like she needed to. She put the novel down on the side table, still open to the page she was reading, and followed him up the half stairway to the bedroom area. When she reached his bedroom, she knocked on the closed door.

"Dad?"

"Yup," he said.

She entered the room to find him sitting on his bed. "What's going on?" she asked.

He motioned for her to sit down beside him on his bed. "It's nothing, Rebecca."

She waited for him to continue.

"Sometime after you left, you know, with the Stimpsons, I went back to that clinic. I was angry—very angry. So I reported them and had them shut it down. I don't know what happened to the staff. Maybe they just moved on to the next small town and started up all over again. I didn't care; I was glad to see them go. But then, the women here had nowhere to go."

Rebecca nodded for him to continue.

"So I helped a young girl," he continued. "Someone like you back then, actually. And after a while, the word got out."

Rebecca didn't know what to say, so she sat quietly.

"Look," he said, "I don't want to upset you, especially on this particular week. And to be honest, I don't like what they're doing. But these women have no money, and they have no support. So they have no options. But they are strong, independent survivors. With just a little bit of help, they manage just fine." He looked at her directly and smiled, hopefully. "So I help them. The way I should have helped you."

She watched him as she thought about her own experience: the fear, the terror, and the guilt—it all came rushing back. She swallowed, almost audibly.

"I should have done better for you. You should have known you could come to me . . . I should have been there. It's been a big regret of mine for a long time."

"I'm sorry, too," she said. "But Dad, that was my mistake, not yours."

"I'll never really see it that way," he said. "That's just part of being a dad."

They sat there on the bed together in silence, reflecting. She wanted to undo the past along with the problems she'd created for herself and him. But that simply wasn't an option. She wondered if it would have been different if she'd had a mother then. It could have been; she didn't know. She'd never had a mother and had often wondered what that would be like. She'd always wanted to be a mother, but she knew that wasn't likely an option—at least, not with a child of her own. There were things her father would never understand about girls, women, and, she presumed, motherhood. But she also knew, almost innately, that if she were so lucky as to have a child, she'd want to be the mother that her father had been to her. She couldn't explain what that meant, even if she wanted to. But that didn't change its truth.

Her father put his arm around her the way he always did when she was a child, and she again felt the safety of his comfort and love. Recognizing there was nothing more to say, she kissed him gently on the head before shutting the door behind her as she left.

Back at the Four Seasons, Elena woke to the smell of fresh coffee and the warmth of the morning sun streaming through the balcony window in the hotel suite she shared with Richard. She reached over for him but noticed that he was gone. On his pillow was a note: *Went for a beach run; back for breakfast.* She climbed out of bed, put on her robe, and poured herself a cup of the coffee he'd made before leaving. It was going to be a beautiful day but also a workday. Richard had another transaction to work on, and she'd been assigned to do the background research. But at the moment, she had the place to herself. She took her coffee out to the balcony and sat at the small wicker table overlooking the sandy beach.

After finishing the coffee, she decided to take a quick shower and get ready for the day. While drying her hair, she heard Richard's key unlock the bedroom door of their hotel room. He entered the room, soaked in sweat. In his gym shorts and T-shirt, he looked as sexy as ever.

"Morning," he said. "Ready for another day?"

"Yeah, a little," she answered.

"Let me take a quick shower?"

"Sure," she said.

While he showered, she pulled out some shorts, a blouse, and her sandals. She had to work, but she didn't need to get dressed up while on vacation in Mexico. She put on her clothes, and within moments, Richard returned from the bathroom in his towel, which he dropped while standing in front of her.

"No sense rushing off," he said.

His firm body was still wet with the shower water, and the hair on his chest and legs clung against his skin. His message was clear: He wanted the sex they'd skipped after their disagreement on the fishing trip the day before and, as she thought about it, after the family dinner the night before that. But she was already dressed, ready to go, and for some reason, she had no desire or interest, anyway.

"Rain check?" she asked. "How about tonight?" She reached for her toiletry bag, which contained the antacids she'd purchased.

"What about this?" he said, looking down at himself.

"It'll still be there then," she said. "No doubt about it." She smiled, encouragingly.

He looked frustrated, struggling for the right words. "Remind me again," he asked, "why we came here?"

"To meet my family." She smiled.

"Right," he answered. He smirked and held his finger in the air as if acknowledging the point. Then he picked up his iPad and went into the bathroom he'd just left and locked the door.

After a few minutes, she could hear him satisfying himself. It made her feel guilty. She didn't know what she was supposed to do. She didn't understand how relationships worked in the United States. For that matter, she didn't understand how relationships worked in Mexico, either. She decided she'd just have to make it up to him later.

"I'm going to head down to the restaurant," she said through the closed door. "I'll see you there." Then she left, thinking he'd be better off having some privacy, anyway.

Downstairs, she ordered a light meal of yogurt, granola, and another coffee. The breakfast was served on a veranda that looked out across the sea cliffs and ocean. The view was from a different angle than that of the palapa of her home, but the landscape was much the same. It didn't take long for her to eat what she wanted of the meal, so she lingered a while, waiting for Richard to join her.

She felt guilty about deferring him, but she felt frustrated with him as well. *No*, she thought, *more like disappointed*. After a rough day on the boat, he hadn't bothered to ask her how she was. Did he care? She knew she'd handled it poorly, but she'd clearly been seasick. That night, he'd gotten even angrier about not having sex. And while she felt somewhat better now, she still didn't feel great. When she finished the coffee from the small pot they'd left on her table, she realized Richard was probably stuck working. She signed the bill to their room and headed toward their suite.

When she arrived at their room, she knocked before entering. When Richard didn't answer, she opened the door and saw him, now fully dressed, packing his suitcase.

"You're back," he said. "Last minute change of plan."

"You're leaving?"

"Just got a call. I'm needed for a pitch on the new transaction—you know, the Galbraith deal?"

"Can't someone else do it?" she asked, knowing that new business client pitches in person were an important part of his job but also a regular occurrence—something typically skipped for a vacation, particularly over Christmas.

"No can do," he said.

"Seriously?" she asked sarcastically.

"Seriously," he answered. "Besides, mission accomplished here, right?" He continued packing as he spoke without looking up.

"Mission?" she asked.

"Yeah, to meet your family. I did that." He looked at her sternly before harshly zipping the suitcase he'd never really unpacked.

"But we're here for a week—it's been only a couple of days."

"Yeah?" he said. "Well, I came down here to fuck in the sand. That was the deal. At least, that's what I thought."

The deal? she thought. *Was everything a transaction with him?* She repeated his words in her mind and watched the suppressed anger on his face, highlighted by the stern ridge lines of his brow.

"Richard," she pleaded, "just slow down. There's plenty of time for sex. The point was for me to spend time with my family and for you to get to know them."

"Your point, my sweet, not mine." He set the suitcase down and started scrolling through the email on his phone. "I'm gonna get some work done back home. Might as well, right?"

"What does this mean?" she asked.

"You mean, are we breaking up? No, not if you don't want to," he answered, while again looking down at his suitcase.

She didn't respond.

"But does it matter?" he asked. "I mean, really?"

"Of course it matters!" she answered.

"Well, weren't we going to do that at some point, anyway?" he asked.

"What do you mean?"

Richard stopped for a minute to tuck in his shirt. Then he lifted his suitcase from the rack and looked directly into her eyes. "Elena, I'm just not sure what's going on anymore. You seem to think I'm here to court your family in some type of pre-marriage bonding ceremony. Well, I'm not."

When she didn't answer, he continued, "You're just not being realistic, Elena."

Again, she didn't respond.

"I mean, you're an analyst. That's a two-year program at Goldman. You're almost at the end of that cycle."

"So?" she asked.

"So, you do what all of the other girls at Goldman do: They leave."

Elena felt her brow tighten. Richard had said *girls*, but he'd meant *analysts*. Apparently, in his mind, they were the same. He was wrong, of course, but also right. It was a two-year analyst program. At the end of it, most analysts went back to business school for an MBA, or they went to work for a company, usually in the industry where they'd gained expertise during their investment banking term. Occasionally, Goldman would promote a very impressive analyst to stay as an associate. That's what had happened with Richard, anyway. Did she think she was on that same track? *Apparently not*, she realized.

"Richard, this is more than that, and you know it!" She looked into his eyes, seeking an understanding and waiting for a more reasonable response.

"Look," he said, sitting next to her while reassuringly taking her hand. "I gotta go back now—but no worries!"

Elena wasn't sure exactly what he was saying. She repeated his words in her mind and considered the alternatives. After her analyst position with Goldman ended, she could have gone to business school in New York City at Columbia or NYU and kept dating him. Or she could have taken a job at another firm in the city and kept dating him. And for Richard, she would have. Was he simply anticipating her leaving him then? Or just telling her those weren't options for him? It wasn't entirely clear.

Elena nodded affirmatively but reflexively removed her hand from his.

Richard stood. "This place is great," he added. "I'm assuming you'll just want to stay here. You know, the Four Seasons is always a win."

Again, she didn't answer. She knew he expected her to acquiesce. After all, that's what she'd always done. But for some reason, this time she couldn't.

When she didn't reply, he continued. "Anyway, I've gone ahead and prepaid the room for the balance of the week. Put whatever meals and the like you want on the card, too." He stood up, reached down for his bag, and gave her a quick kiss on the forehead. "See you back at the shop," he said from the door, as it closed behind him.

"See you back at the shop," she said to the now-closed door.

Elena looked at the dark wooden trim of that door while considering what to do. She felt hurt, anxious, and confused. Yes, the Four Seasons was a win—much nicer than her family home in Sayulita. But this hotel wasn't her home, and going home was exactly why she'd come. She pulled her suitcase from the back of the closet and unzipped it. Once she'd finished packing, she firmly zipped her suitcase closed, turned off the light, and left.

Chapter 12

Later that afternoon, Rebecca pulled the bag of art supplies from the back of the bedroom closet of her childhood home. After the conversation with her father earlier that morning and the many difficult memories it brought back, her body tightened with anxiety and stress. Feeling tired of her novel, she took the painting bag along with her easel to the living room palapa. She decided to paint the sea and a whale. But she didn't want it to be a realistic work. *Something more fantasy-magical,* she thought. Then she remembered Lento's painting of the dancing mariachis and the gunslinging pigs that hung in her childhood bedroom. Maybe something like Puerto Vallarta's own Lento? *Perfect,* she concluded.

She set up her easel near the railing of the deck and placed her paint on the table next to it. The day was already heating up, but it was still cool enough to be comfortable, especially under the shade of the palapa. She set the canvas on the table and started to sketch out the painting. She began with the ocean, framed by the cliffs of the same bluffs that surrounded their home. After a while, she added the whales, smiling while spouting, of course, before realizing that wasn't enough. On the beach, she sketched one of the cantinas, with a bar and beach chairs in front. She decided to make the Americans sitting on the beach lobster red and chuckled to herself with amusement.

After completing the rough outline, Rebecca scanned the charcoal sketch to assess it. *Not happy enough*, she thought, *or magical*. And it definitely was not her happy childhood vision of Mexico. She decided to add some mariachis. She sketched a fat one with a viola de gamba, a midsize man with a violin, and a tall, skinny one with a trombone. Then she dressed them in black with traditional sombreros and tight suits with white lace shirts. It was better, but it was still missing something. So she changed the musicians from men to mariachi dogs, blissfully playing while singing romantically to the sunburned American women, with one dog staring at one of the woman's large, red breasts. *We'll call that one Richard*, she thought, chuckling to herself.

When she heard the front door of the home opening after a short knock, she put down the charcoal and turned to see who it was.

"Elena?" she asked.

"Yup, me," Elena said, walking into the entrance corridor while towing her black Travelpro suitcase behind her.

Rebecca got up to help her. "Where's Richard?" she asked.

"Went back—had to work," Elena casually answered.

Rebecca frowned. "I'm sorry."

"All good," Elena said. "That's the job—twenty-four seven, including vacations." She smiled, but the tension in her face belied her tone. When the handle of her suitcase didn't seamlessly retract, Elena banged on the top, forcing it back in. "There."

"Then we just get to have more of you," Rebecca said, placing her sister's suitcase next to the entry table under the mirror.

Elena walked into the living room. "You're painting?" Elena said, noticing the easel on the palapa deck. She turned and walked toward it.

"Filling dead time," Rebecca answered, moving the sketch aside. "You know, according to Dad, it's a 'skip day.'"

"Let me see?" Elena asked, touching the easel while scanning its contents.

Rebecca picked up a paintbrush and turned the sketch around. Then she watched to see Elena's reaction, hoping for a favorable response.

"I don't know," Elena said. "Are those dogs singing to the woman?"

Rebecca nodded.

"And she likes it?"

Rebecca smiled.

"So, the fat American woman is being seduced by a chorus of Mexican dogs?" When Rebecca hesitated, Elena continued. "That's really not politically correct, Rebecca—don't you think? I mean, it's fun, but don't quit your day job." Elena smiled at her joke.

Rebecca grinned back but felt a little hurt. She didn't know what to say about the comment on the painting, so she responded to the job quip instead. "Actually, I've been thinking about just that," she started.

"What?"

"Quitting McKenzie."

"Seriously?" Elena answered. "That's the most prestigious global consulting firm out there, and you make even more money than I do!"

"I spend my days and nights in an incredible office with very smart people," Rebecca said. "But it's not satisfying—well, not to me, anyway."

"How so?"

"Well, most of our work is modeling synergies," Rebecca said.

"Yeah, that's what I do, too," Elena answered. "What's the big deal?"

"My specialty is life science HR—the RIFs, basically."

Elena nodded.

Rebecca knew that she didn't need to explain to Elena that a RIF was a "reduction in force," or the termination of employees who were deemed to be redundant. But she also didn't want to suggest that there was anything wrong with Elena's job. As she'd noted, Elena in many ways did the same thing. Sensing her sister's irritation but not knowing what to say, Rebecca didn't respond.

"You know that's necessary," Elena said. "It's not like we're the villains in the story."

"Right," Rebecca said.

She well knew that the efficiencies she modeled would be realized one way or another. If her clients didn't "effect" the necessary reductions, through a merger or an internal reorganization, a competitor would, forcing her client to "effect" them anyway, losing market share if not viability in the meantime. She'd spent four years studying economics at Stanford, learning the difference between "positive economics" (assessing things as they are) and "normative economics" (assessing the fairness of how things should be). The problem was that her job was all about positive economics, but to her, it was not at all *positive*.

"The thing is," Rebecca continued, "I don't think I want to anymore."

She considered the words as they left her lips for the first time. Did she mean it? She wasn't sure. But she thought she might be. Earlier that week, she'd noticed that one of the small shops in town was closing. After walking through it briefly, she'd thought it would be the perfect place for an art store. Already in her mind, she'd imagined rows of native pottery along the shelves, as well as beads and other jewelry along the side walls, leaving ample space in the rear and behind the counter for several of her own paintings. With the rent being surprisingly modest, she would need to sell only a couple of paintings each year to make it all work, with sales of the local jewelry and pottery covering the cost of a small staff.

Rebecca watched her sister's reaction as she spoke. Elena didn't say anything, but Rebecca could tell she wasn't supportive of the idea.

"I'm sorry, Rebecca, but that's so narcissistic," Elena said slowly.

"What?" Rebecca said. "Why?"

Elena pressed her lips, thinking. "You do pretty much the same thing I do, but now it's not *satisfying* for you. Seriously?" She chuckled, while rolling her eyes.

Rebecca thought that her sister's tone was ironic and condescending. "Wow, that's pretty harsh, don't you think?"

"But true?" Elena pressed. "Sometimes I'd like to quit too when it's not *satisfying*." As she spoke, she used her index fingers this time to indicate quotation marks, thereby marking her sarcasm. "But I can't. Why? Because I need the money. You know, Grandma Stimpson didn't leave *me* a trust."

Rebecca thought the condescension was too much. "You're being ridiculous," she responded. "Why are you so upset? It's just a job—and it's *my* job!"

"Because you have a Stanford education and a job at McKenzie," Elena continued, without hesitation. "Do you know how many Latino kids would kill for that opportunity? And you don't care. Not a bit."

Rebecca listened carefully to her sister's words. She knew Elena was professionally driven and not at all afraid of being aggressive. But harshly judgmental and critical, too? This was too much. After all, it was her job and her life; she could do what she wanted.

"Don't give me that politically correct lecture," Rebecca said. "You went to Boston College, and they gave you a scholarship that paid for it."

"Yes, but I earned admission, worked in the school cafeteria, and borrowed a lot."

The implied accusations had become overt—and downright rude. Rebecca felt her fingers clutch the paintbrush. "My test scores were in the ninety-ninth plus percentile. Were yours?" Rebecca answered defensively.

"So, they aren't doing legacy admits at Stanford anymore?" Elena answered rhetorically.

"Or diversity admits at Boston College?" Rebecca countered. "You know, more affirmative action? Except you're not a poor Latina girl, are you, Elena? You're not even Latina, really. You're just half, using anything—or should I say anyone?—to climb your way to the top."

Rebecca knew she'd gone too far when she saw Francisco emerge from the bedrooms. He descended several stairs before he stopped behind Elena. Rebecca presumed that he'd heard most of their conversation. They hadn't been yelling, but they had been direct with each other. She knew she should have stopped Elena from speaking further, but for some reason, she just didn't care.

"You take everything around you, Rebecca," Elena said. "You take it, consume it, and then drop it."

Rebecca nodded, almost encouraging her.

"Dad gave you everything," Elena continued. "He brought us here and loved us equally—even if you technically weren't his."

Rebecca felt the anger in her brow rise as her face flushed. "But I *am* his," she said quietly and slowly. "Why can't you accept that?"

"Because *you don't*," Elena said.

When Rebecca didn't respond, Elena continued. "You left him, and you left me. Why? Because you wanted to be with your rich, White grandparents. You chose *them*, not *us*." As she spoke, her color reddened from her anger, but her eyes started to tear from her pain.

Rebecca felt calm but furious as she considered what to say. She knew Elena was dead wrong, but she could tell there was no convincing her. "You know what, Elena? Maybe on some level, you're right. But maybe it doesn't matter anymore," she said. "Because I don't think you'll ever get over all that, and frankly, I don't want to hear about it anymore."

When Elena had nothing further to say and turned to get her suitcase, she saw Francisco covering his face while sitting on the stairs. She pulled the handle of the suitcase up but then stopped when he didn't move as she approached. She turned away from him, and with her free hand, quickly dried her eyes in a pointless effort to hide her emotion.

After a moment, Francisco removed his hands and looked down at them from the stairs where he continued to sit.

"You asked why I wanted you to come home together," he said. "Well, this is it."

Rebecca didn't respond; Elena remained silent as well.

"Time is precious. You are precious. And this family is precious. You know, relationships don't just exist—they're built." He paused. "The two of you love each other more than you realize. You need each other even more. But time is running out. So, the question is this: What are *you* going to do about it?"

"Dad, you need to understand . . ." Elena started. But when he raised his hand, she stopped.

"You're both incredibly beautiful, intelligent women, and you both know it. You're just different. Your personalities, perspectives, interests, and aspirations are different. You're sisters who don't look alike. But at your core, you're the same. I know that because I know you—each of you. And right now, you need each other. Why can't you see it?"

Rebecca didn't answer, because she knew she shouldn't. Elena said nothing as well.

Unwilling to give up, he continued. "Try to hear what I'm telling you. The mistakes we made yesterday and ten years ago are all ancient history. Relationships ebb and flow. They're like the tides that rise and fall. But they're only constant if you're persistent. You think that the stories created in your minds are true. But I'm here to tell you they are not." He stopped for a minute to collect his thoughts. "The question is, what decisions are you going to make today, tomorrow, and the next day?"

"I know, Dad," Rebecca started, "but . . ." He again raised his hand to silence her.

"All I ask is that you think on it. Carefully." Then he turned and walked back up to his bedroom.

Rebecca looked at Elena, who continued gazing at the stairway he'd just left. "You could have told me he was sitting there," Elena said. Then she followed him up, turning into her old room on the right before firmly shutting the door.

"I guess," Rebecca answered, after her sister left. Then she put down her paintbrush, picked up her coffee cup, and walked up the stairs toward her own bedroom.

It was just a fight, Rebecca thought, after closing the door to her bedroom. So why was her father making such a big deal out of it? They'd had a million of them; this one was nothing new. Besides, he was right: their relationship did ebb and flow. That was part of what made it real. But for some reason, this time it felt like the tide wasn't returning. Simply put, there was no denying that they'd grown apart, and as each year passed, the distance was growing. *Maybe that's the inevitable part of growing up and leaving home,* she thought. *Maybe we just need to get used to it. Maybe Dad does, too.*

As she sat on her childhood bed and stared pointlessly at the blank wall, her anger quickly passed, and a sadness replaced it. Why was Elena so frustrated with her, and how did they get there? Her thoughts returned to that time in high school before she'd left Sayulita, nine years earlier. She tried to refocus, but she couldn't.

Miguel was a high school senior at the American School of Puerto Vallarta and Elena's first real crush. Rebecca, like all of the other sophomore girls at the high school, thought he was a catch. While he was at best a B- student, he was captain of the soccer team, and his father was the manager of the Fiesta Americana Hotel. He wasn't particularly tall, but he wasn't short, either. More importantly, his lighter skin color and angular facial features hinted at a Spanish lineage often associated with a privileged class in Mexico. Rebecca thought he was handsome. At the beginning of the school year, she hadn't had much interest in responding to his overtures. After all, he made them to all of the pretty girls, including her twin sister. But when Elena had started focusing on him in return, something changed. It all began after English class.

English had always been pretty easy for her, as well as Elena. Their father was Mexican, but he spoke perfect English, albeit with an accent, and he generally spoke English to them at home. That week, she'd delayed writing her essay on *The Great Gatsby*, which she considered to be a silly story of a spoiled rich man in the United States. By contrast, Elena had written her essay several days in advance and had rewritten it after getting comments from their father. Instead, Rebecca had hastily finished hers at school, only moments before it was due, and was relieved to be done after turning it in. Several weeks later, she didn't feel that way when Elena got an A+, and she got C-.

"What'd you get?" Elena asked.

"Why are you asking?" Rebecca asked. "Is it because you got an A, like you always do, and want me to know it?"

"I did get an A," Elena answered. "How about you?"

"I didn't get an A," Rebecca said. "Does that make you feel better?"

"Whatever," Elena answered, walking toward the outdoor cafeteria to have lunch with her friends.

"Whatever," Rebecca parroted.

Rebecca knew there wasn't any more time to improve her grade for the semester, and their father wouldn't be happy when he saw the resulting C+ on her report card. But there wasn't much to be done about it. So, like her girlfriends, she focused instead on the boys. And when Miguel started raising his eyebrows and smiling when he passed her, she noticed him. One day, when she looked back, he stopped.

"Hey," he said. "Wanna have lunch sometime?"

"No, thanks," she said, before shyly rushing away.

While her answer was no, his interest intrigued her. So she started giving him more attention. Then he started dropping notes into her locker. The second time he approached her, she said no as well, but she encouragingly smiled back. Several days later, he told her he was only interested in her. She smiled but again shook her head without speaking. Unwilling to give up, he asked her a third time several days later. That was right after semester grades had come out, and her father, after getting the report card, had responded as she'd anticipated: with kind understanding but clear disappointment. So this time when Miguel asked her, her answer changed. "Sure," she said.

Rebecca followed Miguel to the outdoor cafeteria line and then to a table directly in front of her sister. She watched as Elena scowled at them while chatting quietly to her friends, who also stole peeks at the two of them. With Miguel, Rebecca felt good, successful, vindicated, and validated. Elena was probably smarter than she was. And maybe her father loved Elena more than he loved her. But as a blonde, she was prettier, or at least the boys thought so—all of them, including Miguel. So she laughed excessively when he talked about his soccer team as they walked.

Over the next week, Rebecca continued giving Miguel her attention and watching his interest in her sister wane. He started to seem so handsome—and sexy. His hair was thick, and his eyebrows were full. His chest was broad, and his legs were lean and muscular. And he was actually taller than her—one of only a few boys in their school who passed this test. She really liked that. But it was his persistence that made it clear that he was committed to her. Indeed, while he had his choice of girls at the school, he'd chosen her above everyone else, including Elena.

"Do you want to skip lunch today?" Miguel asked, several days later. "Maybe go to the beach and hang out?"

"I dunno. What about Elena?" she asked.

"Who?"

"My sister," she answered. "I thought you liked her."

"Oh," he said. "No, she's not my type."

Rebecca wasn't entirely convinced.

"It wasn't anything, and it ended. We never even kissed," Miguel added.

Rebecca nodded. She believed him, but she still had her doubts. Maybe it didn't matter anyway. So she considered his offer. She didn't like the idea of getting in trouble. But the beach was just a couple of blocks from their school, and a walk there and back wouldn't take long.

"Sure," she said.

Miguel took her hand, and they left the school grounds. When they got to the beach, they sat together, and he started kissing her. The warmth of the sun and the strength of his body against hers felt powerful and satisfying. She thought it was all so romantic. She was a woman, and she had a handsome boyfriend. She felt energized, kissing him on the beach, and wonderfully naughty, doing it during school. After a while, she felt the electrical charge of his hand on her breast, first on top of her dress and then underneath it, gently massaging her.

"Hey," he said. "Wanna head up where it's private?" He nodded to the bushes forming a line of cover along the edge of the beach.

She looked in the direction he pointed. It was only a little way from where they were. Besides, she didn't want someone to see them in the open and get caught.

"Okay," she said.

Rebecca followed him along a small path to a sandy clearing area surrounded by bushes and palms. He sat her down and again started kissing her, this time moving quickly to her breasts. He was a senior. He was in control. And she liked it. He was sexy, and he made her feel so good. When he took off his shirt and put his chest against her own, she felt connected. The feeling only increased when he unzipped the back of her dress, fully exposing her breasts. She could tell that they excited him even more.

He continued kissing her, deeply and passionately. She felt her body instinctively cling to his. Then he lifted her dress and started massaging her legs, first at the thigh, before moving upward. She'd never done that, and she'd never felt anything like it. So she didn't notice him unzip his own pants. But she did notice how he continued firmly holding her body, connecting them. At first, it hurt, but then it didn't. He was so handsome, so sexy, and so incredible. *This is what it means to be a woman*, she thought. Within what seemed like seconds, she felt his body tighten and convulse before his motion stopped. Then he rolled off her.

"Wow," he said. "You're so hot."

Was it over? She hoped not. But she didn't know how to respond when he zipped his pants back up, having never actually removed them, and reached for his shirt. She followed his lead, pulling her panties up and her sundress down, realizing that it had never left her body but instead had remained crumpled about her waist. She stood up and reached for the zipper of her dress, thinking that he might help, but he didn't.

Fear gripped her as she realized what had happened. "Did you wear anything or pull out?" she asked.

"I think so," he said. "Yeah, I did."

But by the uncertainty of his answer, she knew the truth.

During the next weeks, Miguel repeatedly asked her to go with him to the beach again, but she consistently refused. Then he started talking to Elena again. After a while, Rebecca saw him leave with another girl during lunch instead, and she realized what had happened. She was not special to him or unique. Elena wasn't, either. He just liked one thing: having sex with the prettiest girl on campus. And if he couldn't have her, another girl—pretty much any girl—would do.

Rebecca thought about what had happened a decade earlier. With hindsight, she wondered if a larger truth was becoming apparent: Elena had judgment, but she didn't. So, as she sat on her childhood bed, Rebecca wondered if Elena was right about Miguel, Richard, McKenzie, the Stimpsons—and all the rest of it. More importantly, she wondered if Elena was right about her.

Did it matter? She wasn't sure. They'd had sisterly spats a million times, and they'd always gotten over them. But this time, something was different—or so it seemed. Perhaps that was all ancient history, as her father had said. But Rebecca could sense that something was changing, and that change was starting to feel permanent.

Chapter 13

THE NEXT DAY, FRANCISCO WATCHED HIS HANDS TIGHTLY GRIP THE steering wheel of his tan Jeep as he headed into Puerto Vallarta on errands. He knew that Rebecca and Elena had often fought in their childhood. He also knew that the fight they'd just had was one of their worst, if not *the* worst. While he'd hoped that such a confrontation would be avoided, he'd always believed it was unavoidable—a hurdle that had to be jumped before continuing along life's track. Less clear to him was the path to resolution on that track. It was depressing, maybe even heartbreaking. But he'd done what he could, and it was out of his control. Had he failed them? He didn't know. Maybe it didn't matter. Their relationship together mattered a lot to him. *But did it matter to them?* he wondered. They'd have to figure that out.

He turned his attention to his own agenda for the day. He'd intended but failed to complete the to-dos on his short list before the girls had arrived. He knew exactly what he needed to do; he just didn't want to do it. So, when he reached his destination in central Puerto Vallarta and turned off the ignition of his Jeep, he slowly and reluctantly opened the door to the funeral home called Rosario's.

The store was dark and small, with a variety of caskets lining the windows or hanging on racks facing out to the street. Others were placed around the small perimeter of the store. When he entered, he could smell paprika chicken, a common dish that could be purchased fully prepared at most grocery stores in Mexico.

"Can I help you?" a gentleman asked, wiping the food from his face as he spoke.

"Yeah," Francisco answered. "I'd like to make advance arrangements for a passing—my passing."

"I understand," the salesman said. "Do you have an immediate need?"

Francisco ignored the question. "Do you embalm and the like here?"

"Certainly," the man said. "We provide complete services."

"How does it work?"

"Well, we have a variety of packages," the man started. "May I suggest that we start with the caskets?"

Francisco listened as the salesman showed him the various choices and described the price ranges of each option. Some caskets were relatively simple, but most were quite elaborate, with carved exteriors and silk-covered interiors. All of them seemed pretty expensive and somewhat pointless.

As he listened to the salesman, Francisco started to feel afraid. There was something about the physical reality of the caskets that made his death feel tangible and permanent. While he remained a person of faith, he'd long given up the concept of being judged and going to someplace like hell. For him, that theology made no sense—at least not as categorically applied to married gays. Sure, he'd made his mistakes, no doubt. But he'd done his best, and that would be good enough. He felt certain of this.

As he thought about it further, he realized it wasn't death itself that frightened him. Instead, it was the fact that he would continue in the afterlife without his daughters. That simple reality was a void that terrified him. And of course, he also felt afraid for his girls. He couldn't change the reality of his death, but he could change the timing of it. More importantly, he could discuss his intentions with them. And after all, didn't they deserve that? It seemed harsh not to, and perhaps it was. But he knew that having a discussion in advance with them about his intentions couldn't possibly be productive. Far more likely was that it would be harmful. He'd just have to pray that they'd understand.

So, as he looked again at the various caskets, he did so with a renewed confidence. Simply put, he'd made up his mind, and his fear didn't change anything. How could it? His cancer was real as the casket his hand now rested upon, and his death was as certain as the cancer that now filled his body. And while he had infinite respect for those courageous enough to fight death to the last breath, he knew he was not among them. Instead, he would quickly and quietly go out on his own terms.

Francisco refocused his attention on the salesman, who described the embalming process and the related fees. "These services are provided in the back room," he noted, "for a fixed fee." The salesman further explained how those services included pickup of the deceased as well as transportation to and from the burial site. They did not include a limousine, should that be desired, or police escorts for a motorcade to the burial site. He noted, however, that they would offer a 10 percent discount if the casket were purchased from them. Francisco just smiled. He'd lived in Mexico long enough to know that everything was negotiable, even funeral services.

"What about burial?" Francisco asked.

The attendant then explained the various cemeteries around town with "availability." Most of them were about a half hour from central Puerto Vallarta, though there was an older one just above the hotel zone. Having no deceased family in the area, Francisco had never been there but had seen it while driving by. He thought it was pretty creepy. Why anyone found a cemetery to be restful eluded him.

"Let me think on it," Francisco said. "Give me your card. I'll make a decision and call you back later today."

"Wonderful," the salesman said, while handing Francisco his card. "By the way, we do provide an additional discount for the presale for multiple 'residents.' Will you be looking to find an eternal resting place for one or for two?"

"One," Francisco said. "Just one."

After leaving the store, Francisco opened the door of his Jeep and started it. He turned on the air-conditioning, a year-round necessity in Puerto Vallarta, before resting his head on the steering wheel to think. It was too fast and too much. *It wasn't supposed to be one*, he thought. *It was supposed to be two. It was always supposed to be two.*

That dark irony was not lost on him. Francisco vividly remembered Derek's funeral services twenty-three years earlier. They had been held in a Protestant church in Atherton, where the Stimpsons still lived. Derek's mother had planned everything, and Francisco had been grateful at the time for that. He'd been unable then to focus on anything other than tending to the twins. But he remembered regretting that decision as soon as the funeral services began.

Anticipating a large gathering, the Stimpsons held the viewing of the body the night before the funeral. Francisco saw Derek's lifeless body, covered in makeup, in a smaller chamber adjoining the chapel. Derek didn't have any siblings, but his parents, as well as his aunts, uncles, and cousins, formed a greeting line next to the casket. Francisco and the girls simply walked through it along with the other invited guests. It all seemed so odd to him, but he wasn't Protestant and didn't want to object to their customs. Obviously, they were as grief-stricken as he was.

The funeral was held the next day. Like the rest of the family, Francisco arrived with his toddler twins about an hour before the services were to begin. He'd had to buy a black suit the day before; he'd never owned a suit, let alone a black one. It was way too shiny, and the tailoring, literally done overnight, left the fabric drooping on his shoulders and hanging over the back of his shoes. He knew that Derek would have laughed. The girls wore yellow and blue sundresses with matching hats. Francisco thought their outfits were tacky, but Derek's mother, Beverly, had purchased them and was quite insistent that at least Rebecca wear hers. He pulled the girls one by one from their car seats and headed toward the chapel entrance from the adjacent parking lot.

Once they'd entered, a man he didn't know in a dark suit with a green striped tie greeted him. "Are you here for the Stimpson services?"

"Yes," Francisco answered.

The man handed Francisco a program. "The family is meeting in the chapel parlor," he said. "The guests are to find places in the chapel itself."

"Thank you," Francisco said, taking the girls' hands and proceeding slowly with them to the parlor where the body apparently was resting.

Ben and Beverly waited at the entrance to the parlor door; the other members of the family had already entered.

"Hi, Francisco," Beverly said. "Rebecca looks great. Thanks for getting her into the new dress."

"They do look great," he said proudly.

"Francisco," Ben started, pulling him aside. "This is the room where the family says goodbye to the deceased. First, we say a prayer together, and then we each have an opportunity to individually say goodbye to Derek at the casket. Then the pallbearers will move the casket into the chapel for the funeral services."

"Thanks," Francisco said, proceeding toward the parlor.

He noticed Beverly scowling before Ben gently pressed him on the chest. "It's just for the *family*, Francisco."

Francisco looked at him, puzzled, before realizing what he'd said. "I see," he answered.

Ben then pointed to the main chapel. Francisco turned around and headed in the other direction with the girls until Beverly gently stopped them.

"Rebecca," she said, bending down to his daughter's level, "would you like to come with us to say goodbye to your dad?"

Francisco was caught off guard, unable to comprehend the meaning of Beverly's words. Although Rebecca nodded automatically, the question was pointless. As a two-year-old, she couldn't possibly understand. But when Beverly took Rebecca's hand and led her in the other direction to the "family's room," Francisco realized exactly what was happening. He wasn't part of Derek's family; Elena wasn't, either. But Rebecca was. He thought about grabbing Rebecca and pulling her back but realized it was the wrong place and time for a scene. He didn't want to upset Derek's parents. More importantly, he didn't want to frighten the girls. He turned with Elena and went into the empty chapel, finding a place on a long wooden bench toward the front.

The whole situation seemed surreal to him. Was Derek really gone? Was Francisco a widow, a widower, or just a friend? The Stimpsons had told him that the service was going to be a family affair. But the crowd that was entering wasn't small. He realized that the chapel was completely full when they opened a partition in the back for overflow seating. He looked at the faces of the people attending. He didn't know any of them, but they all knew each other. None of Derek's gay friends were there, because Francisco hadn't invited them. Beverly had told him not to. After a while, Francisco realized that the spectators were all members of the Stimpsons' church, of Derek's church—at least, they had been when he was a child.

The organ music began, and the pallbearers entered, wheeling in Derek's casket between them. Ben and Beverly followed with Rebecca in tow. The rest of the family, all in black, followed them as they proceeded to the front of the chapel before sitting in the two front rows of benches, designated as "Reserved."

"Is that his girl?" the woman sitting next to Francisco asked her husband while nodding at Rebecca.

"I think so," the man said.

"So cute. But where's his wife? I didn't know he was married."

"He's not," the man said.

Francisco clutched Elena's hand as the presiding pastor walked to the pulpit and welcomed them "at this time of tragic reflection." There was a hymn, which everyone sang, and then a few words from Ben about the tragedy. Several of Derek's high school friends then spoke, recalling stories of their youth. Francisco listened with amazement. He could tell that they were not Derek's friends; they were his acquaintances. Moreover, they really knew nothing about Derek after their time together in high school—more than ten years earlier. It all was cold and distant, even alienating.

Francisco regretted not taking a more active role in the funeral planning. Derek would have loved hearing from his group of friends from medical school, from his practice, or better, their gay friends from San Francisco that he always called their "girlfriends." While the minister spoke warmly about Derek's life, it wasn't really about Derek. As an adult, Derek had never gone to church, especially a church that had campaigned for years against gay marriage. Derek had spent his time helping children as a pediatrician and donating his services to the free medical clinic. Derek loved to tell off-color jokes, to drink cocktails on Saturday nights, and, most of all, to be Francisco's husband and the father of their two children.

After a while, the minister's speech turned to the church's doctrine on life after death and in heaven, where, apparently, they all believed Derek would go. The minister then turned his attention to the family. "We'd like to extend our deepest sympathy to Ben, Beverly, and Derek's daughter, Rebecca," he said, looking down at them in the front row. "We know this is a terrible time of loss, but God works in mysterious ways. We also know that, despite leaving this beautiful daughter, Derek died unwed. But through our faith, we know that this is a temporal issue. Because in the afterlife, Derek will have the opportunity to find an eternal companion, and he will be able to live joyfully with his celestial wife for time and all eternity, along with his daughter, Rebecca, when in the fullness of time, her turn comes. Until then, we take solace in our faith."

Francisco looked at the pastor, wondering what that meant until it dawned on him: They believed that in heaven, Derek would find a woman whom he would marry, and they would live together forever. And when Rebecca passed, she would join Derek and that woman. In the meantime, and apparently in the afterlife as well, he and Elena were on their own. Francisco felt an emptiness envelop him—an emptiness more powerful than anything he'd ever felt before. Derek was dead, but he and Elena were very much alive. To these people, however, they both were invisible.

After the minister ended his speech, there was a closing hymn, which everyone sang, and a final prayer. Then the casket was removed by the pallbearers, followed by the family, including Rebecca, while the organ played another hymn Francisco had never heard. Francisco and Elena, along with the rest of the congregation, were then directed to leave, row by row, until the chapel was empty.

Francisco stood in front of the chapel, holding Elena, and waiting for Beverly to return with Rebecca. The service hadn't been about Derek, and it certainly hadn't been about his family. It had been about the child the Stimpsons had wanted or believed they'd had: a projection, a fantasy, an illusion. Francisco realized that, to some extent, Derek had enabled this by living a double life—not to be elusive or mean to Francisco, but simply to keep the peace with his parents and to shelter him from them. Francisco had met the Stimpsons only a couple of times. Derek had primarily just called them on the phone or taken the girls down a couple of times to visit. Francisco wondered if that myth had been the only relationship they were able to sustain with him—the only Derek they'd been able to tolerate. Francisco felt a hollow darkness start in his chest before filling his being. It was one thing to be hated and despised. As a gay man, he'd felt that for a lifetime. But it was far worse to be ignored and shunned—erased, as if never having existed.

"It was a lovely service, Beverly," Francisco said when Beverly freed up. "Thank you." He appreciated her efforts, even if not the service itself.

"You're welcome," she said.

"Let's go, Rebecca." Francisco reached to take his daughter from Beverly, who continued holding her.

"She can ride with us to the burial," Beverly said. "We've got plenty of room."

"We're good," Francisco responded. "She probably needs a diaper change, anyway."

"I really don't mind—" Beverly started.

"We'll see you there," Francisco responded, cutting her off and taking Rebecca from her.

Beverly again looked at Ben, this time more sternly.

Ben pulled Francisco aside. "Francisco, we'd really like to have Rebecca come with us to the burial services," he said. "After all, as part of our family, she'll be living with us from now on; we might as well help her start with the transition."

"The *transition*?" he asked. When Ben didn't respond, the import of his words settled into Francisco's mind.

"Francisco," Beverly started, reaching for Rebecca, "you need to realize—"

Francisco cut her off again. "We'll see you at the burial," he said, holding Rebecca tightly to his chest while defensively gripping Elena's small hand.

After putting Rebecca down, Francisco walked to the car with the girls toddling slowly beside him. He squeezed their fingers tightly, trying to stop the shaking in his own hands. Then he fastened them into their car seats and started driving to the cemetery.

After a little over a mile, he pulled to the side of the road and stopped. *No*, he thought. *No way.* He turned the Audi around and headed toward their home in San Francisco. There would be no such "transition" for either of his girls. He just had to figure out how to make sure that didn't happen.

Francisco lifted his head off the steering wheel of the Jeep that was still parked in front of Rosario's funeral home in Puerto Vallarta. *That's all in the distant past*, he thought. And yet it wasn't. Put bluntly, the Stimpsons had succeeded. With their money and their power, they'd taken his daughter and divided his family. It just took them a while to do it. And now, his time had run out.

Regardless, now he had to deal with the future. The sharp, periodic pain in his abdomen could no longer be ignored, and a glance at his face in the rearview mirror confirmed that the discolor of his skin could no longer be explained by exposure to the sun. He turned his Jeep off and walked back into Rosario's. The salesman returned with paprika from the chicken again on his lips. When Francisco pointed to his own lips, the man quickly wiped the juices off with his hand and then dried it on his pants.

"Did you already come to a decision?" he asked.

"Yes," Francisco answered. "I think cremation will work. Can you just put that on my credit card now?"

The man started to protest, probably frustrated by the loss of a larger sale, but Francisco immediately raised his hand to terminate the pitch. "If you don't mind, I'll just take cremation and an urn. For one."

After completing the sale, Francisco placed the urn in the back of the Jeep and headed out to the pharmacy—his last errand of the day. He knew that if he, like the tourists, went to one of the corner drugstores, he could get exactly what he needed without the hassle of a prescription.

I'll just stop quickly before heading home, he thought. *No problem.*

Chapter 14

Rebecca wasn't surprised when her father had suggested that they have a family dinner at Barcelona Tapas and attend the *Ballet Folklórico de México (Folk Ballet)* at the *Teatro Vallarta (Vallarta Theater)* afterward. In their youth, the family had often eaten at the restaurant and then gone to the theater. What was disappointing was that their father had decided not to join them. She guessed it was because of the argument she'd had with Elena. She wanted to make things right with her sister, but she really didn't know how. Unable to sleep the night before, she felt anxious about the dinner. She couldn't tell what Elena was thinking, but she, too, seemed uncomfortable.

As Rebecca and Elena rode together in the small yellow taxi from Sayulita to Puerto Vallarta, neither of them spoke. But Rebecca's spirits lifted when they reached the cobblestone streets of old Puerto Vallarta and passed under the multicolored Christmas banners on each block. Made of faux garland in alternating colors of red and green, they welcomed everyone with *Bienvenidos* and *Feliz Navidad*, written in script. As the taxi passed by the Malecon, she remembered the many times they'd walked as children under the enormous green wooden Christmas tree and through the multicolored soldiers before playing on the giant toy rocking horses. The decorations were dated and tired, looking like something from the '50s, and their enormity was simply ridiculous.

But nobody cared. They captured the Mexican joy of the season and continued to delight the children who danced among them.

Barcelona Tapas was an upscale restaurant frequented both by the locals and the tourists located in the foothills overlooking central Puerto Vallarta. The restaurant was surrounded by traditional Mexican homes, haphazardly built along the hillside and accessed by narrow and steep cobblestone streets. It wasn't unusual to see families watching television through the windowless openings of their living rooms right next to the sidewalk or to pass street vendors selling tacos or other Mexican delights from the gas stoves of their portable stands. But for Rebecca, the quaint chaos of old town Vallarta dripped with delightful charm. For her, it was both authentic and real.

In Puerto Vallarta, buildings often didn't just spring up; instead, they evolved. Barcelona Tapas was no exception. What had started as a nice-but-nothing-special restaurant on the top floor of an old hotel had become, year after year, brick by brick, newer, nicer, and ultimately an upscale dining establishment. Rebecca noticed that this year, they were finally adding an elevator to take patrons up the four stories to the rooftop bar. But like much of the construction in Mexico, the elevator remained a work in progress.

After climbing up the four floors, they reached the bar and dining area of the restaurant. The restaurant was fully decorated for the season, with a Christmas tree at the top and lighted garland strung along the bar area as well as the balcony railing. As always, the views from the outdoor patio were spectacular, making the hike up, as well as the long ride from Sayulita to Puerto Vallarta, well worth it. To the left of the restaurant balcony was a giant crown, literally, at the top of the principal town cathedral. Below them were the informal and haphazardly placed residential and commercial buildings of Puerto Vallarta that they'd passed coming up. Behind these buildings were the Malecon, the beach, and the ocean.

A hostess quickly approached and welcomed them to the restaurant. She then took them to a table placed next to a glass railing overlooking the city and ocean.

"I wish Dad had come," Elena said.

"Me, too," Rebecca answered. "Can I see his note?"

Elena rummaged through her purse before handing the envelope with their father's note to her sister.

"Doesn't say much, does it?"

"No," Elena answered.

"Well, we're here, and I'm happy about it."

"Yeah," Elena said. "But did you notice there're four tickets in the envelope?"

Rebecca looked more carefully at the theater tickets. "For Richard and him?"

"That's what I'm thinking."

"My guess?" Rebecca suggested. "He skipped dinner because he doesn't want to see us fight again."

"Or, he wants to give us some time to make up?" Elena asked.

"You're right," Rebecca said.

The waiter approached their table and asked them in English what they'd like to drink. They both immediately laughed, and the waiter looked confused.

"Sangria to start?" Elena asked Rebecca. "Maybe that nonalcoholic kind we used to drink as kids?"

"Sure," Rebecca nodded. "But a margarita wouldn't hurt, would it?"

Elena smiled. She conveyed the order in Spanish to the waiter, who wrote it all down and left.

"So now even the locals presume we're American?" Rebecca asked, referring to the waiter.

"I guess so," Elena answered. "How can they tell? Weren't we speaking in Spanish?"

"Maybe it's our clothes," Rebecca said.

After but a moment, the waiter returned with their drinks: two margaritas, both rimmed with salt and accompanied by a fresh lime. He set the pitcher of sangria next to the margaritas.

"Have you decided what you'd like to order?" he asked.

The restaurant served small plates, or tapas, in the Spanish style. Rebecca doubted that there was much about them that was truly very Spanish, let alone from Barcelona, but it didn't matter; the food was always very good there.

They selected tequila shrimp, Iberian ham, gazpacho, glazed salmon, and short ribs. Within minutes, a number of waiters brought them their first dishes.

"The service here is always so much better than in the States, don't you think?" Rebecca asked.

"Way better," Elena responded. "The food is fresh, and the staff is actually nice."

"I love the short ribs," Rebecca said, spearing another piece of the dish with her fork and taking a small bite of it.

"Me, too!" Elena said. "Good comfort food—not pretentious."

Rebecca noticed that her sister's glass was untouched. "You're skipping the margaritas tonight?"

"They look great," Elena said. "But I'm just going to stick with the sangria."

As they ate, the waiters brought additional tapas, one by one, and cleared their plates as they finished.

"So," Rebecca said, "are we going to make up? You know, we always do."

"I'm sorry," Elena started. "There was a lot going on. My tantrum wasn't really about you."

"Thanks," Rebecca said. "I'm sorry, too. But I do want to talk through some of it, if you're okay with that."

"I guess so," Elena nodded, listening more intently. "Is this gonna be scary?"

"No," Rebecca answered. She took a moment to collect her thoughts and then continued. "I know you didn't mean a lot of what you said last night, but at some level, I think you did, too."

"Rebecca, that really wasn't about you . . ." Elena started, before Rebecca raised her hand slightly to cut her off.

"I need to say this, Elena, and it needs to be thorough."

Rebecca paused again, and Elena waited for her to continue.

"You were more or less right, Elena. So I need to tell you that I'm sorry," Rebecca said. "I didn't say it before; I should have. I've needed to say it for a long time, and you've deserved to hear it."

"Nonsense," Elena said. I still can't believe some of what I said. It's embarrassing."

Rebecca took a long breath and then continued. "You know that time was really tough for me. But you were right: I did steal Miguel, and it was wrong."

Elena softly chuckled. "Miguel? Good grief!"

"I know," Rebecca said. "That's all so silly now. But we can't ignore the fact that I did run away—I just left both of you. I shouldn't have."

Elena listened as she spoke, waiting for her to continue, after seeming to notice that Rebecca wanted to.

"It's hard for me to understand why I left exactly," Rebecca continued. "I was only sixteen—who thinks clearly then?"

Elena nodded again.

"I wish I had a better explanation, but we both know I don't."

"I understand, and it's done," Elena said. "Forget about it. I have."

"Maybe. But I still haven't yet," Rebecca continued. "I think I felt alone and different. Maybe I still do. You and Dad? You're cut from the same cloth. I wasn't. Sometimes, I felt like I was watching a movie. The characters were everyone else, and you and Dad were the stars. I was just a spectator, accepted and loved but separate."

"I know sometimes you feel that way," Elena said, "but I don't really understand why."

"Maybe it's just my excuse for unacceptable behavior. I don't know." Rebecca paused again to collect her thoughts. "Maybe the one thing I really had was the boys' attention. But when you started to like Miguel and he noticed, I was jealous. Sure, that's silly; I understand that now. But then, I felt like I was the spectator again—the outsider."

Elena nodded, listening carefully to her sister's words.

"What's scary is that even now with Richard, I'm not one hundred percent certain it's different."

"I know what you're saying," Elena said. "But believe me, Richard isn't your issue."

"At some level back then, I felt like I was losing you," Rebecca said. "Maybe it's the twin thing. I don't know. But it didn't feel good. And then it all got so much worse. You know, after the procedure, Dad couldn't even look me in the eye anymore. After a while, it felt like I couldn't stand it. So, when the Stimpsons gave me a quick and easy exit, I took it."

Elena took her sister's hand as it rested on the table. "I remember. I'm sorry."

"This is my apology," Rebecca said, smiling, "and now it's sounding like an explanation or an excuse. That's not my point. The point is that you were always there for me, Elena, even when I really didn't deserve it. I just wanted you to know that I count on that, and I'll always be there for you, too. I can do better. I'm committed to it."

Elena slowly exhaled. "I know," she said. "And I'm sorry, too. Truly. You know, we were really sad when we realized you were gone. At first, it was terrifying; Dad went crazy. Then he found your note and figured it out." She grinned. "You know, he kept blaming himself for not getting you an iPhone so that we could call you. Anyway, it hurt a lot for both of us."

Rebecca nodded, waiting for her sister to finish.

"I guess I'm still insecure about it all—that fear of being upstaged and abandoned," Elena continued. "I know you won't, but I wonder if the feeling is still there."

"I did that to you—to both of you," Rebecca said.

"I really didn't get the outsider stuff back then, but I do now," Elena continued. "I hadn't felt that until I moved to the United States and became the outsider. You know, sometimes people just presume I'm undocumented and that my father's a migrant farmworker. Then they tell me how much they support our plight. It's incredibly uncomfortable."

The waiter returned to clear their plates and to refill their water glasses. "*Uno mas?*" he asked.

"I pretty sure I could use another margarita," Rebecca said. When Elena declined, he instead refilled her sangria glass from the pitcher.

Elena paused before continuing. "You know, I wasn't going to tell you, but Richard didn't just head back to work; he kind of left."

Rebecca felt her fingers tighten around her fork. Her instincts about Richard had never been good, and she instantly felt protective. "Really?" she asked. "For good?"

"No. Maybe. Well, it's complicated." She smirked at her contradictory thoughts.

"What does that mean?" Rebecca asked.

"Well, we didn't break up," Elena said. "But there's clearly a directional issue. At the moment, I don't know what it means."

"I'm sorry," Rebecca said. "But you'll figure it out, I'm sure." She wanted to share her instincts about Richard. But at the moment, it didn't seem appropriate. She watched her sister, looking for a clue as to how to react.

Rebecca knew there was more going on with her twin. There was nothing wrong with the water at the Vista Linda, and the seasickness didn't make sense, either. After all, they'd spent their childhood on boats in the ocean. Rebecca glanced down at Elena's margarita, which remained untouched.

Elena caught her glance and responded. "It's not that I don't want to drink with you," she said. "But everything feels unsettled at the moment."

Rebecca nodded but didn't respond, again searching Elena's face for guidance.

"You know, I can see exactly what you're thinking, and you're right," Elena said. "It's very early, but I think I've missed my cycle."

Rebecca nodded. "I wasn't going to say anything, but I do know you pretty well," she said, taking her sister's hand. "Does Richard know? Is that why he left?"

"No," Elena said. "I'm just figuring it out myself. Maybe I'm overreacting, and maybe I'm in denial. I haven't taken a test. I guess I'll just deal with it when I'm back in the States—I mean, if I have to."

Rebecca nodded but again didn't know what to say. "I understand," she eventually said softly, while averting her eyes. "Believe me, I do." She looked back up and warmly smiled. "I don't have any advice, but I know you'll figure it all out, Elena. You have good judgment. I've seen it my whole life, and I respect it."

Elena nodded. "*Gracias*," she said.

"Maybe just give it some time for now," Rebecca said.

Elena nodded again without comment.

"Just know that I'm here for you—just like you always were for me."

"I know. I really do," Elena said, smiling. "Hopefully, it will all be a nonissue."

"Agreed," Rebecca said.

With the coming of the evening, the city's lights replaced the last rays of the sunset. Framed by the deep darkness of the sea, they sparkled magically throughout the town and all along the coastline. In the distance, Rebecca saw the twinkling lights of several boats, taking tourists out for an evening meal at sea or bringing back the last catch of the day. After a while, a spectacular flash of light beamed across the skyline near the coastline, followed promptly by a boom.

"Time for the evening fireworks?" Elena said. "I still love them!"

They both turned their chairs slightly to watch the fireworks stream over the ocean before bursting into mushrooms of multicolored light. In addition to bedazzling the evening sky, the fireworks reflected magically over the dark waves of the ocean below. Punctuating their bursts were the "Oohs" and "Aahs" of the restaurant patrons, as they stopped their dinner conversations to watch the brilliant display.

"A symbol of our own breakthrough?" Rebecca said with a wink.

"Well, yes," Elena answered, "but for the fact that they do them every night here—and have forever . . ."

"Maybe more of Dad's scheming—you know, sending us here, now?" Rebecca asked.

"I wouldn't be surprised," Elena responded. "Wouldn't be surprised at all . . ." She raised her eyebrow with a half grin.

"Hey," Elena continued, changing the subject. "What's up with him, anyway? Do you know?"

"What do you mean?" Rebecca said.

"Well, he doesn't look so good, and he seems particularly focused on, well, us."

"He's getting older and misses us, I'm sure. But I agree. He seems so sensitive—definitely off his game."

Elena nodded.

After the fireworks ended and the tapas stopped coming, the restaurant staff cleaned their table and refilled their water glasses. The sisters continued to talk. Having cleared the brush, they talked about everything as much as nothing. They shared recent photos, complained about their jobs, and reflected on the simple moments of their childhood—things like getting lost in the mall or collecting seashells on the beach. And as they casually spoke, the volume of their memories and the significance of their bond rekindled. Rebecca knew the comfort she felt was due in part to the tequila in the margaritas. But through the warmth in her sister's eyes and the passion of her voice, Rebecca could tell that Elena felt exactly the same way—and always would.

While the restaurant had nearly emptied, Rebecca realized that the waiter hadn't delivered their check. "It's great the way they never ask you to leave," she said. When she motioned to the waiter, he quickly left them their check along with two small homemade ice cream cones and a Bailey's shot on the house.

"This helped me," Elena said, taking a bite of one of the cones. "Thank you."

"It may take some time. But I want you to know that you're my person," Rebecca said, smiling. "Dad is, too. I need you, and I rely on you. That's not ever going to change for me."

"You're my person, too," Elena said, smiling back. "And Dad, of course."

Rebecca squeezed her sister's hand before noticing the time on her watch.

Elena caught her sister's glance and withdrew her arm to check the time herself. "I guess we missed the *Ballet Folklórico*?" she said.

"I think so," Rebecca answered. "We've been here for quite a while."

"Well, we've seen it about a thousand times, right?" Elena said.

"Yeah, I think we're safe on that one," Rebecca answered.

Rebecca picked up the check that the waiter had left on the table. After paying the tab with the waiter's portable electronic credit machine, they left the restaurant and headed home in a small yellow taxicab.

As they drove in silence through the cobblestone streets of Puerto Vallarta and then along the highway to Sayulita, Rebecca thought again about what Elena had said when they'd argued the day earlier. Over dinner, she'd explained why she'd left Sayulita. But she hadn't explained why she never went back after sneaking away. Even after the years, she still felt disappointed in herself.

It was a mistake, she thought. *A big one.* As she considered it further, she realized that the Stimpson red flags had been there all along. She'd just chosen to ignore them when she was sixteen, nine years earlier.

A large iron gate marked the entrance of the Stimpsons' driveway in Atherton. That gate made clear that wealthy people owned the home and that others were not welcome without an invitation. Like old Puerto Vallarta, the Stimpsons' driveway was covered with cobblestones. But unlike the charming and haphazard stones covering the streets in Puerto Vallarta, the stones in Atherton were neatly arranged and symmetrically placed. It seemed to Rebecca like everything in Atherton was like that: symmetrical, ordered, and controlled. On both sides of the driveway were expansive lawns of varying but equal proportions, banked by various trees. Oaks spread their curving branches mischievously across the driveway, each placed about twenty-five feet from the other, and redwoods towered into the sky, grouped in twos or threes, first on the left, and then on the right. Ahead was the huge house, rising three stories tall, painted in beige-gray, with brightly colored blue trim and matching shutters. From the street, none of it was visible. But once inside the gates, the house appeared majestically, almost as if it were a castle.

At sixteen, Rebecca felt humbled as she walked with her grandparents for the first time into the dramatic entry hall. Panes of glass extended in front of her from floor to ceiling; marble floors ran in all directions, and a semicircular stairway led to the second of the three floors.

"Don't be shy," her grandmother said. "This is your house, too, you know."

After a while, pride replaced her feelings of inadequacy. These were her grandparents, and she was their granddaughter. She wasn't just a worker or guest. Was she rich, too?

"Ben, can you grab her bags while I take her up to her room?" her grandmother said.

Rebecca followed her grandmother up the staircase made of rich, dark wood and proceeded along a corridor to a large bedroom on the right. The floors, covered with some type of Asian rugs, were made of the same dark wood as the staircase, and the tall windows, framed with thick burgundy curtains, looked over the gardens in the back of the house. There was a large bed, twice the size of her bed at home, covered with fluffy pillows and a fancy bedspread, which all matched perfectly. And in the back, there was a large bathroom with beige marble floors, a giant shower, two sinks, and two toilets. Rebecca walked to the second toilet, wondering why the room had two.

"It's a bidet," her grandmother said. "It's like a sink to clean in, if you want."

Rebecca looked at it, still puzzled, before grinning when she figured it out.

"Why don't you take a shower," her grandmother suggested, "while I make you something to eat?" Her grandmother pointed to where the towels were. "Put your clothes in the dresser. When you're done, just continue down the same hall and come down the back stairs. That's where the kitchen is."

"Thanks, Grandma," Rebecca said.

Her grandmother hugged her firmly. "You can't imagine how happy we are to have you here and to hear you call me *Grandma*!"

She left, and Rebecca collapsed on the bed. It all seemed like a fantasy. She couldn't imagine that people actually lived in places like this—normal people, *her* family. She unpacked her few belongings, took a quick shower, and then followed her grandmother's instructions to the kitchen.

"There you are," her grandmother said. "And all cleaned up. Here, I made you a sandwich for now. Turkey okay? You'll have to teach me what you like and don't like. I can't wait!"

After she finished the snack, her grandfather took her around the house. She could see from the entrance that it was big, but she didn't understand how big until she walked through it. In the basement, there was a gym, a theater, a wine cellar, a game room, and an extra bedroom with its own bathroom. On the main floor was the entry hall, the kitchen, the master bedroom, two offices, a butler pantry, a laundry room, a living room, a family room, a library, a dining room, and an in-law unit, which just looked to her like another bedroom, mini kitchen, and bathroom with its own door going outside. Upstairs was her bedroom, three other bedrooms, and a knitting or children's room, each with its own bathroom. Behind the house was a large yard with a fireplace, a sitting area, a swimming pool, a tennis court, and a pool house, which included two additional bedrooms. The enormity of it was overwhelming.

"I've never seen anything like this," Rebecca said to her grandparents when they returned to the kitchen.

Rebecca watched her grandparents' faces brighten with the love they felt for her. She knew her father would be angry with her, but she didn't regret for a moment coming with them.

The next morning, Rebecca's grandparents approached her in the living room. She could tell it was serious when her grandfather took a seat next to the cream-colored sofa, and her grandmother took the adjoining seat.

"Rebecca," Ben said, "we want to talk to you about something important."

She looked at him and then her grandmother while anxiously waiting to hear what they had to say.

"We want you to stay here, to move in," he continued.

Rebecca instantly felt a knot in her stomach. "But I don't live here," she said. "This is just a vacation."

"You can live here if you want," he said. "And we hope you will."

She tried to listen but had trouble concentrating on the meaning of their words. She placed her hands under her legs and focused on her grandfather as he spoke.

"The reality is that we can provide you with enormous opportunities and experiences that, well, just don't exist in Mexico," he said. "You are an American citizen, and you're our granddaughter. So these things are your birthright."

She was happy that they liked her, but she wasn't sure she understood what they were suggesting.

"I've already made a couple of calls," Ben continued. "Sacred Heart will take you now for high school; you can start as a student there next week. If you do well, I'm pretty sure Stanford will take you, too."

"Stanford?"

"Stanford is the university around the corner. It's probably the best in the world—unless you're a Harvard fan."

She nodded again, wondering what he meant.

"I have friends on the board there," he continued. "It's not a sure thing; you'll have to get some good grades. But with hard work, I'm pretty sure you could go. The admissions committee will love your abduction story."

She wasn't sure how to respond. She felt insecure. "Can Elena and Dad come?" she asked. "I know that's more people, but there's tons of room here. You'd really like them, too. I know it!"

Her grandmother looked nervously at her husband, who nodded for her to respond. "I don't think that will work," she said. "Your father isn't a citizen, and he's wanted for child abduction and grand theft. Elena probably is a citizen, but you wouldn't want her to leave your dad there alone, would you?"

"Maybe she could come for the summer—maybe for a year?" Rebecca asked. "We're twins, you know."

"I know you were born at the same time, but you're really not twins," Ben said. "Elena isn't our granddaughter. But you are."

"We searched everywhere for you," Beverly continued. "Tell her, Ben! We even hired a PI. But they wouldn't do anything to help us in Mexico—at least, not without a bribe. They just kept telling us to fill out a form."

"We found Francisco's parents after a while, but they'd cut him off—completely," Ben added. "Had no idea where he was, the little gold digger."

"Ben," her grandmother countered, taking his hand.

Rebecca knew her father's situation was more complex than they suggested, but that didn't really change their offer. "I don't want to leave them," she said. "I think they'd miss me."

"They will," her grandmother said. "I'm sure of it. But if you go back, we'll miss you, too."

"You'll be missed either way," her grandfather said, taking her hand and looking at her grandmother. "The question is, what's right for you?"

"We think spending a year here with us is right," Beverly said. "After that, you can stay or go."

Rebecca looked at them, puzzled. "Can't I go back now?"

"We feel very strongly that you shouldn't," her grandfather said. "We want you to at least give it a try here with us—for a year."

"Think about it," her grandmother said. "I'm happy to call your dad and explain it all to him. I'm sure he will agree."

Over the next several days, her grandparents took her to Sacred Heart High School, Stanford University, the San Francisco Symphony, and the 49ers football game. It was incredible, all of it. And they were right: There was nothing like it in Sayulita or Puerto Vallarta—maybe not even in Mexico. Her grandparents were rich, really rich. She used to think that her family in Mexico was rich; relative to many Mexicans, they were. Now, she understood that they were relatively poor. But how could she just leave them? She instinctively understood that the Stimpsons just wouldn't let her go home. At some level, theirs wasn't an offer to stay; it was a requirement. But for now, she wasn't sure she wanted to go home anyway. Elena was still mad at her, and her father was disappointed in her. Her grandparents just wanted her for who she was: their granddaughter. She liked that.

After speaking again with the Stimpsons, Rebecca reluctantly picked up the phone to call her father in Mexico. She knew he was worried and would be disappointed, but she didn't want her grandparents to tell him that she would be staying for a while. It was an hour later in Puerto Vallarta, so she was pretty sure he'd be home.

"*Hola*," Francisco said, after answering the phone.

"*Hola*, Daddy," Rebecca said. "It's me."

"It's so good to hear your voice, Rebecca! We've been so worried about you. Are you all right?"

"Yes, I'm fine. I'm here with Grandma and Grandpa in the United States."

"I know," he said. "I got your note. They called me the day after you left and sent me several texts." He didn't say anything more, but she was sure he was mad.

"I'm sorry, Dad," she said. "I just wanted to see what it was like here and to know my grandparents."

"I understand," he said. "We miss you."

"I know," she said. "But I'm getting to see all kinds of things here."

"Tell me about it," he said.

"Well, they live in this mansion with beautiful gardens and four cars, even though they don't have any kids."

"Yes," he responded. "They were in that same place when I lived up there. It's pretty incredible, isn't it?"

"Yes," she continued. "I got to go with them to the San Francisco Symphony and the Museum of Modern Art. It's all so clean, new, and incredible! Yesterday, they took me to Stanford. It's just a couple of blocks from their house, but it looks Mexican."

"Yes, it's built in the Spanish style. San Francisco is pretty incredible, too, isn't it? I'm so glad you're getting to see it; I just wish I could have taken you." A sadness replaced the anger in his voice.

"Me, too," she said.

The line went quiet, so she carefully considered her next words. "They told me, Dad, that I could go to high school here at Sacred Heart. It's Catholic, so I'm sure you'd like it. It's just a couple of blocks from their house, so I could ride Poppy's old bike or even just walk instead of taking the bus for an hour, like I do there. It's got everything: a swimming pool, tennis courts, a football stadium, a soccer field, a theater, and a whole art gallery, where they teach the students how to make ceramics and even how to paint. If I went, I could learn so much and do all of those things."

The phone remained silent for a while before Francisco responded. "Is that what you want, honey?" he asked.

"If I stay, I can work on my English. Then I won't get bad grades on my essays anymore," she suggested. When he didn't respond, she continued, "The American School in Puerto Vallarta doesn't have any of those things. And the students aren't as smart. Everyone at Sacred Heart goes to school at the universities when they graduate; they told me."

"I don't know if the students here aren't as smart, Rebecca," he said, "but they're right. The education there is probably better."

Rebecca considered what he was saying but didn't immediately answer. "It's only for a year," she continued. "One school year. Then I'll come back."

"Is that what you're trying to tell me—that you want to go to school there?" he asked.

"I don't know," she answered. "What do you think?"

When again he didn't immediately answer, she wondered what he was thinking. Perhaps she was making a mistake.

"There certainly are many more opportunities up there than there are here, particularly with extremely wealthy people like Poppy's parents," he said. "If that's what you want to do, I will support you for a year. But we will miss you—a lot. And you must come home after a year."

Rebecca felt overwhelmed with excitement. "Thanks, Dad," she said. "You're the best. I love you so much!"

"Call me every week," he said. "And get a phone so you can text me every night before you go to bed, okay?"

"Okay," she answered. "Night, Dad. I love you."

"Good night, Rebecca. We love you, too."

Rebecca felt a deep sense of relief when the conversation ended. She was going to continue this most incredible adventure, and her dad was letting her do it. But when the line didn't go dead, and instead she could hear him quietly weeping at the other end, she wondered what she'd done.

When the taxi approached the entrance to their family home in Sayulita after the long drive from the restaurant in Puerto Vallarta, Rebecca tried to refocus her attention on the present. After her dinner with Elena at Barcelona Tapas, she felt a new sense of resolution with her sister. But she knew that she still lacked resolution with her father. She never should have left him or her sister in the first place. She knew that now, and to be honest, she'd known it then. But to make matters worse, she never did go back. Instead, she stayed and did just as the Stimpsons had suggested because, as she'd later told her father, it was her senior year, and she didn't want to lose her friends.

Perhaps for the first time as an adult, she fully comprehended the gravity of what she'd done in her youth and the emotional harm she'd caused, both to her sister and her father. But she also knew there were pieces of the puzzle that were missing—things she still didn't fully understand. She would need to collect her thoughts further and then speak with her father. As with Elena, the conversation with her father was long overdue, but it was not one that could be avoided any longer.

Chapter 15

Rebecca finished the breakfast dishes with Consuela while her father and Elena read their iPads on the palapa deck. It was going to be another beautiful day in Sayulita, but, as usual, a hot one. After their dinner the prior night, Rebecca had an idea, and when she'd explained it to her sister, Elena had quickly bought in. Now, she just needed to execute it.

"Consuela," Rebecca asked, "whatever happened to that karaoke machine we used to keep at the restaurant?"

"*No sé,*" Consuela answered. "Why?"

"We were thinking of a surprise for Dad at dinner tonight."

"I love surprises," she said. "Will you sing? Your father will love it. *Seguro.*" (Certainly.)

"We're thinking about it."

"I will ask Guillermo to find it and set it up. It must be here somewhere."

After Consuela left, Rebecca put away the last plate and wiped down the countertop. Save for some discoloring near the faucet, the granite was exactly the same as it had been when she was a child. She scanned the kitchen and living room of the palapa before looking up toward the bedrooms, Consuela's apartment, and then the restaurant. They were all right on the beach, with incredible views of the Pacific Coast.

Rebecca felt apprehensive, and she knew why. While her father's home wasn't a mansion like the Stimpsons', the fact of the matter was that it didn't make sense for him to own it. And while taking them to Mexico as toddlers might have been justified, she'd never been comfortable with the secrets: hiding their background and identities, eliminating contact with her grandparents, prohibiting them from using their middle names, and avoiding any travel to the States.

She watched her father as he read his iPad on the deck. She knew that she owed him an apology, just as she'd owed Elena an apology. But for her to really apologize to him, she needed to hear the whole story from him. And, like it or not, it seemed like the time to hear the whole story was now. So, when Elena went back to her bedroom, Rebecca walked over to her father on the palapa deck, taking the coffeepot with her.

"Refill?" she asked him.

"I'm good, but thanks," he said.

She set the coffee on the table before taking the wicker chair next to him on the deck.

"How's my favorite twin?" he asked. "I hear you patched things up last night?"

"We did," she answered. "At least, we started to."

"And?"

"There's real baggage there, and most of it's my fault," she said. "It's going to take time, but we're making progress. There was a lot unsaid that needed to be said. I don't think Elena and I could have had our conversation a year or two ago, and it wouldn't have worked remotely. Maybe it just needed to all come out first. I hope so."

"That really does make me happy—the resolution and the hope, not the fight."

She smiled but continued looking at her father.

"I see that's not it," he said. "So, what's on your mind?"

"To be honest, there's some stuff I'd like to discuss with you, too," she said.

He put down his iPad and turned his attention to her, inviting her to continue. "*Dime.*" *(Tell me).*

"Remind me, Dad," she asked. "When did you buy this place?"

"Well, let's see," Francisco said, looking up. "We got here when you were about two, and Jose died when you were about four. You didn't know Jose, but he was the prior owner."

"But how'd you pay for it?" Elena asked. She was being direct, but that seemed unavoidable to her.

Her father looked puzzled by the question but didn't hesitate to respond. "Derek left some money—actually, a lot of money. After he died, I took it when I came back to Mexico with you girls and used it to buy the house and restaurant from Jose a couple of years later. But you know this already, right?"

She nodded but persisted. "So, you needed the money to leave?" she suggested, offering him a solution to the issue. "You know, the Stimpsons told me you stole all of Derek's money when you left."

"Ah, so that's what this is about. Well, I'm not surprised they'd say that," he said. "But no, I didn't really need the money to leave."

"Okay," she responded, hoping for further clarification.

"Legally, it was tricky. Derek and I were married, at least in our minds," he started. "Well, certainly in my mind, anyway. You know, I couldn't marry him legally, so I couldn't get citizenship and work up there. And when you girls came along, one of us had to stay home to take care of you, anyway. Since Derek was a doctor and I couldn't work, the 'mom' job went to me. That's all changed now, but you have to remember, the laws were very different for gays back then."

She watched him as he spoke. He wasn't embarrassed and didn't seem at all uncomfortable or concerned. It surprised her.

"Anyway, when Derek died without a will up there, most of his money would have gone to me, and the balance would have gone to you—if we'd been legally married."

"I get it," she said.

"Since Derek died without a will and we weren't legally married, I suppose that all of the money technically was yours. He hadn't yet adopted Elena, so as his only legal child, you would have inherited all of it. I'd never thought about that, but since I used the money to buy this place, I suppose it's actually yours."

She glanced around the living room, which formed only a small part of their home. It was significant, but it wasn't hers, regardless of the legalities. "Then I give it to you," she said without hesitation.

He chuckled.

"But tell me, how were you able to get the money?" she asked. "I presume he didn't just have it in a drawer."

"No," Francisco said. "He put his savings into an investment account, but he set it up with signing authority for both of us. I didn't know that until he died. So, when I realized we had to leave quickly, I transferred it to our joint bank account. Then I wired it to an old bank account I still had from my college days in Mexico City. Later, I withdrew it all over a short period in cash, so they couldn't trace it back here."

She nodded again. "And that's why we had to be secretive?"

"Yes, there's been a lot of hiding. I don't know if that was necessary or not. My guess now is that the Stimpsons didn't pursue it—or the Mexican authorities didn't help them."

"I think it was some of both," she said. "Grandpa tried, but he hit a dead end."

Francisco nodded. "Well, there you have it. Was it legally mine by law? No, it was Derek's. Was it mine because he'd actually given it to me? No, it wasn't. Did I take it anyway because I knew you'd need it? Kind of, but not necessarily. And is that what Derek would have wanted? Well, we'll never really know. *I* think so, but the *Stimpsons* don't. The laws up there don't, either."

Rebecca thought his answers made perfect sense. The fact of the matter was that he didn't know what Derek wanted with certainty, and he wasn't at all ashamed to say so. She refilled his coffee cup before turning to her other question, the important one.

"Did you ever legally adopt me?" she asked. It was a tough question, but she was entitled to know, and she needed to know. "I know you couldn't in the United States, but did you ever actually do it in Mexico?"

He shook his head. "You know how you came about. But no, I couldn't legally adopt you, here or there, and I'm so sorry about that," he said, as tears filled his eyes. "I felt like the risk of losing you after making a governmental filing was just too great." He tried to dry his eyes quickly before continuing. "But I *know* you're my daughter, Rebecca. I'll never be able to explain exactly what that means to you—or anyone else. I understand that. But I'm *certain* it's true."

She sadly nodded. "You know," she said, "the Stimpsons see you as a child abductor and a thief. They claim there's a warrant outstanding for your arrest up there."

"I suppose that's right," he said. "But that's not so interesting to me. What is, is how you see me—what story do *you* believe?"

She thought about the question. From the Simpsons' perspective, and the law, for that matter, he was an illegal immigrant, a child abductor, and a thief—someone to be locked up or deported. But from her perspective, he was not. As she considered it further, she knew, with certainty, that there was nothing the Stimpsons or anyone else could do to change her view. And at some level, she realized, she'd always known it.

"I see you as I always have," she said. "You're the father who would do anything for his girls."

He smiled before reaching over to kiss her forehead. "Thank you," he said. "That means everything to me." Then he quickly dried his eyes again.

As the surf rushed below, they sat together in comfortable silence. After again collecting her thoughts, Rebecca proceeded with her apology.

"So I want to tell you I'm sorry, Dad. Sorry for all of it."

"What?"

"I'm sorry I left. I'm sorrier I didn't come back when I said I would. I should have." She could feel the tears welling up as she spoke but tried to contain them.

"I'm not," he answered. "I'm not sorry for any of it."

She was surprised by his answer and again felt confused. "You don't understand," she continued, trying to explain. "I was . . ."

"Young and confused," he said. "You were sixteen, your boyfriend dumped you, and you felt like you didn't fit in." He smiled. "You know, I see more than you think."

"I guess that's right," she said, looking down at the coffee table.

"There's not a day that goes by when I don't think about all of that and wonder what I did wrong. What I should have done. And what a better father would have done."

"Why?"

"Because I've always wondered if I'd made a mistake bringing you down here in the first place. Let's be honest: You did, too. You needed to figure that out."

She thought about what he'd said but couldn't think of how to respond.

"You've been given an enormous opportunity," he continued. "You were able to obtain a high school education that was superior to your sister's, and the Stimpsons paid for you to attend a premier global university. I don't regret your taking advantage of all of that—not for a second. Elena shouldn't, either."

She silently nodded again.

"Maybe taking you was selfish of me," he said. "But after losing Derek, it seemed particularly important to have you grow up together as a family, even if that meant raising you without any money in Mexico. I'll never know if my decision was wrong. But I can't imagine raising two more beautiful women—despite all of it."

For the first time, Rebecca thought she fully understood. While he had no concern about the ethics of *what* he'd done, he remained deeply concerned about *why* he'd done it: Was it for him, or was it for her? Apparently, he'd agonized about his decision to bring her to Mexico for years, and even now, he remained troubled by its effects on her well-being. The realization made her feel sad—very sad.

"It's different here, but in many ways, better," Rebecca said, seeking to comfort him. "We have a simpler life, a slower life. Spending time with family and friends here is not only a pleasure, it's recognized as important and prioritized. It's okay if you don't go to the fanciest college or have the most important job. Here, you don't have to spend every moment making money or climbing somebody else's ladder of achievement, relentlessly. Pointlessly? And here, you don't worry so much about following a rule or even a law that just doesn't make sense."

While she'd directed her words to her father, she quickly realized that they weren't necessarily tied to him or any other person. Nor did they necessarily speak to Mexico or any other place. They were values, his values. And they were her values, too. At some level, she wanted him to understand that. Realizing that she'd been somewhat vague, she decided to be more specific.

"More to the point," she added, after catching his eyes, "in Mexico, I got to have a dad, and that dad is pretty darn incredible."

Francisco beamed, even as his eyes started to tear again. He quickly dried them before responding. "Thank you. Maybe I needed to hear that?" he asked, as his moist eyes brightened with delight.

She took his free hand and smiled. "Maybe I needed to say it," she answered.

She kissed him on the cheek, and he hugged her firmly. As he did, she felt surrounded by the warm security of his affection in his home—their family home. She knew she'd hurt him before—she'd hurt him a lot. But she thought their conversation had helped. *At least it's a start,* she thought.

Rebecca began to clear the coffeepot and cups from the table. But as she placed them on a tray, she realized that he wasn't done. "Something else?" she asked.

"Yes, actually," he said tentatively.

She nodded and sat back down to listen.

"I don't want to undermine your relationship with the Stimpsons," he said. "But I do want you to be careful."

"Why?"

"The Stimpsons offer a lot, but it comes with strings. At least, that was Derek's opinion. The Stimpsons very much have a worldview. You see that in the way they characterize me, you, gays, race, money. Balancing their demands was tough for Derek; with time, it might have become impossible."

"And you think that's true for me, too?" she asked.

"I'm not saying that," he answered, "because I don't know. I hope not. But you'll have to figure that out."

His thoughts resonated with her. Perhaps it was his approach. He clearly had an opinion, a view. But he didn't have answers. He left those for her to discover. *He'd always been that way*, she realized. It was a simple confidence in who and what he was. He didn't need to do anything or impress anyone. Nor did he need to convince her or anyone else of anything. He was a simple man who'd lived a simple life. For her, he wasn't just a father; he was a role model.

She wanted to continue the conversation. She wanted to ask him about himself—and a thousand other things. She enjoyed talking with him; she'd missed their moments together. But in his eyes, she could see he was getting tired. So she decided to let him rest before catching up with him further.

"Thanks, Dad," she said. "I'd rehearsed this apology for hours, maybe even years. But it feels like I just got another pep talk."

"Good." He hugged her. "That's my job. Have no regrets with me, because I think you're awesome."

As she stood to leave, she saw her leather briefcase sitting next to the art bag that was hanging on her easel. She smiled as she examined the sketch of the painting she'd started, and wondered if he'd given her the courage to do what she increasingly felt she should.

Chapter 16

Later that night, Rebecca walked up to the restaurant's roof deck, looking for Consuela. She and Elena had planned the evening's dinner for their father at his restaurant. She checked her phone for the time: 7:15 p.m. The table was set, and they'd made all of the arrangements for the evening with the restaurant chef. That evening, the staff would prepare the restaurant's finest cuisine, and they'd have the roof deck to themselves. Rebecca thought everything was done until she realized she hadn't followed up on the karaoke machine.

"Consuela," Rebecca called quietly, "are you up here?"

"*Sí, sí,*" Consuela answered. "I'm coming up now."

"Did you find it?" she asked. "The machine?"

"*Sí,*" Consuela answered. "Guillermo fixed it up. It hadn't been used for a while, but it still works fine. Do you want to try it?"

"Where is it, and what do we need to do?"

Consuela lifted a tablecloth from a rectangular object sitting near the rooftop railing. "Right here. And here are the microphones," she added, pointing to two remote mikes on top of the machine.

Rebecca turned one on. "Testing, one, two, three," she said. The adjoining speakers amplified the sound from her voice.

"Guillermo already set up the song. Just tell him when you're ready."

"Okay," Rebecca said nervously.

"You will sing beautifully," she said, "just like you play piano."

"That's what I'm afraid of," Rebecca answered. She kept the mikes out but recovered the machine. "Do you have any tape? Something strong?"

Consuela went down to the restaurant and returned with some silver duct tape. "Here."

"Thanks." Rebecca took the microphones and taped one under her chair and Elena's.

"*¿Está bien?*" Consuela asked. *(It's okay?)*

Rebecca nodded.

"Consuela?" she asked, changing the subject. "Is Dad okay?"

"Okay?" Consuela asked.

"You know, depressed . . . maybe sick?"

Consuela looked away. "*No sé nada,*" she said, taking a towel and wiping the drops off the water pitcher. *(I don't know anything.)*

"I mean . . ." Rebecca started.

"*¡Habla con tu padre!*" *(Talk to your father!)*

Consuela didn't look up before finishing and then turned to go back down the stairs. While doing so, she passed Elena and Francisco coming up.

"What's up with Consuela?" Francisco asked.

"You tell me," Rebecca said, scrutinizing him as she spoke.

He shrugged. "I see the sun's starting to set, which means it's margarita time!"

Francisco found the pitcher the bartender had left them and poured the margaritas into the salted glasses over ice. "*Salud,*" he said, as they raised their glasses to the sunset that marked the completion of another day.

They finished their drinks over pleasant conversation before taking their places at the table, which was decorated in festive, vibrant floral patterns. In the center was a bird of paradise plant surrounded by multicolored plates and light-blue glasses—all benefits of dining in the restaurant they owned.

After their appetizers of soft crab and shrimp were served, a lively discussion began. When they'd finished the first course, Francisco gently tapped his water glass with his fork to gather their attention.

"Hey," he started. "I know I told you not to worry about gifts, because, of course, your coming is the best gift imaginable. But I did get a couple, anyway, so I hope you won't mind if I hand them out."

"Dad, you tricked us?" Elena said, smirking. "And Christmas Day has already passed!"

Without responding, he stood and walked over to the bar area before returning with three packages, which he handed to Consuela, Guillermo, and Elena. Rebecca presumed he'd inadvertently forgotten her, but when he returned to his seat and waited, she realized he hadn't.

Consuela opened her present first, which was haphazardly wrapped with golden paper—clearly Francisco's handiwork. "Ay," she said, once it was open. "A salsa dress and dance shoes?"

"Yes. You know, she's graduated to the next level in her class," he explained to the others.

Consuela smiled as she held the dress up to her chest. "I love it," she said. "Now I will dance even better!"

Guillermo opened his present next. It was a large, heavy rectangle that was poorly wrapped like Consuela's. "A tackle and bait box?" he asked, even before he'd finished opening it.

Francisco nodded. "I think your old one's pretty much dead." He then turned to Guillermo and whispered, "But don't open that secret compartment when Consuela's around." He pointed to a lever at the bottom of the box.

Guillermo opened it anyway, but then quickly shut it. "You know," he whispered back, raising his eyebrows mischievously, "Herradura is my favorite." Then he smirked at Consuela as she frowned, knowing well that she'd heard them.

Finally, Elena picked up her gift, a small, light rectangular box. "I'm so curious," she said as she unwrapped it. The box itself was black, and when she lifted the lid, the pearls of a necklace sparkled up at her.

"My God—is it real? Mikimoto?" She paused, confused. "Dad, it's too much. And not fair," she added, looking at Rebecca.

"You're right," Francisco said, also looking askance at Rebecca while raising an eyebrow. "I gave Rebecca some money to buy something nice for you in San Francisco. But I'm pretty sure I didn't pay for that..."

"Seriously?" Elena said, looking again at Rebecca.

Seeing her sister's delight, Rebecca grinned. "Sometimes a girl needs a confidence boost for those key nights out," she said. "I hope you like it."

"I know, but..." Elena started. "The Stimpsons?"

Rebecca chuckled. "No. My bonus." She smiled. "Money comes and goes," she said. "But family doesn't."

Elena opened the necklace and quickly fastened it about her neck. "Ah—I can't believe this!" she squealed. "Thank you both. *Gracias*, Rebecca."

From her sister's eyes, Rebecca could see that Elena was visibly touched. And as she walked around the table to give Rebecca a hug, Francisco grinned with delight.

While Rebecca enjoyed seeing her family's pleasure with their gifts, she couldn't help feeling left out. Was it a rekindling of the same feeling she'd felt in her youth—the one she thought she'd finally laid to rest? She hoped not. She again looked at her father hopefully, but he declined to make eye contact and instead just continued to grin. Then she noticed that the others were also grinning.

"I guess I've been naughty this year?" she said, trying to chuckle with them.

But when Rebecca caught her sister's gaze, she noticed that Elena's eyes kept darting to the right. Then Elena used her index finger to discreetly point in the same direction. When Rebecca didn't respond, Francisco stood up, walked to the bar, and pulled out a large red ribbon. Everyone watched as he passed, and Consuela started to giggle. He then walked to the other end of the room and stuck it on the aqua-green surfboard that was resting unnoticed in the corner against a wall. When he returned to the table, he wore a mischievous grin.

"*Feliz Navidad*, Rebecca," he said.

Rebecca felt her face brighten and then flush. She walked to the surfboard and pressed her palm against it; she could tell it was a nice one. Then she looked back at her family, who were laughing at her, clearly having been in on her father's prank.

"I love it," she said, grinning. "I really do!"

"I know your old one's cracked. They call this one a Shortie," her father said. "Apparently, it's the new thing—faster, but tougher to ride. Pablo at the surf shop was pretty sure you could handle it. He's waiting for you to take a test ride with him when you have a minute. But he'll trade it for another, if you like."

She continued to run her hands along the board's edges, wondering what it would be like to ride it while remembering the many days she'd spent surfing in her youth. Her dad had picked it out for her because he knew her. And he knew what would make her feel special, connected, and loved. *Well, he's right,* she thought.

She walked back to the table and hugged her father. "Thanks, Dad," she said. "It's perfect."

After clearing their plates, the staff served their main course: a dorado, presented head and all, glazed with a tequila-lime sauce and grilled over an open fire.

"We need to thank Guillermo for this beauty," Francisco said. "He caught it for us this morning."

Rebecca looked at Consuela, seeking confirmation.

"*Es verdad*," Consuela agreed, as Guillermo nodded.

Francisco served each of them a healthy portion of the white meat. While doing so, Rebecca could see that he was happy and content. She knew there was nothing that made him happier than having a wonderful meal with his family. As she thought about it, she realized that it had always been that way. When they were well and together, he was at peace. And when there were issues and conflict, he was not. All he wanted, she realized, perhaps for the first time, was their happiness. He thrived on it.

But Rebecca could also see that that wasn't the whole picture. He'd looked visibly tired earlier in the day when they'd spoken. Now, small beads of sweat formed on his brow, which he regularly wiped. And his color under the light of the palapa looked off—more yellow than tan. She didn't want to overreact, but she was starting to feel real concern. She'd let him evade her questions before, and she wasn't going to confront him now. But she was sure something wasn't right, and she wasn't willing to wait much longer.

When they'd finished the main course, Rebecca nodded to Guillermo, who got up and walked behind the karaoke machine without removing its cover. As her father watched him, trying to ascertain what he was doing, Rebecca discreetly reached under her seat and turned on her mike while hiding it carefully in her lap. When the music on the karaoke machine softly began, it took Francisco only a moment to recognize it.

"What the hell? *Beaches*?!" He paused. "Are you kidding me?"

Rebecca smiled as she raised the mike and stood to sing.

"Oh, dear," Francisco said, interrupting her. "Seriously?"

Rebecca ignored him while lilting gently to the music and singing, "Ohh" as the instrumental introduction repeated. When the first verse started, she dramatically sang along to the words, as if she were serious. Then, after completing the first line, she started acting out the words of the song, just as Derek had done in the same room to the same song, twenty-plus years earlier—except that she sang directly to her father and only to him. So, when she sang about his being *cold* when she'd left, she held her body with a shiver, and when she sang about his always being in her *shadow*, she turned and looked behind her, as if to see him. Similarly, when singing about *sunlight*, she pointed to the sky and then him, and when the text turned to his *smile*, she gently touched her father's cheek. While her affectations were completely serious, their exaggeration created an ironic effect that was clearly intended to be comical.

"You're singing the same song Derek sang to court me. Why?" Francisco asked.

Elena then took her mike from under her seat and started the next verse, ignoring him.

"Oh, no," Francisco said. "You're in on this, too?" He grinned with anticipation.

Elena smiled as she began the next verse, acting out the words just as her sister had done. So, when she sang about Francisco's being her *strength*, she flexed her thin, little bicep, exposed by her sleeveless dress. When she sang about his *beautiful face*, she looked directly into his eyes, watching him as he grinned with the delight of the surprise and the memory of the music. And when the screen described his *pain*, she contorted her face with exaggerated effect before *hiding* it with her hand and smiling peekaboo, just as he had when they were children—all while keeping a watchful eye on the words as they scrolled down the karaoke screen.

When the vocals stopped for an instrumental interlude, Guillermo applauded, and Consuela giggled quietly while waiting for the sisters to continue. As the next verse of the song began, Rebecca and Elena walked to each side of their dad. This time, they searched for him, while singing about his going *unnoticed*. Then they sang about how they'd like to be just like him because he was their *hero*. After standing again and walking to opposite sides of the table, they then sang about how they could fly *like an eagle*, and, as they did, they raised their arms softly, as if in flight, because he was the *wind beneath their wings*.

As the verse returned to the chorus, the word *fly* repeated, and when text on the karaoke machine read *high*, they walked faster and then stood on their toes, lifting their "wings" gently with a slight increase in speed.

"You realize you look absolutely ridiculous," Francisco said. "Like levitating lunatics."

Rebecca didn't care, and she knew Elena didn't, either. They were singing for him together because they understood that their happiness together was what gave him happiness. And on that night, that was the only thing they cared about. So they smiled at each other as they sang while trying not to giggle.

As the coda started, the sisters continued singing to the melody. But this time, they ignored the text on the screen and instead changed the lyrics. First, they thanked him for wanting them. Then they thanked him for raising them. And finally, they thanked him for loving them.

Rebecca knew they weren't great—certainly worse than Derek, she presumed. But she thought they weren't all that bad, either. Regardless, she could see that Elena was also having fun with it, and their father's elation felt infectious. As the verse concluded, they circled the table one last time and returned to his side. Then they sat gently on each of his knees and thanked him again for being the *wind beneath their wings*.

"Wait," he said when they'd finished. "You're not going to fart on me like Derek did, are you?"

Of course, they knew exactly what he meant but only silently smiled, as the instrumental music cadenced to a conclusion. Consuela and Guillermo then stood and vigorously applauded, as did the rest of the restaurant staff, who had all come out to see what was happening. She and Elena then stood and took deeply exaggerated bows before kissing their father on his forehead and returning to their seats.

"Bravo!" Francisco said, while the restaurant staff whistled with enthusiastic approval.

The sisters stood for another bow and then clicked their mikes together as if in a high-five.

"Thank you," he said again. "Thank you, indeed."

"Boy—that's such a relief to be done," Elena said, after returning to her seat.

"I know," Rebecca added, taking a sip of her margarita. "I'd been stressed about that all day."

Francisco chuckled. "I'd forgotten I'd told you that story. When was that?"

"Uh, maybe a thousand times?" Elena answered.

"Well, bravo," he said. "I guess you learned something from those piano lessons after all?"

Rebecca laughed. "I doubt it."

"We learned from you how not to be afraid," Elena said.

"And to have fun," Rebecca added.

"From Derek, you mean," Francisco said. "He was the fearless one—and the musician."

The conversation continued as Francisco remembered those events and retold the same story, yet again. From the delight of his expression, Rebecca could see that their little performance had worked. It had been twenty-three years since Derek had died, but her father was still completely in love with him.

And as he spoke, he didn't seem to be worried about his daughters, nor was he even focused on them. Instead, he'd simply enjoyed their company and the meal. While it had been but a moment, the moment seemed significant. And in that moment, something had changed. When she caught Elena's eye, she could see the same reaction from her twin. So she discreetly raised her glass, and they silently toasted each other with the acknowledgment of their success.

After a while, the restaurant staff served the dessert: fresh berries over custard with a selection of liquors and cheeses. When the staff refilled their glasses, her father redirected the conversation.

"Thank you for coming back home," he said, looking at the twins. Then he shifted his gaze. "And to you, Consuela, Guillermo, for helping this family and me for a lifetime." Consuela blushed before she started to tear up. "And who could forget the incredible entertainment?" He smiled, again focusing on Rebecca and Elena. "We've had some struggles over many years and across this continent. But we've had much more fun. And we've always been a family. You can't imagine how happy that makes me."

When he paused for a bit too long, the resulting silence quickly became uncomfortable. Rebecca watched him and then the others at the table. She could tell from his body language that there was something more, so she waited. Guillermo looked down at his hands, which he nervously fidgeted, and Consuela's eyes filled with tears as quickly as she dabbed them away with her napkin. After a moment, Francisco started to speak but then again stopped. When his voice resumed, his lower lip quivered, just slightly, and then he stopped a third time. Recognizing he had something important to say, they waited for what seemed like a minute, maybe even two, before he gathered his composure and continued.

"So, I want you to know that I've lived a full and satisfying life, with few regrets. I hope you will forgive me for my many flaws. I know that I've made mistakes. I want you to know that I'm sorry."

"Okay, Dad," Elena said. "We get it!"

"I know, Dad," Rebecca added. "We already did all that." She could tell that what he had to say mattered, but she also felt anxious about his endless delays and obfuscation.

He raised a finger to silence them and looked down briefly before reestablishing eye contact.

"The thing is, there's something I need to tell you, and I just don't know how to do it." He cleared his voice and again paused. "The thing is," he stated, speaking clearly this time, "I don't have a lot of time left."

Rebecca felt her heart sink. She looked at her sister and saw the same reaction on Elena's face. "You're serious, aren't you?" Rebecca asked.

"What exactly do you mean?" Elena asked urgently.

"Cancer," he said. "Pancreatic."

When they didn't respond, he continued. "Terminal. Less than six months, realistically—and not good ones."

Rebecca watched him and listened, feeling stunned. She'd seen some of the signs and sensed that something was amiss. But that didn't alter the feeling of terror that gripped her body as tears clouded her vision. She looked at Elena and again saw the same reaction from her twin. Consuela then started crying. When she couldn't stop, she got up from the table and left the room. Guillermo just kept looking down, still fidgeting.

"We still have a couple more days before you leave," he said, smiling. "So there's plenty of time to feel sad and process all of this. I know it's a lot I'm springing on you. I know my life is going to be a short one—shorter than you and I would have liked. But I also know that I've done what I wanted to do in life: I've lived it the way I wanted to live it. I got to be a father, something that seemed impossible as a gay man in Mexico. And I got to marry the love of my life, Derek. So, while I'm not ready to go, I'm okay with going. And I'm ready to see Derek again. In heaven."

Rebecca heard the words but failed to comprehend them. She could see that Elena was also overwhelmed. Noticing their reaction, Francisco repeatedly tried to comfort them. But his voice trembled with emotion, and then his words just stopped. When he couldn't stop his eyes from tearing, he stood from his seat, touched Guillermo's hand, and then kissed Rebecca and Elena on their foreheads. "We'll talk more in the morning," he said. And then he left.

Elena was stunned. She could see that Rebecca was as well. Guillermo, obviously uncomfortable, quickly followed his wife and left the room.

"You didn't know?" Elena asked her sister, as they remained at the dinner table.

"No," Rebecca answered.

"I thought we had the surprise for the evening," she said. "Wow."

And then there was silence.

Elena looked at his empty chair at the table, imagining how it would be without him, permanently. She couldn't. And after a moment, she realized she shouldn't. Her father was a smart man, but he wasn't educated in the way the world worked, at least not in the United States. Maybe he didn't understand. She was certain there were options—there always were options—that just needed investigation. She would persuade him to try; he had to try.

After considering the situation a bit longer, she walked back to their home next to the restaurant to find him while Rebecca returned to her bedroom. When he wasn't in the living room, she went up to his bedroom. While the door was closed, she could faintly hear him inside. She knocked and waited for a minute.

When she entered, she could see that his eyes were red. "Dad," she started, "can we discuss this? I need to process it, as you said."

Francisco quickly dried his eyes and took a deep breath. Then he directed her to sit next to him on the bed. "Yes," he answered. "I knew you'd be the tough one for me."

"Did Consuela know?"

"Yes," he confessed. "Guillermo, too. But I asked them to keep it quiet."

"Why?" she asked. "Why all the secrecy? It sounds like you've known this for months!"

"I have," he answered. "As I mentioned, that's a big part of why I asked you both to come down: to enjoy a wonderful week, while I still could, and then to process it."

"That's why you sent us to dinner alone last night?"

He grinned. "More processing—yours."

"Why didn't you come with us?"

"Because then you wouldn't have done the work you needed to do," he said.

She nodded. "I'm just not ready. You really do need to fight this—you know, explore all options."

"Those are two different points, Elena," he said. "I've been to several clinics, including the primary cancer facility in Mexico City. It's late-stage and inoperable. While chemo is technically an option, it's not a viable one and, in my case, virtually pointless."

"I believe you, but . . ."

"They've sent all of my data up to Sloan Kettering in New York City. There has never been any difference of opinion."

"Experimental treatments? Have you looked into those?"

"Yes," he answered. "But no, that's not for me."

She watched him as he spoke. While his words were calm and tranquil, she could see more than sadness and anxiety in his expression.

"It hurts sometimes, doesn't it?"

He slowly nodded.

She could see the truth in his reaction but still felt like she was hitting a wall.

"I know," he said. "I'd like to have more time with you. There is so much I'd still like to see; your lives are really just beginning. Where will you go to business school? Who will you marry? Where will you live? Will you have children? Will they look like me?" He smiled.

He paused for a moment and then continued. "You know," he added, "your sister probably can't bear children . . . but you can."

She looked into his eyes, searching for his intent. Then she felt him take her hand while he moved next to her on the bed.

"Just promise me, you'll think about what you really want in a partner." He smiled. "You know, you deserve the best and only the best."

"You didn't like Richard?" She removed her hand reflexively.

"I didn't say that," he answered. "But do you?" He gently took her hand again and waited to hear her thoughts.

"I don't know," she said. "Maybe."

"Does he cherish you?" he asked. "And respect you?"

She wanted to explain but couldn't think of the right words. There was so much he understood—and so much he didn't.

"Well, you'll have to figure that out. Just be the woman you want to be. You know, I've always been so very proud of that girl."

She dried her eyes and tried to smile. As she hugged him, she could feel him struggling to keep his body from trembling.

"I love you so much," he said.

"And I love you," she answered.

Recognizing that her efforts were pointless and unable to control her own emotions further, she released him slowly and then left his bedroom.

Chapter 17

ELENA OPENED THE TRUNK AND PUT HER BACKPACK INTO THE TAN Jeep that was parked in front of their home in Sayulita. Rebecca set hers next to Elena's, and Francisco shut the Jeep's hatch before climbing into the driver's seat. Elena wasn't thrilled about spending the day zip-lining from mountain cliffs. But it was her father's idea, so she'd quickly accepted the invitation. Clearly, it brought back fond family memories to him; they were fond memories for all of them.

"Are you all up for this?" Francisco asked, looking to his right at Elena and then back at Rebecca in the rearview mirror.

"Yup," Rebecca.

When Elena nodded as well, he responded, "Good."

Francisco started the engine, put the Jeep into gear, and they drove off. Elena gazed from the Jeep's window as they left her childhood home and headed toward the Puerto Vallarta marina, where they would travel by boat another hour south to the canyon jungles for the zip lines. As children, they'd loved taking the day trip to the zip lines with their father. She wondered why going now felt so different. Maybe it was because everything had seemed so permanent as a child. But as an adult, it all seemed so transient: the day zip-lining, the week together over Christmas, their happy lives as children in Sayulita, and her father's life.

As the Jeep accelerated onto the main highway, Elena continued to think about how quickly the time had passed. Gone were the lazy days of playing in the sand and bodysurfing on the beach along with the carefree life of her childhood home. She'd loved that life; she loved her father. Sure, there had been hardships and struggles. But when confronted with the certainty of his passing, she could barely remember any of it. Instead, she felt gripped with anxiety at the prospect of losing everything she really loved: her family home, a life with her sister, and her dad's very existence. She felt her hand clutch the handrail of the Jeep.

Elena had left that life for college in the United States and replaced it. But with what? The frantic profession as an investment banker on Wall Street while dating someone who didn't respect her. Why? To prove herself capable. To whom? Well, not her father—at least, not anymore. And for what? To make money, or worse, compete with her twin—a sister who had no desire to compete with anyone. It all seemed so pointless. Her direction seemed pointless.

As the road passed the hills of the jungle area overlooking the vast expanse of the sea, Elena considered what she'd done. She'd spent a lifetime trying to prove herself equal: equal to the memory of her White father, Derek, the American doctor she'd never known; equal to her White sister, Rebecca, who, with her fair skin, blonde hair, and blue eyes, was the one the boys always wanted the most; and equal to her father's expectations, as he sought to provide them with everything they'd lost by leaving the States. She'd spent years trying to satisfy her ambition and insecurities. She enjoyed the life she'd built in the United States. And after living there for years, she'd found her confidence—at least, she'd started to. But she'd been a fool.

"There it is," Rebecca said, "our old high school, the American School."

Elena looked at the dilapidated walls, crumbling with painted stucco in disrepair, topped with barbed wire for security. From the street, it looked as much like a prison as a high school. As they passed it, she realized, for the first time, how run-down the place was despite being a top private school in the area. Having lived in the States among the successful and the elite at Goldman, she'd adopted their perspective—the Stimpsons' perspective, Richard's perspective.

What she understood now, however, was what she'd given up: a culture of acceptance, kindness, community, and love. Where meals with the family were treasured. Where it was okay to arrive a little late, but leaving early was not acceptable. Where friendship meant real friendship, not an accident or convenience of work, time, or place. And where coming home for Christmas was mandatory, not optional. Why? Because relationships were what mattered most. These were the things her father was talking about after her argument with Rebecca. And these were the things her father had spent a lifetime trying to teach them by example. Sure, it was stereotypical and romanticized, at least in part. Of course, there were plenty of exceptions. But like Rebecca, Elena missed it—all of it. And now, the thought of living without it—without him, her father—felt like living in a collapsing black hole.

Francisco continued driving past the school to the marina, where the various tourist boats departed each morning. He parked the Jeep in the adjacent lot and pulled their bags from the hatch. "I already have the tickets," he said, "so we can head through the entry gates and toward the boat dock in the back."

After a short walk through the marina, they boarded a transit vessel along with the other passengers. Once it had cleared the buoys, the boat moderately increased its pace. The sea was calm, making the journey smooth and exhilarating in the fresh morning air. From the boat, they saw the towering hotels and condominiums lining the sandy beaches and then the long boardwalk of the Malecon. They continued past the historic Romantic Zone and proceeded south, down the tropical coast toward Mismaloya.

Francisco took Elena's hand and smiled. "Tell me a story about when you were little," he said. "Something that made you happy."

"That's our line—what we used to ask you!" she said.

"I know. Things change." He smiled.

"Wow," she answered. "There's a million things—all coming at once."

"Anything special?" he asked.

Elena thought about the question. It was a day to reflect happily—that was what her father wanted and needed. So she searched her mind for a memory he'd enjoy. As she did, she realized that she was adopting his approach, focusing on his needs rather than hers. As he'd said, things change. It was a gross understatement.

"Machu Pichu," she answered. "For sure."

"I remember," he said.

"We took the bus up to the clifftop first thing in the morning," she started.

"And we fought for the window seat," Rebecca said, joining the conversation.

Elena had no recollection of what had happened with the window. For her, the memory had been erased, but for Rebecca, apparently, it remained. "I don't remember that," she said, "but I remember how magical Machu Pichu was when we reached the top of the mountain."

"Like . . ." Francisco said, encouraging her to continue.

"Like the incredible beauty of what must have been palapas covering their small huts, with water streaming from the mountains through their small open pipes—and the views overlooking the peaks of an endless tropical jungle," Elena answered.

"Like how it's not ruined," Rebecca continued, "because the place was lost over time and then rediscovered. When you think about it, you realize they must have had so little. But they lived harmoniously for hundreds of years in a primitive world that we now envy."

"I remember," Francisco said. "It was an incredible vacation—once in a lifetime."

The boat breached the crest of a large wave, spraying water on the passengers sitting on that side of the boat, including Rebecca and her father. Elena thought that Rebecca looked ridiculous, now soaked in her silly orange life jacket next to her father in his. As she watched her sister, she remembered what she'd seemed to have forgotten: how inseparable they'd been and always would be. How she loved her more than life itself. And how she would do literally anything for her. But she couldn't stop wondering what would happen to them, to their family, when he was gone. Would this life and their relationship become the ancient history their father had been talking about? The thought seemed almost unbearable.

After another fifteen minutes or so, the boat stopped on the coast beyond

Mismaloya, and they disembarked. Following a short ride in canopied trucks, they arrived at Los Veranos for the zip lines. They checked in at a registration desk and walked past some monkeys and other exotic animals on the grounds.

"Do you remember the monkeys throwing their wet food on you that one time we came here?" Francisco said. "It took me an hour to wash it all off, and then you both ran right back to their cages again."

Rebecca nodded. "We rode all the way home covered in it, and it stank."

Elena smiled.

A guide then handed them release forms. Elena was about to sign hers without much thought, but then she reconsidered. She quickly scanned the document for pregnancy disclosures but saw none. So she pulled the guide aside and asked him. He seemed surprised that she would even ask. If she were pregnant, she wasn't showing at all. Was she being ridiculous? He pointed out how the harness didn't press on the abdomen but warned her against spinning or going upside down. She smiled. There was absolutely no chance of that.

After signing their release forms and gearing up with their guide, they started walking along the jungle trail to the first zip line launching pad. When they arrived, their guide checked Elena's helmet and body gear, including her gloves and the cable hooks.

"Knee up," he said before fastening her hooks to the pulley that hung from a long cable spanning the valley of the vast jungle below. "Ready?"

Elena nodded before he gently released her. She sailed comfortably over the dense jungle while the water of the river rapids crashed noisily below. She felt the warm air woosh across her face as she continued along the long cable line, seemingly miles above the jungle terrain. She felt frightened but invigorated, as if injected with new life. After what seemed like an instant, she arrived at the landing station, where another guide caught her. He helped her detach from the cable and quickly moved her off the landing pad. Rebecca followed on the same cable, and shortly after that, her father also arrived at the landing pad. It certainly wasn't a dangerous or extreme course, but they all had the same exhilarated thrill written on their faces.

They continued hiking along the modest inclines of the trail and zipping down and across the river below. The jungle was beautiful; the air was warm but fresh; and the vistas were incredible. Elena counted the lines one by one. There were eighteen, like a golf course, but the experience was so much better. But as they progressed, Elena realized that their father was falling farther and farther behind. While he tried to hide his fatigue, the lather of the sweat on his brow and his inability to fully catch his breath exposed the significance of his illness. Even when they slowed their pace, the wait for him didn't change; in fact, it only increased with each line—a sharp contrast to the way he'd sprinted through those same trails in their youth. Twice, the guides directed them to pause so that other groups could complete the course without waiting, and at the eleventh line, the guide suggested that they take a detour and skip the next six. Elena quickly accepted the offer, and Rebecca redirected Francisco without objection. As she watched him, she understood why the hike had been important to him: That day would be their last on the zip lines together.

After taking the detour, they arrived at the last line. Elena noticed that it was a short and almost level line that appeared to function primarily as a transport across the river and back to the main entrance area.

"It's a race," the guide explained.

Francisco smiled when the guides lined up his twins on the two competing lines.

"You know I'm going to beat you," Rebecca said.

"You know you can't," Elena responded. She pulled her guide over and whispered into his ear while her sister was being hooked into the second cable line. The two guides then counted, gently rocking the sisters' bodies back and forth, before releasing them: "One, two, three!" But when Elena's guide released her, Rebecca's waited and then only nudged her enough to get her started.

"Hey!" Rebecca said, as she slowly trailed her sister down the last line. "You cheated!"

"Of course," Elena said, yelling back up at her. "Did you think I'd let you win?"

Rebecca laughed as she slowly trudged down the zip line. "Not a chance," she answered quietly to herself.

After landing safely and removing the gear, they found a seat at the restaurant under a palapa overlooking the river at the base of the valley. While Elena was feeling a little tired, the rich oxygen from the lush tropical jungle felt invigorating. She took a deep breath while listening to the rush of the river, as it passed over large boulders before settling into the tranquility of a small swimming hole beneath the restaurant.

Once they were seated, a waitress came and took their orders for lunch. After she left, their conversation continued.

"So, how about you, Rebecca?" Francisco said. "Tell me a story about when you were little?"

Elena watched her sister think while the waiter took their orders before bringing them tropical fruit drinks.

"I liked it when we went to the Palacio de Bellas Artes in Mexico City," she said.

"What did we see?" Francisco asked.

"*Don Giovanni*," Rebecca answered. "I remember the Mozart opera but really liked the Rivera painting inside."

"What do you remember?" Francisco asked.

Even as he spoke, Elena noticed that beads of sweat were still forming on his brow, and his questions and answers were short, almost truncated. And while they'd been seated at the restaurant for a while and served their drinks, he still seemed tired.

"Well, the building was incredible," she started. "It was much more interesting than the opera house in San Francisco. His painting made the place unique."

"Which one was it?" Elena asked.

"*El Hombre Controlador del Universo*," Rebecca answered in Spanish. "They translate it to *The Man at the Crossroads*, but it seems more accurate to say *The Man Controlling the Universe*."

"Remind me," Francisco said. "I remember going, but not much more."

"The mural was originally painted for Rockefeller Center in New York City during the Great Depression," she continued. "The Rockefellers didn't like it, so they fired Rivera and painted over it. Rivera recreated the work in Mexico for the opera house, where it became a national treasure."

"Whitewashed, literally. Why'd they do it?" Elena asked.

"It depicted various scientific discoveries made possible by the 'working man.' The problem was that 'man' was depicted as Latino in a Soviet May Day parade along with a portrait of Lenin."

"Yeah," Elena said, "that's not going to work so well in Manhattan—even now."

"Even now?" Francisco asked. "Still so judgmental; so much hate."

No one answered. After the waitress returned with their meals, the conversation resumed.

"How about you, Dad?" Rebecca asked, changing the subject. "Tell us a story—something you remember that made you happy."

Francisco paused, apparently considering his options. "How about the story of how you were created?"

Elena looked curiously at Rebecca. They knew the story, so she wasn't sure why he wanted to tell it again. Feeling finished with her lunch, she put down her fork to give him her full attention; Rebecca did the same.

"You know," he started, "Derek and I considered ourselves married, and we wanted to have kids. Back then, surrogacy was pretty much illegal, even for straight people. But surrogacy was nothing new. You know, the Old Testament tells the first story: 'When Sarah couldn't have a child of her own for her husband, Abraham, their servant, Hagar, had a child for her.'" He looked directly at Elena as he spoke.

"Dad, are you quoting the Bible on us?" Rebecca asked.

Francisco laughed. "Yeah, I guess I am. Does that make it seem more legit?" He again glanced over at Elena before continuing. "Anyway, when we were young, the law hadn't caught up with ideas like gay marriage or surrogacy, and as you well know, the Catholic church still hasn't. So, we found Elizabeth. You've seen pictures of your surrogate mother but have never met her. She was a tall, Swedish woman, who liked the idea of helping gay guys have a baby."

"We know all this, Dad," Elena said. She didn't understand why he was revisiting all of this on that particular day, but she could tell that he wanted to continue with his story.

"Obviously, we weren't going to have sex with her," he said. "So, on the donation day, Derek and I went into his clinic to leave a sample, if you know what I mean, to have them do the insemination artificially." He raised his eyebrows for dramatic effect. "Anyway, the nurse gave each of us a small plastic cup with a lid, just like the ones you get when you leave a urine specimen, and sent us into separate rooms. I didn't have any problem in my room. In fact, I did a double just to make sure it was all good."

"Way too much detail!" Rebecca said, showing her teeth with an anxious grin as Elena shook her head and then put her hands to her head.

"But Derek didn't have the same luck," he continued. "Apparently, most of his ended up on the floor, not the cup." He smiled while reflecting.

"That's disgusting," Elena said, laughing. "So disgusting."

"Dad," Rebecca protested, looking up, "too much information."

"Anyway," he continued, ignoring their interruptions, "my cup was good, but his only had a dribble."

"Okay, okay," Elena said. "We got it. End of story."

Francisco nodded but tenaciously continued. "So, when they combined the samples per our instruction, it wasn't exactly a level playing field in terms of who would end up being the father of our child. You see, we didn't want to decide whose genetic material was used. We decided that you would be raised as ours, jointly and equally, regardless."

The waitress then returned and asked them if they wanted anything else. When they declined, she took their plates and wiped down their table.

"But," Rebecca added, "you ended up with a twin from each of you. So all's well that ends well: You fathered Elena, and Derek fathered me."

Francisco nodded in a way that acknowledged the comment without necessarily affirming it. Elena wondered why. She knew that her father's parents were Mexican of Spanish-European descent. And that Derek's parents were English and German. But as she thought further, she realized they'd never visited Francisco's parents, so they'd never actually seen them. After having been abandoned when he came out, Francisco didn't keep any photos of them around the house. Nor did he seem at all interested in notifying them of his diagnosis now.

"You don't actually know for sure," Rebecca said, "do you?" She looked at him directly and waited apprehensively for his response.

"No," Francisco answered. "We didn't want to, and I still don't." He smiled while raising his eyebrows. When Rebecca didn't respond, he continued. "I know what your birth certificates say legally, but as I told you before, we just made that up." Then he paused. "As you know, I've always thought Rebecca was Derek's and I'm close to certain that Elena's mine, but in fact, I do not know the genetics of either of you."

Elena saw the glimmer of understanding flash through Rebecca's eyes.

"Actually, you told us that your mother's family going way back was from Southern France," Rebecca said.

Francisco nodded. "That's my understanding. At least in part."

The waitress returned with their check, and the family at the table behind them got up to leave. Elena watched her sister as she processed the new information he'd given them. A gentle breeze disrupted Rebecca's blonde hair, which she nervously brushed from her face with little success.

Rebecca returned her hand to her lap and looked directly at Francisco. "Do I look like your mother?" she asked.

Elena thought that was the key question. And that was the question they'd never contemplated. Rebecca brushed her hair away again. Elena and her sister watched their father think carefully before answering.

"Not really," he said. "You know, I haven't seen her since I was a teenager. But she did have blue eyes."

When they didn't respond, he continued. "So I guess the question is, does it matter?"

Elena watched as Rebecca looked at him, thinking. "I don't know," she said. "It's a lot to take in."

"But Dad," Elena said directly, "don't you think you should have told her this earlier? She might not even be related to the Stimpsons..."

"Probably," he said. "But when? Would it have made things better or worse? I've always told you the truth I know and believe: that you both have two fathers, Derek and me."

Elena could see the discomfort on Rebecca's face. Her teeth were clenched, and her lips were pressed. Elena looked to her father for help, but he seemed to have nothing to offer her.

"I don't know," Rebecca said.

"You know, Rebecca, they have those DNA tests now," Elena suggested. "We can take a hair from you into a lab. Dad can, too. Then you'll know."

Rebecca nodded apprehensively.

Francisco motioned for the waitress to return. When she did, he asked her for an envelope from their office. They sat silently once she'd left. When she returned, Francisco plucked a hair from the top of his head, put it in the envelope, sealed it, and handed it to Rebecca.

"Now you can," he said. "If you want to."

Rebeca took the envelope and put it into her backpack, scrutinizing him for a hint of his desires as she did so. But he only smiled in response.

"Well, whatever!" She laughed in an apparent effort to deflect the tension.

Francisco then motioned for the waitress to take the check. When she returned with the change, she again refilled their water glasses. While the other patrons played with the animals or swam in the river pool, Elena and her family continued to relax at the restaurant. After a bit, Francisco resumed the conversation.

"It's strange," he said. "You know, that story—these stories. After a while, many of the facts quit mattering."

"What do you mean, Dad?" Elena said.

"It's not that the stories aren't real or that some aren't better than others."

When they didn't respond, Francisco continued. "Blurring," he said. "That's kind of how I think of it. Maybe you forget. Maybe sometimes you want to forget. I'm sorry I didn't deal with this sooner, Rebecca. I should have. So maybe I'm just rationalizing. But over time, many facts become details, and then they quit mattering. What does matter, at least to me, are the times we've spent together, like today. These are the stories of my life and the stories that I love. Maybe they're partly fiction, by design, or by inadvertently forgetting the difficult facts or times while reconstructing the good ones. I don't know; it doesn't matter. Because with hindsight, you refocus the binoculars of memory to remove certain details and find clarity—fictional clarity. Our stories together, as we create and recreate them, are what make us who we are. They mean the world to me. They are my truth. Thank you for making them with me. Thank you for living them with me."

Francisco took another drink of his water and then smiled at them before chuckling. "Well, that's the silly stuff that sticks with me now, anyway."

Elena felt sad listening to him speak. She watched as her sister turned away, hiding her reaction while considering her father's words. They were contradictory, maybe oxymoronic. But were they accurate?

As they sat in the outdoor patio of the restaurant and chatted about unrelated topics, Elena continued to consider his concept of *fictional clarity*. It certainly wasn't true in the business world of numbers and balance sheets where she lived. But then again, was it? Was it any different, really, from the *pro forma adjustments* she and Rebecca ran on financial statements at work: taking out the synergy costs or combining revenue to make a new financial history that would allow a marketable business going forward? *A fiction of sorts created for a company to succeed*, she thought. *Or for a struggling family to thrive.*

"They're waving for us to return to the trucks," Francisco said. "Shall we head back?" He took his credit card from the table, signed the receipt, and they left.

Chapter 18

After the long day in the jungle on the zip lines, Francisco and his twins returned to their home in Sayulita. The hiking, sun, and travel had made for a fun and enjoyable day, precisely as he'd planned. At times, the conversation had been uncomfortable. But he'd completed his objectives, and he thought it had all gone about as well as it could have. While he felt exhausted, he gathered his energy and put on his happy face. His girls were scheduled to return to the States the next day, and he very much wanted their last memories of him and their home to be satisfying.

After unpacking, showering, and relaxing for the balance of the afternoon, the family enjoyed a simple evening meal of the tacos, carnitas, and guacamole that Consuela had made earlier and left for them before returning to her in-law unit. When they'd finished eating and cleaning up the dishes, they went to the living room to watch the evening's sunset.

"Ah," Francisco said. "We're late. The sun's almost set, and we don't have our margaritas in hand."

He walked from the living room to the kitchen and quickly poured the tequila—Herradura Reposado, of course—with a fresh lime and triple sec into the glasses Consuela had left for them.

"Please tell me you don't want some gringo drink like those negronis!"

Elena smiled while ignoring him. "Better hurry, Dad. The sun's hitting the horizon."

"I'm hurrying!" he said.

He tossed it all into the blender, salted the thick, blue-rimmed margarita glasses, dropped the lime on top of each, and quickly walked with all three glasses back to the living area, handing one to each of his girls.

"Another perfect Sayulita sunset," he said, looking out at the vista and down at his drink. "*¡Salud!*"

They clicked their glasses, laughing, as the radiant yellow, orange, and red colors of the vibrant sun turned into rich green, purple, and blue reflections of the clouds. He and Rebecca took a deep drink while Elena casually held hers.

"The colors," Rebecca said. "They're so vibrant tonight. They radiate against the clouds."

"Alpenglow or *enrosadira*," Francisco said. "It's that vibrant, panoramic reddish glow that appears on the clouds from the last rays of the sun. I think the word comes from a view of the sun shining against the mountains like the Swiss Alps."

"I think it's a sign," Elena said. "I'm trying to think of what, but nothing's coming to mind."

"Maybe a satisfying sense of the natural beauty and peace," Francisco suggested, "that comes once in a while simply from the certainty of the passage of time."

"Uh, yeah—no. Too much," Rebecca said, as they laughed.

Elena nodded. "Maybe something inspirational for my favorite budding artist?" She smiled, and Rebecca nodded.

Francisco grinned. "Now *that* makes sense."

As they spoke, the vibrant colors of the evening were replaced with the darkness of night, as the shimmering moonlight reflected peacefully over the calm ocean. For the rest of the evening, they simply lived. They reflected on the day zip-lining and on their many childhood memories. They teased each other ruthlessly and hugged each other lovingly. They discussed things they'd enjoyed long ago, omitted the things that had hurt, and celebrated the wonder of life, their lives—their blurring. They were a family, comfortably enjoying the simple pleasure of each other's existence, without expectations or demands but with full acceptance of their faults and differences. They were rewriting their stories, one by one, and each version was improving. And with that resolution, their resolution, came a new sense of happiness. A clarity.

Francisco looked down at the coffee table and then at the margarita glasses. He noticed again that two of them were empty, his and Rebecca's, while Elena's remained untouched. She hadn't actually told him anything, so he'd continued serving her. Was she just being cautious, or did she now actually know? If so, he wondered what she'd do. Regardless, he had the wisdom to understand that further sharing of his opinions on the topic wouldn't be helpful, that sharing them could instead be harmful, and that any decision made would have to be hers. Simply put, his time in life for instructing her had ended. But it didn't matter. Not to him, anyway. They were good children, now grown women. Elena would make the right decision for her, and that was all that mattered.

After a while, Rebecca turned the conversation to a more serious topic. "Dad," she started, "we've been talking."

"Uh-oh," Francisco said.

"We think one of us should stay for a while, you know, to help you," Elena continued.

He nodded. "I was afraid of that," he said. "So, who drew the short straw?" He chuckled.

"I'd like to stay, actually," Rebecca said, looking at her sister. "Frankly, I don't want to go back, knowing you're here alone."

"Actually, I'd like to stay," Elena countered. "Goldman Sachs isn't going to fall apart if their most junior analyst is gone for a few months."

Francisco returned his focus to his daughters but didn't hesitate to respond to their proposal. "That, my dear twins, is exactly what I don't want," he said. "I raised you to live your lives, not walk away from them. And I don't need anyone to care for me—except maybe Consuela and Guillermo."

"Dad, this is something I want to do. I think it's something I need to do. I feel like . . ." Rebecca started before he raised his hand to politely cut her off.

"We don't have to do anything in life," he responded, "except die." He smiled. "Unfortunately, that's exactly what I've got to deal with. I'm too young, and it's not fair—I get that. But I'm okay with this. Frankly, I've got to be, and you do, too."

He smiled again before continuing. "By now, you know that I have no problem saying exactly what I want and need, generally, and from each of you." It was his parenting voice: firm, direct, and authoritative. He'd used the voice when they were children to let them know there would be no more negotiation. He couldn't direct them much anymore, but he could still play the parent card.

"I told you before what I wanted: I wanted you to spend a week together with me, while I still felt good. And you did. To be honest, I also wanted the two of you to spend this time with each other. And you did that, too."

"Dad, I already canceled my flight," Elena said, interrupting him.

"I did, too," Rebecca added, looking at her sister with surprise.

"Maybe we could rotate weeks with you, or come every other month for a while," Elena added. She looked over at Rebecca, who quickly nodded.

Francisco could tell they'd already discussed most of this and had jointly reached a decision. He very much appreciated their concern and commitment. But he did not agree. He slowly shook his head, indicating his objection, before explaining.

"Girls, nothing will upset me more than knowing that you're not living your lives to the fullest," he said. "That's what I've always wanted, and it's important to me. No, it's *critical* to me."

While they nodded with acknowledgment, it was clear to him that they still didn't agree. And from the depth of the concern he saw in their faces, Francisco could tell that their conviction was firm. As far as he was concerned, having them stay any longer was counterproductive. But he could tell that they weren't listening: One or both of them intended to stay until he eventually died naturally, which could be months out and possibly even longer. It was generous and kind of them. But for him, it just wasn't okay.

Francisco paused for a moment to again consider his options. Accelerating his exit by a couple of days now felt a little fast—not for him, but for them. They'd still be here in the home when he left, which he hadn't anticipated, and after all, it had only been a couple of days since Christmas. But if he stayed, their conversations and interaction, like his body and their lives in the States, would devolve, day by day, week by week, exactly as he'd feared. And as each day passed, it would only get worse. Did that matter? *Yes*, he thought. It mattered to him. And while he would have liked to process his thinking with them, he well knew that was pointless. Simply put, they lacked impartiality. More importantly, it was his decision, and he'd already made it. Yes, it was a little faster than he'd anticipated. But he was ready.

Having made up his mind, he turned his attention back to his twins and smiled. "Then, if you don't mind, I'm exhausted and ready to pack it in," he said.

Rebecca and Elena smiled back and nodded. Oh, how he loved those smiles. While they were adults, grown women, he couldn't help but see through the veneer of their age to their youthful beings, their spirits, their essence. Rebecca, with the beautiful blonde hair she'd never cut as a child and bright blue eyes that simply couldn't find fault, was and always would be so trusting, empathetic, bright, and artistic. Elena, with her deep brown eyes and strong angular face, was always so driven and would forever be rational and ambitious but also kind and forgiving.

He wondered what would become of them—where their lives would lead them, with whom, and how? They'd grown into strong, independent, confident women who would make their own decisions, some good and some bad. But they'd find solutions to the adversity that life would inevitably deal them. He knew that. He hoped they would experience joy; he thought they would. There was so much he would miss. He hated it. But he knew they'd be fine; he knew they'd thrive.

"Thanks for coming, girls," he deliberately said. "The two of you are the ideal daughters—my wildest dreams come true. I hope you'll always know and remember that. And take care of each other." He could feel his eyes tearing, so he knew he needed to make it quick. "I understand you won't be leaving tomorrow anymore. And I don't want to be melodramatic. But I'm going to say goodbye now as if you were, while I'm healthy, and tipsy, and then not worry about it again."

He paused and smiled before continuing. "Thank you for the perfect week, my dearest twins," he said. "Thank you for the perfect life."

From the expression on their faces, he saw a combination of concern and puzzlement. He wasn't surprised, but it did make him feel sad. In an effort to gather his composure and deflect the tension, he took the pitcher of margaritas and their glasses back to the kitchen and placed them into the dishwasher. When he returned, he hugged each of them, feeling the slight quiver of Elena first and then Rebecca, as they processed the moment's sadness. Then he reassuringly smiled and kissed them gently on the head before returning to his bedroom.

"Night," he said, in the same casual voice he used every night before putting them to bed. "Love you."

"Love you, too, Dad," they replied, just as they always had when he'd tucked them in.

As he climbed the half staircase from the living room to his bedroom, he again felt the pain in his body. He'd noticed that it had become generalized in the evenings; even the tequila didn't dull it anymore. He wanted to think it was from the long day, but he knew that wasn't really true. It had increased daily, since the time he'd sent the text to his daughters months earlier, asking them to come one last time. They had, and he'd now completed his objectives, save one. It was too early for him—way too early. But it wasn't really up to him. Just as it hadn't been up to Derek so many years earlier.

He took a quick shower, his second for the day, before putting on his boxer shorts, the same ones he always slept in. When the steam cleared, he caught his reflection in the mirror. He still looked pretty darn good, all things considered. Sure, the rippled abs were gone. But the hair was all still there, for the most part, and the wrinkles were modest, despite living his life in the Mexican sun. He knew, however, that the reflection masked his reality. The color of his face was increasingly yellow. His body mass was rapidly shrinking. In his abdomen, the pain, once sporadic, had become consistent and at times was both blunt and sharp. And in his eyes, the exhaustion of his body was now transparent. Sure, he had a little more time, if he really wanted it. But it wasn't the kind of time he wanted. He folded his wet towel neatly and squeegeed the shower, as he always had. Then he filled his glass with water and pulled from the medicine cabinet the pills he'd purchased from the corner drugstore earlier in the week.

He felt confident but also anxious. So he decided to play some music. He put in his earbuds and scrolled through his iPhone for something to listen to. He searched for something calming before selecting Eric Clapton's "Tears in Heaven." He knew the piece well. It seemed perfect.

Francisco pushed the "Play" button, and the music started with a simple accompaniment of an acoustic guitar before the artist's voice softly entered above it. Francisco had always loved the piece and immediately remembered the melody. But this time, he listened more carefully to the lyrics. They described the premature death of a loved one, now in heaven. Feeling the intense sorrow of that loss, the singer hopes, when reunited, to again find comfort, simply by seeing the familiar face of his loved one and by again holding hands. It wasn't Derek's song, but Francisco knew Derek would have liked it. It was the song Francisco had sung to Derek from time to time after his death, when the struggles of life seemed overwhelming, and the loneliness of living without him felt unbearable. Francisco knew that Derek had patiently been waiting for him in heaven. Francisco wondered if Derek had also been watching him—watching the three of them—and listening. As in the song, Derek, too, was taken away at a young age. It still made no sense to Francisco. He realized now that it never would.

Like Derek, Francisco didn't yet belong in heaven. He wasn't ready to leave life, his girls, or any of it. *For Christ's sake*, he thought, *I'm not even sixty.* But he was ready to be with Derek again, and he knew Derek would be there, waiting for him, as he always had been. On some level—maybe instinctive, maybe spiritual—he knew this to be so from the depths of his being.

After the chorus, the second verse began as the music progressed. The comforting sound of the artist's quiet, masculine voice over the acoustic guitar continued, but to Francisco, somehow, this time, it seemed different. This time, Francisco heard Derek's voice in the words, recognizing him, calling him, and comforting him.

Francisco took a deep breath, testing his resolve. It remained firm. It was right for him. And he knew it. He opened the bottle of pills he'd bought and tossed back the opioids—all of them. He took a full drink of the water and then another. Then he listened, as Derek's voice anticipated the uncertain but satisfying peace of being reunited in heaven, free of conflict, free of pain, and free of tears.

As the song ended, Francisco removed his earbuds, turned off the lights, and gently rested his head on the pillow. It felt soft and inviting. Within minutes, he felt the comfort of the medicine and the satisfaction of his decision. *No*, he thought. *Not my decision, but rather, my life.* He'd lived a full and rich life. He'd felt love. He'd given love. He'd contributed. And he'd made a difference. He had no regrets. It was good. His comfort only grew as his thumb gently rubbed the inside of the wedding ring on his finger—the ring he'd never removed. And when he reflexively opened his hand, he felt only the warm grasp of Derek's large fingers firmly taking his. Taking him. He smiled to himself before closing his eyes for the last time. The final time.

Chapter 19

REBECCA WATCHED THE WAVES BREAK AGAINST THE SAND OF THE Sayulita beach from the living room deck of their palapa while drinking her morning coffee. The rhythmic repetition of the sound was quietly soothing, and the air was still fresh and crisp from the morning's arrival. She glanced at her phone: 9:30 a.m. She looked at the urn that now held her father's ashes. At 10:00 a.m., they would take his ashes and scatter them at sea, as he'd requested. While she had been shocked the morning following his passing, she wasn't at all surprised that he'd left. Nor was she surprised that he'd handled all of the arrangements, including his timing. It wasn't the Christmas she'd expected, but it was the Christmas he'd wanted. She felt so thankful to have given it to him, and she knew that Elena was thankful, too. Still, the harsh reality of his absence weighed heavily upon her. She watched as Consuela busied herself in the kitchen before leaving for the restaurant.

"Guillermo's getting the boat ready?" she asked.

"He's at the restaurant," Consuela answered.

Rebecca nodded. "Why?"

Consuela continued wiping the already clean counters without answering.

"Consuela, are you okay?"

"*Sí, sí.*" She nodded, while wiping more vigorously but refusing to make eye contact. "He will be here in time for the funeral."

"Funeral?" Rebecca asked.

"*Sí,*" Consuela responded, as if the information were nothing new.

"I thought Dad didn't want a service? Isn't that what he told you?"

"*Sí,*" she answered. "But the people are already coming." She nodded to the group gathering on the beach below their home.

Rebecca walked to the edge of the palapa deck and looked down. People were quietly congregating, speaking in soft voices, while looking up toward the palapa of their house. Guillermo then entered the living room carrying the two karaoke microphones.

"All ready," he said.

Elena entered, and Rebecca looked at her. "Did you know they were planning a funeral?"

"I didn't," Elena answered as Rebecca pointed to the mikes in Guillermo's hands and the growing crowd of locals gathering below. "But I think it's a great idea."

Rebecca realized that Guillermo had moved the speakers from the karaoke machine to the sides of the balcony deck of their living room between some tropical plants. On the beach below were long tables that women were filling with all kinds of food. Next to them were more tables with what looked like coffee, sangria, and lemonade. The tables were covered in white linens, with birds of paradise and other tropical plants serving as centerpieces. Rows and rows of white plates were stacked at the ends of each table. It was informal yet elegant. Apparently, they were expecting a large crowd.

"How many people are you planning on, Consuela?" Rebecca asked.

"I don't know," she answered. "We didn't plan it. Those people did, with the restaurant staff."

Rebecca watched as the crowd continued to assemble. By 10:00 a.m., the people were flooding the beach and filling it from the base below their palapa to more than half the distance back to the bank of the sea.

"Who are they?" Elena asked. "I recognize a face or two, but that's it."

"The restaurant staff," Guillermo said. "They're using their Christmas bonus to pay for it."

"Plus, your father's friends and the people he helped at the food bank—he had a lot, you know," Consuela added.

"I didn't," Rebecca said. "But there are hundreds."

"I'm curious," Elena asked. "Who will donate to the food bank now?"

Guillermo shrugged. "The new owner of the restaurant, hopefully," he said.

"And you and Consuela?" Elena asked.

"Maybe we can work for the new owner, too," Guillermo answered. "But your dad left us some money, just in case."

Rebecca nodded, wondering how all that would work. She looked down at the people assembling and then at Consuela before asking, "They're not just from the food bank, are they? You know, the women?"

Consuela looked across the faces of the women in the growing crowd below. "No," she said. "They're also the women your father helped." She crossed her chest.

Rebecca could feel Elena looking questioningly at her, but she avoided her sister's eyes, choosing instead to scan the faces of the women below. She wondered who would help them now. The absence of an answer was troubling.

"I think you should say something; they'd like that." Guillermo picked up a mike and extended it to Rebecca and Elena, waiting for them to decide who would take it.

Rebecca shook her head while looking hopefully at Elena. "Do you mind?" she asked.

"No," Elena said, "I don't mind." She took the microphone and looked down at the crowd below.

"*Gracias*," she started, speaking of course in Spanish. "Thanks to all of you for joining us in an informal memorial service for my father, Francisco Montoya."

Rebecca could see that Elena was gathering her thoughts as she cleared her voice. Rebecca took a sip of her coffee and sat down in a chair Guillermo had pulled over immediately to the left of her sister.

"For those of you who don't know me, I'm Elena Stimpson Montoya, and this is my twin sister, Rebecca Stimpson Montoya. We are Francisco's children, his daughters."

She waited for a moment while the crowd below stopped milling around and quieted down.

"My father was a strong man who lived during difficult times. But he was also a happy person who embraced life to its fullest in what I like to think of as the Mexican spirit," she continued, looking out at the many people below. "I'm sure there's much I will never know about him, but I'd like to share some thoughts with you.

"Dad was born in Mexico City, the son of a wealthy family that, in prior generations, had owned vast tracts of land through the Spanish encomienda system. His father was a district governor, among other positions. He is survived by his mother and father, who continue to live in Mexico City, and his daughters, Rebecca and me.

"I know this, factually, but I have never met Dad's family. This is because they abandoned him when he was in college, when he came out as gay. Things have changed since then and gotten better. But that was how it was for him, and it wasn't easy.

"Almost thirty years ago, my father found his lifetime companion, Derek, at this restaurant. They fell in love and moved to the United States. They couldn't legally marry then, so they took their vows privately. But it didn't stop them from living their dream. It wasn't long until my dad, Francisco, and his husband, Derek, started a family with my sister and me."

Elena stopped for a moment, apparently to collect her thoughts. Consuela handed her a glass of water, and she took a quick drink before continuing.

"I don't have memories of Derek, my other dad, because he was murdered in what now is referred to as a hate crime. Derek died because he was gay; because he loved his husband; because they chose to have children; and because he wanted his family to be treated the same as anyone else. That act of hate took away Dad's husband and our other father—the father we never knew. So, Dad raised us alone here in Mexico."

Elena was interrupted when a large wave crashed against the shore's bank. She looked over the beach to see what it was and then down at the crowd, which remained silent and focused on her.

"My father wanted to be buried next to his husband, Derek, in the United States. But we know that Derek's parents would never allow that. Because doing so would be a public admission that their son was gay; that he was married to a man; that his husband wasn't wealthy or connected; that his husband was, in their words, an illegal alien and a criminal; and that his husband was a Mexican. I intentionally repeat these words, these facts, because they need to be said, and they need to be heard. During the last two decades, my father never returned to the United States to see the burial site of his loved one, his husband, because he couldn't. My father never talked about these things; that wasn't his way. Instead, he chose to focus on being honorable and good. As he'd wished, we will scatter his ashes in the bay that gave him so much joy and in the company of his family and friends, whom he loved, and who gave him so much love.

"While Catholic, Dad adopted some of the views of the afterlife held by Derek's church—views he learned at Derek's funeral so many years ago. Like them, Dad believed that in heaven, he would be reunited with Derek, his husband, and they would live together for time and all eternity. That faith, like the Catholic faith, has not and may never recognize my dads' wedding, so they would never condone the idea that my dads would be together again. But Dad knew that God did, and that was all that mattered to him."

Rebecca knew that many of the spectators were deeply Catholic, so she wondered how they would react. But in their attentive faces, she only saw sympathy and kindness. She turned her attention back to her sister, who continued speaking.

"I'm not so religious, but I know with certainty that my dads are together now, in heaven, looking down on us, watching over us, and happy to be reunited. In life, so many things get confusing, or 'blurry,' as Dad would say. But relationships, family, and friends built on love are not situationally true or ambiguous; they are categorically good. In the long run, giving and receiving love was all that really mattered to him."

As Elena continued to speak, Rebecca realized how much her sister had grown up. The days of fighting over a bus seat or a boy were long gone. They'd been replaced with the confidence, composure, and elegance of an educated, sophisticated, and compassionate woman—a natural speaker and a natural leader. Rebecca could see this in each word of her sister's impromptu but articulate tribute. The crowd below could, too. She grinned with pride as the tears welled and then fell from her eyes. She knew that her father would have felt exactly the same way.

"My father lived a life of significant adversity that was scarred by hate, but he never allowed it to poison him. Instead, he lived a life of love. I know this, and I try to follow his example. You know this, too, and that's why you're here. Let's remember him today, recognizing his loss, but feeling the happiness and love he would have wanted for all of us at this time and forever.

"Thank you for supporting my father. Thank you for supporting us."

As Elena handed Guillermo the mike, he nodded to the right, and the restaurant's mariachi sinfonia came into the living room in full traditional attire. They began with a tranquil piece with a simple melody. But after a while, the darker, somber feeling of the day was replaced by the joy of their festive music: the trumpets, the violins, the violas, the bass, and the rich, dynamic voices of the mariachi singers. Rebecca watched her father's friends and the local residents enjoy the festivities. Families danced with young children. Couples embraced. Women gathered to chat. And men headed to the bar area for the sangria and cerveza. They were all together, young and old, rich and poor, recognizing death but celebrating life. And their vibrancy only increased when the mariachis started playing everyone's favorite song, "¡Viva México!"

"Well, what do you think?" Rebecca asked Elena.

"He would have loved it," Elena answered. "I'm sure of it."

"Me, too," Rebecca answered. "I love this home, this beach, this town, these people—this happy place that he built for us; this life he created for us."

"I know," Elena answered.

"And I hate that he's gone."

They silently watched the crowd below and enjoyed the refreshments Consuela brought them from the beach.

"You know, I've started to wonder again if maybe it's better for me here," Rebecca said. "At least for a while."

"Wow," Elena said. "You mean, you want to move back?"

"Maybe." Rebecca thought about her words and her sister's question. She wasn't sure, and so she didn't elaborate.

"I wish I could stay, too," Elena responded.

The festivities on the beach below continued as the morning sun rose and the day's heat increased. It wasn't long until the *Esperanza* appeared around the bend, heading toward the shore to pick them up. Rebecca watched Guillermo motion to them, signaling that it was time for them to board.

"*Nos vamos*," Consuela said, appearing from the back of the kitchen and indicating that it was time to leave. "He's here."

Rebecca picked up the urn containing her father's cremains and followed Consuela and Elena down the path from their palapa to the beach. When they reached the sand at the bottom, the festive music from the mariachi sinfonia stopped, and they again started playing something softer and more somber. After a few bars, Rebecca recognized the song: "*Vaya con Dios*," or "Go with God," another Mexican favorite. She smiled.

As they left the path and started down the long beach toward Guillermo's boat, the residents stopped talking and dancing, choosing the tranquility of silence instead. Then they lined up spontaneously behind Rebecca and her sister, mostly in single file, and followed the family as they walked from the bluffs beneath their home to the edge of the beach where the *Esperanza* was waiting.

Since there wasn't a dock on the beach, Rebecca entered the water first with the urn, continuing to the back of the boat where the water was almost waist-deep. She handed the urn to Guillermo as the boat bobbed up and down against the waves. He set it inside the boat before reaching down to take her hand and help her up. The spray of the waves, now growing more intense, had soaked her by the time she was inside. But the water was warm, and the sea salt was refreshing. Guillermo pulled Elena up next before reaching for Consuela, whose head was barely visible above the splash of the waves.

"*Ay ya yai*," Consuela said. "I'm drowning!" When the water crested above her shoulders, Guillermo paused before reaching down to pull her up. "You know I can't swim, Guillermo," she continued, once safely lodged inside the boat. "You did that on purpose!"

Guillermo laughed. "You're not drowning. You just haven't been on this boat for years. Besides, when would I get another chance?"

She continued scowling as she dried her body with the towel that he'd handed her before moving to the front of the boat.

With everyone on board, Guillermo started the boat's engine and headed out slowly. Rebecca picked up the urn again and held it firmly before noticing that Elena and Consuela were waving toward the beach. She looked back and saw the local residents, now crowded along the edge of the beach, waving back to them. Seeing them more closely, she was pleased to recognize many of them: Rodrigo and his group from the restaurant, who had worked for her dad for decades; Maribella from the bakery, who had made their festive birthday cakes year after year; Juan, the director of the American School; and Sergio, the lifeguard at the beach. The number of familiar faces grew until the boat's distance made recognition difficult. They were a community, and they had been his friends. Rebecca waved to them vigorously. They were her friends, too.

Guillermo then increased the boat's speed. As their distance from the beach grew, the sound of the mariachi music was replaced by the buzz of the boat's engine. Rebecca continued waving, even after the rest of their group stopped, as if doing so would cause the moment in time to continue—a moment she wanted to last.

"This is my home," Rebecca said softly to herself. "My dad's home—my home."

The boat proceeded for about twenty minutes in moderately choppy waters before stopping in a small and tranquil inlet along the coast to the north. Rebecca recognized it immediately. It was a place they'd regularly visited with Guillermo and her father to play in the ocean as children without the hustle and bustle of the Sayulita beach. Within the inlet was a secluded, sandy beach, where they'd enjoyed many quiet days playing with each other in the ocean or building sandcastles. Behind it were short bluffs, where they'd played hide-and-seek. To the left were familiar rocks, including the one where they'd jumped into the water when their dad wasn't looking. The memories flooded her mind with the recognition that this time in life had ended permanently, along with the fear that somehow that life and the memories of it would be lost, just as her father was now lost. She gripped the urn firmly in what she knew was a pointless attempt to reject that finality.

"Do you still have the water blanket?" Elena asked Guillermo. "Or the water guns?"

"What about those scuba propeller things?" Rebecca added. "You know, the ones that pull you along underwater like James Bond?" The happiness of the memories helped her refocus on the moment.

Guillermo smiled. "No," he said. "They were your toys, so your father gave them away when you grew up."

Grew up, Rebecca thought. *We've grown up. And he died.* She'd struggled against his authority for years, challenging, testing, and leaving him. They both had. And now, seemingly overnight, it was their turn to be the adults.

"It's a lot to live up to," she said. "I don't know if we can."

"I know," Elena said. "We'll try."

Consuela started crying again, and the intensity of her emotions infected all of them with the same dark feelings of sadness. As Rebecca sat, watching, the loss felt overwhelming, swelling throughout her body like the waves that were rocking the boat. She tried to retain her composure, physically and emotionally, by holding the side of the boat while looking to Elena for support. In her sister's penetrating deep brown eyes, their father's eyes, she saw exactly what she knew they both felt, fully, perhaps for the first time: a peaceful acceptance of his life and his passing; a joy in the lives they'd led and the ones they would lead, free from caring about the judgment of those in the north or those in the south; and an acceptance of who they were, as good, decent, and hardworking people, whether they lived in a penthouse on Park Avenue in Manhattan and ran mergers and acquisitions at Goldman Sachs, or lived in a family palapa and chopped carrots in their father's restaurant in Sayulita.

"Are you ready?" Elena asked.

"No," Rebecca answered. "You do it, please." She handed her twin the urn. "You've always been the strong one."

Elena took the urn from her sister and walked to the back of the boat with it. "Goodbye, Dad," she said. "We know you're with Derek again. We know you're happy. Watch over us, as we know you will, and remember that you'll always be in our hearts."

She extended the urn over the side of the boat and slowly poured its contents into the ocean. Then she turned and handed the empty vase to Guillermo before holding Rebecca and quietly weeping. After a moment of silent reflection, Guillermo started the engine. They circled the inlet slowly, once, twice, and a third time before he increased the speed slightly and directed the boat back toward the Sayulita shore.

Elena took her sister's hand. "Don't worry," she said. "We're going to be okay."

"I know," Rebecca responded. "It just doesn't feel like it now."

After regaining her composure, Rebecca quietly slipped to the back of the boat as it proceeded, looking back once more at the inlet that marked the happiness of their childhood lives, and now, the place of her father's burial. She reached into the pocket of her sundress, searching for the envelope her father had given her earlier in the week. Feeling its edges, she removed and opened it. The hair her father had left her was still inside—her DNA sample. Her truth? She knew why he'd given it to her. And she knew why he'd told her about the uncertainty of her conception. He'd thought she needed to know. But as the boat proceeded, trudging back to their home, she realized she did not.

No, Dad, she said silently to herself. *It doesn't matter. It never did. It just took me a while to figure that out.* She brought the hair to her lips and blew it firmly into the wind.

Chapter 20

Back in New York City about a week later, Elena looked at the various options in her clothes closet before heading out for an evening with Richard at his favorite restaurant, Ruminate. After pushing through the closet hangers, packed with far too many dresses in her tiny Manhattan apartment, she decided to go with a navy skirt and low-cut red blouse. She pulled out her navy spiked heels and the Mikimoto pearl choker Rebecca gave her. *Good*, she thought. She set them on her bed while continuing to dry her hair. Then she slipped the clothes on before turning to her makeup. *Something bold*, she thought. She opened her closet door and turned to check it all out in the full-length mirror. At seven, maybe even eight weeks, she was relieved to see she wasn't showing, but she quickly dismissed those thoughts. That evening, she needed to focus on her relationship with Richard. After applying her smoky eye makeup, she selected a deep red shade of lipstick that complimented the blouse and provided a striking contrast against her dark brown hair. *Perfect.*

Elena then walked to the entryway of her apartment and picked up her keys on the table under the mirror before hesitating. She loved wearing fun and, at times, mildly risqué clothes. She knew she looked great in them. And she knew Richard loved the look. But she needed to be careful. Did she want to tease or upset him? *Maybe*, she thought. *Probably*. But was that who she was? No, it wasn't. And that night, her messaging needed to be clear.

She returned to her bedroom and removed the skirt, replacing it with some dress slacks and a blazer. She kicked off the spikes and swapped them for a comfortable navy pump. With the pearls, it still worked. She checked again in the full-length mirror, turning from side to side, before noticing that her hand was trembling slightly. She shook it off and rechecked her appearance. *Now it's perfect*, she thought, as she closed the door and again headed out.

Elena hailed a cab and directed the driver to Ruminate. Within minutes, she found herself at the bar, but Richard hadn't arrived yet. After checking her phone, she realized she was a few minutes late. She lustfully looked at the negronis being served to the patrons. But what she really wanted, she realized, was one of her father's margaritas with his favorite tequila, Herradura Reposado. She missed those margaritas, and she knew why. It had been a little over a week since the funeral, and she most certainly hadn't moved on. But was she ready to settle up? She motioned to the waiter and ordered a Perrier instead. The drink arrived with a hit from one of the professional men at the bar, who apparently had noticed that she was alone.

"Can I buy that for you?" he asked.

"I'm good," she responded, "but thanks." She smiled when he persisted before interrupting him. "I'm sorry, but I'm waiting for someone."

"My name's Carlos," he said, "and I don't mind waiting for a better time." He handed her his card before turning to leave. *Morgan Stanley*, it read.

She thought he was a handsome Latino man—maybe a little pudgy, but in a likable, down-home kind of way. She particularly liked the white of his smile. But his timing was way off. Out of the frying pan and into the fire? *Not me*, she thought. *Not again*.

She finished her drink and checked the time on her phone again. Richard was over forty-five minutes late, as usual. She knew he had a lot on his plate at work. Regardless, that night she needed to be patient, not angry. She returned the phone to her purse before noticing him walking over.

"Sorry I'm late, hon," he said, kissing her cheek while gently squeezing her hand. "Ready to eat?"

"Yes," she replied. She wanted to challenge him on his tardiness but thought better of it. There was plenty of conflict in store for the evening. Why exacerbate it?

The hostess took them to a table in the back—the same one Richard usually insisted upon. She seated them and handed them their menus. Then she gave Richard the wine menu, as she always did. Elena wondered why. Was it his gender? The fact that he always paid? She didn't know but made a mental note: Henceforth, she'd pay for herself, and they'd go to places she could afford. *Enough is enough*, she thought.

Richard ordered cocktails for both of them, as he always had, before engaging with the waiter on the wine selection. They discussed the nose of one wine and the berry aftertaste of another. She liked wine, no doubt. But now, the banter just struck her as senseless drivel. True to form, Richard ordered a Bordeaux, the same one he always ordered, more or less. The waiter then took their dinner orders before leaving them alone.

"What's with the outfit?" Richard said. "It's nice, but it's not like those sexy miniskirts you usually wear."

She nodded and smiled without answering.

"I like those," he added. "Hey, I missed you, hon. I'm glad you're back." He took her hand under the table.

She smiled again. "Thank you. It's been a couple of tough weeks."

"You got that right," he answered. "We got the Galbraith deal. Thankfully, I flew back to sew it up. And we've got a board meeting on Project Aladdin—you know, the Saudi deal? Plus, with you out, we're getting way backed up on the new business pitches. There's probably four or five needing your immediate attention."

Elena took a sip of her water and nodded again. There was a time when she would have been fascinated by his work—the transactions, the money, the prestige. She felt the brush of his leg before it settled firmly against her own. And there was a time when she would have been overwhelmed by him—the incredible body under the Armani suit, the blond hair, and the piercing green eyes. But those days were gone. As he leaned in again to kiss her, she could smell the alcohol on his breath. True to form, he'd been drinking with his friends, she guessed, maybe even with a woman somewhere else.

The waiter brought the wine along with the oysters he liked so much. The truth was, she'd grown to enjoy them as well. At first, the slime factor had bothered her, but over time, that had changed. Now, they tasted salty but delicious.

Richard noticed her perking up and grinned. "Maybe we can get home early and catch up on what we've been missing," he suggested. He looked at her with his deep green eyes.

She smiled, masking her irritation, while searching for the right words. Yes, the oysters were great, but an aphrodisiac was no match for her frustration. *No, not frustration*, she thought. *Maybe disappointment coupled with anger.* It'd been over two weeks since Richard had walked out on her in Sayulita, leaving her alone and humiliated. Since then, nothing had changed his narcissism, even her father's death. When Richard learned of it, he'd blessed her with a text of condolences and some costly flowers, but nothing more, not even a call. He was absent as a mentor; he was a terrible boyfriend; and he'd never be a father of any merit. She was sure of this, but she wasn't surprised anymore. He hadn't changed in the time she'd known him. But she had. And she was sure of this now.

"Richard," she started, "we should talk about it." She pushed the anger back, realizing it had no utility. She focused instead on the message. "My dad just died. I'm grieving."

"Oh, hon," he said. "I'm sorry. I get it. Maybe you should take a little time before heading back to work. Don't they give you bereavement or something? I think they raised it to a month for a parent."

"Actually," she continued, "I'm going to take more than that. I stopped by HR earlier today and told them I wouldn't return at all."

"What?" he said incredulously. "Are you sure?" He paused. "Aren't you taking this a little too seriously?"

"I am taking it seriously," she answered. "Very seriously. But you were right in Mexico: My analyst position ends in a matter of months, anyway, and I'm going to go to business school. So I have a window of time—one that I may not get again for a long time. I'm going to spend it on my family—and on me."

"What does that mean?" he said. "Your father's dead, and your sister lives in California."

"Right," she said.

The conversation paused as the waiters cleared the plates from their appetizers and delivered their main courses. She smiled with reflection while looking down at her short ribs.

"Well, I guess I'd better pass the pitches along to another analyst," Richard continued, while taking a bite of his fish. "Maybe Eric could handle the Saudi deal. But I understand; it will all work out. Don't worry about it."

She was amazed by the way his mind worked. Without missing a beat, he gravitated to solving for work, still missing the central question: How was she? She again felt the rub of his leg under the table. Did he even realize he was doing that? *He has to*, she thought. The contact was far too calculated to be happenstance.

"Where will you apply to business school?" he asked. "I suspect you'll leave the city, but that doesn't mean we can't have fun in the meantime, does it?"

Elena again felt the anger in her body grow. She was too uncomfortable to eat, so instead she took another drink of her water before responding. She wanted to tell him exactly what she felt: that he was a narcissist; that the touch of his leg was repulsive; and that she couldn't imagine spending more time with him, let alone getting in bed with him. But what was the point of that? Would it make her feel better? *Maybe*, she thought, *but only for a minute.* Would it help him self-correct? *No*, she thought. There was zero chance of that.

"Actually, it does," she answered, refocusing. "I'm going to go back to Sayulita to spend some time with my sister. We're going to reconnect there, at least through the end of the summer. We're going to grieve. We're going to be the family we were and still want to be. Because we love each other, and that's what sisters do."

"That's quite a while," he said.

She watched him, trying to gauge his reaction, but she didn't respond. He removed his leg and took a deep drink of his wine as his brow furrowed. Was he getting angry? She'd never seen him actually lose it; that wasn't Richard. But she could see he was irritated.

"Do you know what the GDP of Puerto Vallarta is?" he asked. "Or how many public companies they have down there?"

She raised her eyebrows. Was he trying to persuade her to stay at Goldman? Or to go home with him? Did he realize there was a difference?

"Nor do I," he said. "Why do you think that is?" He took another bite of his fish and chewed it as he spoke.

She knew the question was rhetorical and avoided it. Moreover, the sarcasm was incredibly condescending.

"Look," he said, "let's cut to the chase." He stopped chewing and put his utensils down. "You've done well at Goldman, but you're not unique here. Sure, if you drop out of Goldman now, you'll still get into a great business school looking to fill its diversity quota. But is that all you want? I mean, shit, with your looks and charisma, you could go anywhere, do anything. Seriously, Elena, the sky's the limit. It's time for you to look up, not back."

Seeing that he wasn't through, she didn't respond.

"I mean, for Christ's sake, you can do it—all of it. But you need Goldman to do it right, and you need me, too. And I want to help. Can't you see that? Seriously, Elena, you're not thinking clearly. Why don't you just take a deep breath and consider all of it before you light yourself on fire?"

Elena took another deep drink of the Perrier, pausing to consider the implications of his words. Ironically, they were the same words she'd used to sharply critique her sister when she was thinking of leaving McKenzie. She felt him again take her hand as it rested on the table.

"Elena, we've come so far. Why don't you just think it over?"

We've? she thought. She removed her hand from his and smiled, as her thumb and index finger instinctively touched the pearls of the necklace Rebecca had recently given her.

Elena was surprised by the level of his interest, maybe even flattered. She could tell that he was in his deal mode, and he didn't want to lose. But she'd watched him change the bullets and colors of the PowerPoint slides before, and despite his magic tricks, knew exactly which cup her stone was under. His negotiating started when he wanted something and was determined to get it: a condominium, a bonus, a closing, or sex. The problem was that she wasn't just something. She was a person. A woman. A human being of merit and worth. Sure, the opportunities he described had significant value. And she had no doubt that he could help make them happen for her. But that would mean living his life on his terms. And that, for her, was a deal-breaker.

"Thank you, Richard," she said, looking directly into his eyes and returning her hand to her lap. "For giving me so much. I've learned a lot from you and appreciate all you've done for me. Other than my father, I don't think anyone has taught me as much as you have." She had learned a lot from him; that part was true.

Elena collected her thoughts again before continuing. "You know, my father wasn't educated, professional, or rich," she said. "But he was kind, loving, and wise—wise in the things that mattered. So, he taught me what matters most."

Richard started to protest. She silenced him by simply raising her index finger while looking directly into his eyes—another trick she'd learned from Dad. She noticed that Richard again had stopped eating, but she could tell from his expression that he wasn't hearing her. So she decided to change her approach. She looked down at her untouched short ribs and carefully placed her fork next to her plate while choosing her words.

"It's taken me a while to understand your deal terms, Richard, but I'm pretty sure I understand them now," she started. "You have an incredible job, make a ton of money, and have a lot of very impressive things. The tangible net worth on your balance sheet is unmatched." She paused, noticing that he'd retracted his leg. Then she continued. "I don't have the things that you do, and I probably never will. But the intangibles on my balance sheet—the kindness, the empathy, the love, my family—are immeasurable. Over time, they will bring me a level of happiness and joy that you can't. So, while I understand that the relationship you propose is highly accretive to you, it will never be accretive to me."

When he started to protest, she again raised her hand just slightly, giving her time to finish.

"Simply put, Richard, I'm worth more. Much more."

From the changed look in his eyes and the tightness of his brow, she could tell that he understood: The negotiations were over, and a counteroffer was pointless. Having successfully delivered the message, she paid the check in cash and patiently and respectfully waited for him to respond. When he didn't, she clasped his hand gently on the table, gathered her jacket, and left.

Chapter 21

Rebecca pressed the code into the key deck of the large bronze gates that marked the driveway entrance to the Stimpson home in Atherton. The buzzer beeped, and the gates slowly opened, allowing her to pass. Although her grandparents had suggested that she meet them at the Menlo Circus Club for their usual Sunday dinner, she wanted instead to speak with them at home.

She continued driving past the long lawns that framed each side of the cobblestone driveway and under the oak trees that majestically lined the formal path, forming a canopy of green above. The French provincial home rose grandly as she approached. While it was designed to impress and maybe also intimidate, she loved the ornate wooden detailing, the blue-boarded shutters, the mysterious dormer windows on the third floor, and the natural slate roof. She loved the house; she loved the gardens. And she loved living there. *Who wouldn't?* she thought.

She pressed the door opener on the visor of her car, which lifted a garage door. While the home appeared to have three garages, in fact, it had six, as each door covered an opening for two tandem vehicles, masking its enormity while preserving its charm. She looked at the other cars; now there were three. Had they sold one? She removed her bag and checked for her belongings in the back seat. She grabbed her apartment keys and left the car key in the arm rail. She wondered if her decision was the right one, and she wondered if the outcome would be as she'd anticipated. She hoped not. But it didn't matter; she'd know soon enough. Besides, there was no point in returning the car to San Francisco if she was headed back to Mexico.

"Hello, dear," Beverly said, greeting her in the foyer between the garage and the large kitchen. "Ben, she's here."

Rebecca kissed her grandmother and then her grandfather. They weren't so bad. Maybe this would go better than she'd thought after all.

"Something to drink?" her grandmother asked.

"We're having martinis to start," her grandfather said, lifting his half-empty glass to show her.

"Maybe a wine?" she said. "Actually, I'll take one of those." She pointed to his martini, reconsidering.

"Coming right up," he said. "And no worries, you can just stay here tonight. Tomorrow's Sunday."

Rebecca looked up the back stairway that ran from the kitchen to the bedrooms on the second floor, including her old bedroom, the first door on the left. She'd been happy here, and they'd been good to her. She took the drink her grandfather extended and sat at the kitchen bar, watching her grandmother unpack the take-out food for dinner.

"We went to Draeger's," she said. "I hope you don't mind, but you didn't want to go to the club, and I just wasn't up to cooking a full meal for three, especially on the weekend when I don't have any help."

"No worries," she said.

Beverly unpacked a marinated tri-tip, stuffed baked potato, cashew green beans, and a green salad with beets.

"As usual, your grandmother ordered way too much," Ben said.

Rebecca smiled. "Well, there's always tomorrow to finish it."

Beverly took out the place mats and set the table, while Ben opened a bottle of wine. "Help yourself," she said, motioning for Rebecca to start. "We'll just eat here on the kitchen table; no need to traipse into the dining room."

"Looks great," Rebecca said.

They filled their plates and took their food to the kitchen's casual dining room. While informal, the kitchen table served up to eight, making even the formal table in their Mexican home seem insignificant by comparison. Rebecca paused. Why was she still comparing them? She wasn't sure.

"How was it?" her grandmother asked.

"We worried about you," her grandfather added.

At first, she'd presumed they were talking about the death of her father and the funeral. But from their casual demeanor, it seemed as though they were not. While she'd spoken with them on the phone about the funeral, and they'd sent some lovely flowers to her home in San Francisco, this was the first time she'd seen them in person since her father's passing. So she'd expected his death to be the focus of their conversation, and she'd expected them to comfort her in her time of loss.

"It was hard," she answered tentatively.

Her grandparents nodded but didn't initially respond.

"I just don't think it's safe down there," her grandmother started. "Did you have any problems?"

"It was hard," Rebecca said again. "Really hard, actually."

Her grandparents nodded.

Were they intentionally missing her point? Were they just trying to be nice? Maybe they thought it would be better not to talk about it, unless she brought it up. She couldn't think of what to say, so she just didn't respond.

"Well, back to reality," her grandfather said. "Do you start at work again on Monday?"

She realized that they'd moved on, and now it angered her. They were white-washing: painting over his death as if it were a Rivera. Was this what they'd done to Derek, too? They were kind people, and they loved her. Certainly, they meant her no harm. She searched their faces for an understanding before realizing again that it didn't matter.

"Yes and no," she said. "I wanted to talk to you about that."

"Maybe you should take another week off," her grandmother said. "Maybe you should just stay in your old room for a while and hang out at the pool?"

"You know, we'd love to have you," her grandfather added.

"I know, but that's not quite what I mean." She paused. "The thing is, I've decided I want to paint."

"That's wonderful," her grandmother said. "Will you take the class at the same place next semester?"

"No, I mean really paint. Full time."

"Now Rebecca," her grandfather started. "You're an incredible artist. I love your stuff; everyone does. But it's not a career. You have a career at McKenzie."

"What do they pay you now," her grandmother asked, "two hundred thousand?"

"You know," her grandfather added, "when I started at Chevron—what year was that? Anyway, they offered me twenty thousand a year to start. I was thrilled!"

Rebecca realized their intentions were good, but they still weren't hearing her. So she decided to be more direct and specific. This time, they needed to talk about her, not Ben, Chevron, or her career path.

"I'm leaving McKenzie and going to paint," she said. "I'm going to paint in Mexico, where my father lived."

Her grandparents seemed to physically withdraw as she spoke. It was one of the few times she'd really told them no, so she suspected they felt hurt.

"Ben, tell her that's crazy," her grandmother started but didn't wait for him to respond. "Honey, it's crazy!"

"That's just not how it works," Ben said. "You have to start at the bottom and work your way up. Sure, it's boring and a lot of work, but each day, you learn more, contribute more, build more, and then make more. I know that's hard to hear, but look around you," he said, pointing to the house. "Rome wasn't built in a day!"

"He's right, dear," her grandmother said. "You just have to have patience."

Rebecca nodded autonomically before recognizing she'd need to be even firmer if she wanted to be heard. "You need patience if you're heading in the direction you want to go," Rebecca said. "Otherwise, you're just spinning your wheels." She noticed her grandfather starting to grumble but continued without letting him interrupt. "The thing is, I don't want to be a consultant. I want to paint."

"You know," her grandfather started again, "I was reading that those McKenzie partners now make three million a year, sometimes more. Can you imagine how that would change your life?"

"I can," Rebecca responded. "I've seen it. I've seen them. I don't judge or criticize their business or their lives. I'm impressed, actually. What they do is necessary and important. But it's not me."

"Rebecca," her grandfather continued, now in a stern tone, "you have been given privilege, enormous privilege. We gave it to you. We brought you from that restaurant you lived in down there. We sent you to one of the best high schools in the nation. Then we sent you to the best college in the nation. We did this because we could. Why? Because we earned it."

The words were anticipated, but the fact that they were the exact words Elena had used weeks earlier gave her pause. At some level, they, like Elena, were right. And now, she was perfectly comfortable acknowledging it.

"You know, dear," her grandmother added, "we sent you to Stanford because of our connections. You could have applied to Harvard if you'd wanted to, but it just wasn't a sure thing. That's why Stanford really did make the most sense. Plus, it's just a couple of miles from us here in Atherton." The words were pointless ramblings, but they revealed her grandmother's desperation.

"I'm not going to Mars," Rebecca explained. "I'm just moving to Mexico—a three-hour flight!" She watched the expression on her grandparents' faces. She'd been deferential for years, but now she wasn't. That was new for them. Didn't they understand?

"You're serious," her grandfather said. "You're sure?"

"Yes," she said, nodding.

"You're leaving your friends, your job, and us. Why? So you can live in the restaurant you grew up in and paint silly kids' stuff?"

"Now, Ben," her grandmother said, scolding him before turning to her granddaughter. "But Rebecca, think about what you're saying. *Please?*"

"We helped you escape from that life—the poverty, the drugs, the crime—all of it," her grandfather said. "Don't you get that?"

"You were stolen, Rebecca, and we rescued you," her grandmother added. "I'm just so pleased we found you when we did—before it was too late!"

Rebecca nodded again, as if what they'd said were true, knowing it was not, but recognizing that they couldn't hear anything else. She felt her tears starting to form, but she held them back. Realistically, the conversation was going just as she'd expected; it'd been naive for her to have even hoped otherwise. This was who they were, and the McKenzie partner, or some comparable variation thereof, was the granddaughter they expected—not an artist in Sayulita. Not her.

Sensing that her husband was giving up, her grandmother picked up the slack. "You just need to realize that you're not like them," she said. "You're American; you're White!"

Rebecca nodded again reflexively. Their perspective didn't surprise her; that her grandmother would actually use those words did. And she'd had enough.

"He was my father," she said softly. "And I loved him. I loved him more than you will ever understand, and I always will."

"Damn it, Rebecca, we've already been through that: *Derek* was your father; Francisco was your *abductor*," her grandfather said.

Rebecca bit her lip as he spoke and then carefully chose the words of her response. "You have no business telling me who or what my father was, or who or what I am," she said. "I'm Rebecca Stimpson *Montoya*. My fathers were Derek Stimpson, your son, and Francisco Montoya, his husband. They were gay. No, they weren't legally married, but that's because they couldn't be."

She stopped to collect her thoughts. After deciding she was sure, she continued. "I don't know how it worked with you and Derek, but I can guess. And that's not going to happen to me—at least, not anymore."

"Rebecca," Beverly said, challenging her sternly.

"I am and always will be their daughter, and Elena is and always will be my twin sister. So, if you persist in rejecting my dads, together, or my sister, as such, then you reject me, too."

Rebecca watched her grandparents' reactions as the gravity of the situation settled in. They had a choice because she'd made a choice. Her grandmother's face registered panic, and her grandfather's face registered anger.

"I can't believe you're saying this, Rebecca. I just can't believe it," her grandmother said.

Rebecca stood her ground without wavering.

"If that's how you see it, Ms. *Montoya*," her grandfather said sarcastically, "then perhaps it's time to call it a night."

When they didn't continue, Rebecca slowly got up to leave, hoping they'd stop her. But they didn't. So she picked up her bag and started out.

As she walked alone to the front of the house to leave, she felt abandoned and lost. Her father had died; he was gone. She hadn't begun to process that, let alone understand the significance of his absence. And now, her grandparents were showing her out. She reluctantly opened the thick, wooden door to the entrance of their French provincial mansion. And when she shut it firmly behind her, she knew that the door would not likely open for her again.

Epilogue

Ten years later

Elena scanned the incredible vista from the large palapa of the living room of their family home in Sayulita. That home, once her father's, was the same home she'd grown up in as a child. And now, it along with the Linda Vista were her sister's. The light glimmered magically on the vast horizon of the deep blue Pacific Ocean as the sun began its descent into the darkening clouds of the evening sky. A warm evening breeze gently carried the hint of salt along with the musky scent of the sea. And the waves of the bay, varied in their timing but consistent in their recurrence, slowed as the day came to completion. Elena counted the seconds between each wave while taking a deep, reflective breath.

Elena knew now, with certainty, that she could live and succeed in the world of the north. But she also understood that the sand, the bay, the boats, and this house were as much a part of her being as her hair, blowing gently in the breeze, or her hand, resting lightly on the bamboo rail. Over the years, the weekends she'd spent in Sayulita had quickly turned into weeks and then, at times, even months. And since her father's passing a decade earlier, she'd never missed a Christmas. While she'd lived for what seemed like a lifetime in New York, this simple palapa, nestled on the bluffs over the Sayulita beach, would always be her home—their family home.

"*Buenas tardes,*" Rebecca said, heading to the refrigerator.

"*Buenas tardes,*" Elena answered. "What an incredible day."

"Carlos around?"

"He went into town," Elena responded.

"I'm glad you brought him this time," Rebecca said. "How long's it been for you two now?"

"Married five years. Good ones," Elena answered. "A couple of years after I joined Citibank."

"I remember the wedding," Rebecca said. "He's been a good fit for you—a definite improvement."

Elena smiled, reflecting. It had actually been over a decade since she'd first met Carlos—that same night she'd left Richard at Ruminate. So much had changed since then. After breaking up with Richard and leaving Goldman Sachs, she'd returned to Sayulita and lived with Rebecca through the summer. Looking back, it still amazed her to think that she'd done it to carry a baby.

Elena had agonized about her decision. It went against her very nature. But she'd made the right choice for her, and she was certain of it. That had been a challenging time, a stressful time, and a healing time. But in almost no time, she'd been admitted to the Columbia Business School. And, after graduating, she'd joined the bond placement group at Citibank, rising quickly to the position of managing director. Rebecca, by contrast, had returned to Sayulita and never left, preferring that life to the one she'd lived in San Francisco.

Rebecca took a fresh papaya from the fruit bowl and cut it into slices. "Want one?"

"Sure," Elena answered.

Elena wrapped the papaya with a slice of prosciutto. As she took a bite, she noticed the beach portrait Rebecca had painted of the family over a decade earlier. "You know, you never told me how you came to have the painting," she asked. "You moved it here from the restaurant, but I thought Dad had sold it for you."

"He did, and he didn't," Rebecca said. "When he passed, he left me an envelope in his room along with a box of the various things he'd kept during my lifetime in the storage closet upstairs. The envelope had ten thousand dollars and a note that said, *Live your life. Love, D.*"

"He purchased it for himself—for you?" Elena asked.

"I think it memorialized his family the way he wanted to remember us, even after he'd died," Rebecca said.

Elena smiled, remembering. "What did Dad call that?"

"Fictional clarity. Truth."

Elena turned from her sister, pretending to look at their family portrait in order to hide her reaction. Seeing the hint of her sister's tear, Rebecca responded. "It's always good to have you back," she said. "We're your family, too."

"I know that; I feel it," Elena answered. "I really do." She paused, reflecting. "It was hard at first—coming back here. Maybe too painful, maybe too close. But now, I just feel peace."

"I do, too," Rebecca answered.

Elena took another bite of the papaya. She understood why Rebecca hadn't returned to the States. For Elena, a life in Manhattan worked. But for Rebecca, their father's life in Sayulita had always made sense.

"Whatever happened to the Stimpsons, anyway?" Elena asked, changing the subject.

"They died, one and then the other, a little over a year ago."

"And the world got a little better?" Elena chuckled.

Rebecca smiled. "I'm not saying that," she said. "But they did leave me some money—a lot, actually."

"I'm shocked. I thought they'd written you off when you didn't return."

"They did, but something fell through the cracks of their will. The lawyer called it a 'residual' interest in part of their estate. He said it was because their intended donation to someone else failed. It was something about the strings attached to the gift."

"Huh. That's a mind-bender," Elena said, reflecting. "But with the Stimpsons, there always were strings."

Rebecca nodded. She took another piece of the fruit and then passed the plate back to Elena.

"Now you've made me curious: Did you ever run that DNA test?" Elena asked. "You know, with Dad's hair?"

Rebecca mischievously grinned. "Nope."

"So, the Stimpson inheritance was a mistake?"

"Maybe it was, and maybe it wasn't. Who knows?"

"Well, good for you!" Elena said.

"But it gets even better," Rebecca said. "I'm using the money to open a women's clinic in town with a real medical staff and a doctor—and funds to transport women, if necessary."

"So now you manage Dad's underground railroad for Mexican women?" she asked. "And the Stimpsons are funding it?"

"I'm thinking that the building should bear their name: *The Stimpson Women's Clinic*," she said.

"Our middle name," Elena said.

"*Derek's* name," Rebecca answered, while still grinning. "The doctor of the family."

Elena shook her head and smiled with approval. "Genius," she said. "He would've loved it."

The side door opened, and Consuela entered with a bag of groceries.

"*Buenas tardes*," she said.

"*Buenas tardes*," Elena answered.

While Guillermo seemed unchanged over the years, Consuela's hair had grayed completely, as she'd long since stopped bothering to dye it. Her walk had slowed since Francisco had passed, and her back now curved slightly, making it harder for her to make eye contact, given her short stature. But she remained as vibrant and alive as ever, and her smile was the same.

"For dinner," Consuela started, "we celebrate Elena's last day here with her favorite Mexican meal: grilled *camarones*, ceviche, and fresh dorado tacos. But first, your father's favorite: guacamole and margaritas!"

"*Gracias*, Consuela," Elena said.

"But *we're* cooking tonight," Rebecca countered. "Our treat."

"*¿Están loca?*" she responded. *(Are you crazy?)* "What am I going to do if I can't cook? Talk to you? Or even worse, listen?"

Elena and Rebecca looked at each other before chuckling.

"*Dígame.*" *(Tell me.)* "Do you really want to eat Rebecca's cooking?" Consuela continued. "*Ay ya yai. Creo que no.*" (*I don't think so.*) She rolled her eyes at the absurdity of it.

"Fair point," Elena responded, "I'm thinking no is the right answer."

Rebecca chuckled. "*Excelente.*"

As Consuela chopped the onions for the guacamole and the tomatoes for the pico de gallo, Rebecca and Elena sipped the Herradura margaritas that Consuela had poured over ice with a fresh lime.

"You still like them blended?" Rebecca asked.

"Yup," Elena responded.

Rebecca nodded. "You belong here—even with your gringo margaritas."

"I *belonged* here," Elena responded, before reconsidering. "But maybe. Maybe again someday."

"*¡Salud!*" They clicked their glasses again before taking a deep drink.

Elena felt the cool freshness of the margarita quench her thirst. While they drank their cocktails, they reminisced, casually reflecting on pretty much everything as much as nothing. As they did, Elena felt an enormous sense of satisfaction. Somehow, they'd managed to extend their childhood bond to their lives as adults. Somehow, they'd gotten it right.

Elena turned to the vista, watching the fishing boats as they trudged slowly from the distance of the open sea back to the marina.

"Check it out," Rebecca said, gesturing toward the bay.

"The boats?" Elena asked, noticing them circling in the distance.

Rebecca walked to the dresser, pulled out her father's old binoculars, and scanned the sea while leaning against the railing of the palapa deck.

"I remember how he used to watch the bay for hours," Elena responded. "Dolphins?"

"Nope. A whale. Just to the left of the fishing boats."

"I see it!" Elena answered.

"I think there are two there," Rebecca said.

Rebecca handed the binoculars to her sister. Elena quickly found the whale just as the spray of its blowhole emerged, and the crest of its tail broke the sea's surface. She focused the binoculars to enhance her view. "Ah, you're right. Two!" She could see that one was enormous, and the other was relatively small. *A mother and her calf? Maybe*, she thought. But as quickly as the two emerged, they again descended. And when, after a bit, they did not reappear, the fishing boats continued their journey back. *No*, she thought. *You just need to give them time and have some patience.*

Elena wondered how long the baby whale would take to reach adulthood and when it would return to the bay. She wondered if it would return without its mother, or if she would show him the way, at least the first time. *And so it was*, she thought, *the cycle of life*. The characters evolve over time, but the venue and plot remain unchanged. She hoped so. Because despite the inevitable difficulties and hardships of their lives, they remained beautiful, wondrous, and good. The words, she knew, like the binoculars, were her father's. And they both fit.

"Refill?" Rebecca asked, holding up the margarita pitcher.

"Absolutely," Elena responded.

"Are you liking them more again these days?" Rebecca asked.

"Yes, I think so," Elena said. "They used to just seem bitter; now they seem both bitter and sweet. Have they changed, you know, how you make them?"

"No," Rebecca said. "You've changed."

"We've changed," Elena said. "We grew up?"

"Maybe. I hope so."

They paused momentarily, and Elena caught the vibrancy of her sister's face, framed against the sunset.

"Dad gave us that," Elena said. "Helped us understand."

"To Dad!" They clinked their glasses, turning toward the horizon as the sunset's multicolored hues began to radiate through the clouds and the sun began to set.

"*Enrosadira*," Rebecca said. "Dad's favorite sunset."

"He'd be so happy to see us all here together," Elena said. "For him, it'd be perfect."

"I'll drink to that," Rebeca answered as they clinked their glasses again, this time spilling margaritas on their hands and the table. "Apparently, we'd drink to anything at this point?"

The mess of the spilled drinks seemed only to encourage Consuela. "*Un minuto*," she said, rushing over to refill the glasses rather than reprimand them. "You know, in the States, you have therapy," she said, "but in Mexico, we have margaritas." They chuckled as they took another sip.

Elena could feel the intoxicating warmth of the tequila flow through her body. While tasting the salt rim of the refill, she scanned the beach below as the sunlight diminished and surfers started heading back to shore. Through her father's binoculars, she quickly found the boy she'd been searching for in the distance. He'd caught a wave and was riding it through the tunnel, continuing almost all the way to the beach before flipping casually into the water. His young body was lean and muscular, and he seemed tall for his age. While his skin was brown, his long hair was blond, both naturally and from the salt of the sea. He didn't look like the other boys surfing; he was different. She zoomed in further with the binoculars for a better look. As he continued to approach, she saw, as she knew, that he was strikingly handsome, even in his youth. *But it's the eyes that give him away*, she thought. Those vibrant, penetrating green eyes. *Richard's eyes.* She smiled, knowingly, as the boy reached the path leading up to the palapa.

"Does he ever talk about it?" Elena asked.

"He loves you—you know that," Rebecca answered. "But no, it's not so interesting to him."

Elena nodded. "Luckily, Richard didn't find it so interesting, either."

Rebecca nodded in agreement. They took another drink of their margaritas as the light of the sun disappeared.

"Regrets?" Rebecca asked. She looked directly at Elena, almost scrutinizing her.

"None," Elena quickly answered, looking down at the boy with pleasure. "None whatsoever."

Elena watched her sister, who in turn watched her son. In Rebecca's smile, she could see her sister's simple delight in him. A tear again started in the corner of her eye, as her body radiated with the love she held for both of them.

"Thank you," Rebecca said. "For the best gift of my life."

"You're welcome," Elena answered. "Is it just the margaritas?" she asked, wiping the tear from her eye.

"Probably," Rebecca answered. "Actually, no, it's really not." Rebecca smiled as she leaned over the rail and hollered down. "Cameron, you coming up?" The boy glanced in their direction. "Dinner's ready, and your Aunt Elena's waiting for a goodbye hug."

"On my way, Mom," the boy answered.

Elena watched as her nephew scurried from the beach with his aqua-green surfboard in tow, still roped to his ankle, and headed up the winding path to their home. Elena smiled, remembering the board's origins. When he arrived at the palapa, the sunset reached its peak behind him, even as the vibrant colors of red, orange, yellow, blue, purple, and green streamed over the now-dark ocean floor.

"Hi, Auntie," he said, giving Elena a firm hug in his still-wet swimsuit.

"Hi, Cameron," Elena said. "You know, I was thinking that maybe someday you'd come to the States and visit your favorite aunt for a while."

"You?" he asked. "I hope not. There's no surf in Manhattan!"

Elena trapped him with a hug, holding him firmly under her arm. He playfully started gasping for air while struggling to escape before collapsing on the ground, laughing.

That laugh, she thought. *Dad's.* There was no doubt about it. He was there, with them, after all. Always. And yes, it was perfect, she realized. It was absolutely perfect. But then again, a Sayulita sunset always was perfect, wasn't it?

About the Author

G. Carlos Smith lives with his spouse, their three daughters, and their cat, Edgar, in Woodside, California, and Puerto Vallarta, Mexico. Prior to the arrival of their twins, he was a corporate partner in a global law firm. *Sayulita Sunset* is his second novel. *A Matter of Choice* was his first. He is a graduate of Stanford and Columbia universities.

www.ingramcontent.com/pod-product-compliance
Lightning Source LLC
LaVergne TN
LVHW041910070526
838199LV00051BA/2567